Behind the Story

In 1912, the collector Wilfred Voynich discovered a selection
of ancient books hidden in a chest in Mondragone Castle, Italy.
Among the texts was a manuscript written entirely in code.
It became known as the Voynich Manuscript.

For a century, academics tried to break the code. But not a
single word or phrase in the 245 pages of the
Voynich Manuscript has been read.

In 1944 a group of code-breakers working for the US
government formed a Study Group to try and decipher the text.
They failed. Between 1962 and 1963 a second Study Group was
formed. Eventually Americans joined with British code-breakers
based at Bletchley Park Mansion. They failed.

In 1969 the manuscript was donated to Yale
University and registered simply as 'MS 408'. It is kept hidden
from general view in the Beinecke Rare Book and Manuscript
Library. Since that day, the secret code has remained unbroken.

UNTIL NOW ...

Also by H. L. Dennis

SECRET BREAKERS

1. The Power of Three
2. Orphan of the Flames
3. The Knights of Neustria
4. Tower of the Winds
5. The Pirate's Sword
6. The Circle of Fire

SECRET BREAKERS

ORPHAN OF THE FLAMES

H. L. Dennis

Illustrations by Meggie Dennis

Hodder
Children's
Books

HODDER CHILDREN'S BOOKS

First published in Great Britain in 2012 by Hodder Children's Books
This edition published in 2017 by Hodder and Stoughton

9

A CIP catalogue record for this book
is available from the British Library.

ISBN 978 0 340 99962 2

Typeset in AGaramond Book by Avon DataSet Ltd,
Bidford-on-Avon, Warwickshire

Printed and bound in Great Britain
by Clays Ltd, St Ives plc

The paper and board used in this book
are made from wood from responsible sources

Hodder Children's Books
An imprint of
Hachette Children's Group
Part of Hodder and Stoughton
Carmelite House
50 Victoria Embankment
London EC4Y 0DZ

An Hachette UK Company
www.hachette.co.uk

www.hachettechildrens.co.uk

For
Andrew and Jane
and for Sue and Barrie.
Thank you for all your wisdom
and friendship.

The book that once was white is white no more.
Made black with grease, and thumb'd its pages o'er.
Then, while it still exists, transcribe each page;
Once gone, 'tis lost to every future age.
And if so lost – some fault of ours, 'tis time –
An me! Thou gem of greatest price, adieu!

Taken from the *Liber Albus*

Warning from a Dragon

At fourteen minutes past seven in the evening, the doorbell rang. Brodie didn't think the time was important. Later, she understood it was part of the code.

There was no one there, just a package wrapped in brown paper propped against the 'Sold' sign outside the house. She looked along the street. A car pulled silently away from the kerb but its windows were dark. There wasn't enough light to see inside.

Brodie picked up the parcel. It was heavy and badly wrapped, the paper torn and flapping. She remembered the gift she'd received months ago. A parcel which had begun her secret breaking adventure. This felt different. This felt wrong. There was no note, no explanation, just a small bronze statue of a dragon with a number daubed in thick red paint across its chest. 408.

The dragon was ugly; curling claws and eyes too narrow. It had no wings.

Brodie shivered as a pain bristled on her arm. Weeks ago she'd hurt herself on another ornamental dragon. The graze was still raw. So was the memory of that day. Kerrith waiting for her in the Music Room of the Royal Pavilion, ready to destroy everything Team Veritas had worked for. Brodie remembered how Kerrith had laughed as she stood in the centre of the room on the image of a wingless creature, just like the statue, woven into the carpet. Kerrith said the beast had no need to fly. He was the pendragon. King of them all.

Brodie held the statue. On the back there was a switch. She pressed it with her thumb and the pendragon rocked back its head. Its mouth opened. It breathed flames and its body burned white hot.

Brodie jerked her fingers away and the statue fell from her hand. It clattered across the step, its claws splayed, its mouth still open.

Fire from its throat died. But Brodie could still smell burning.

Then the ground began to shake.

* * *

The Director leant back in his leather chair and fiddled distractedly with the silver cuff links at his wrist.

At precisely 19.14 the phone rang.

The voice at the end of the line was sharp and clipped. 'We're ready to make the connection now, sir.'

The Director leant forward and pressed a red button on a small device near the back of his desk. At first glance the device looked like an audio speaker, but in the rim of the box was a tiny lens, obviously attached to a camera. The Director spoke slowly, as if unsure how well the device would register his words. 'Sir, I'm greatly honoured you have—'

A voice cut him off. 'We've no time for small talk.' The words echoed round the room. 'I need to talk action. Direct action.'

The Director had never met the man who spoke. As far as he knew, no one in the Black Chamber, in which he worked, ever had. The Chairman of Level Five was unseen. All-powerful – but unseen.

'Yes, sir.' The knuckles on the Director's hands whitened and a bead of sweat glistened above his eye. 'Direct action has been taken.'

'You've sent out a warning?'

'Yes, sir. We've made it quite clear they're playing with fire.'

'And you were discreet?'

3

'Completely, sir. Enough to scare them. I singled out a few from the group, but they'll pass the warning on. They won't go back to Station X now.'

'Good. Good.' The Director could hear the pleasure in the Chairman's voice. 'I'd like to see, though, who it was we were dealing with.' There was a whirring noise and the camera lens swivelled in its holdings. 'Who caused such a threat to our operations here.'

The Director was embarrassed. The bead of sweat rolled down the side of his face and splashed on to a thin manila folder resting on the desk. 'The operation was led by Smithies.' He pushed a photograph into the range of the camera. 'He had a team working for him. Sicknote Ingham, a previous employee of the Black Chamber. And Tandi Tandari, Smithies' secretary there.' More photos spilled from the folder. 'And there were three children involved.'

The sound like a disgusted sniff echoed from the speaker. 'Children?'

'Oh yes. They did seem to have exceptional skills.'

The Director took three more photographs and fanned them out across the desk like a hand of playing cards. 'Tusia Petulova,' he said, jabbing at the first with the tip of his finger. 'Junior chess champion. High achiever. All the usual attributes of a code-cracker.

Her grandfather took over from Tiltman as senior GCHQ liaison officer.'

The voice urged him on.

'Hunter Jenkins,' said the Director, sliding the second picture into range. 'Parents profess law at Oxford.'

'Kid of lawyers, eh?' The voice from the desk-top device sounded as if the words left a bad taste in the mouth. 'And the last one?'

'The most intriguing, sir. Another girl. Brodie Bray.'

There was a crackle at the end of the line as if for a second the connection had been lost.

'Bray?'

The Director hesitated. 'Alex's daughter.'

There was a pause. Just a gentle hum lifted like steam from the speaker. 'That's all of them?'

The Director shook his head. 'Bray's grandfather was involved. He bought the huts at Station X. Activated some sort of English Heritage ruling so we can't destroy the building. Meant the outfit would have been safe even though we've withdrawn our support.'

'And the old man had enough funding to keep it going?'

'No, sir. But they had Fabyan III on board.'

'As in, Fabyan of the Riverbanks Labs in Illinois?'

'His great-grandson. A billionaire, sir, with his

5

'great-grandfather's eccentricities and love of the code.'

Air whistled from the speaker. 'Big bucks from the States. Impressive. But that was all?'

'No, sir. Not entirely.'

'Oh?'

'I believe this next recruit was perhaps the most intriguing.' He smirked as he spoke.

The lens on the desk-top box moved as if someone had pressed it forward to zoom.

'They involved Friedman.'

The photograph this time was old and grainy, creased at the corner. Friedman stood as a young man next to two friends.

'An interesting photograph,' the voice said and there was a hesitation the Director hadn't heard before. 'I wonder who took it.'

The Director thought this question an odd one.

'So. They involved Friedman, did they?' He repeated the words as if attempting to make sense of their meaning.

'And how much did *she* know?' he asked slowly. 'The Bray girl?'

'Know, sir? What do you mean?'

'The details about her mother's death.'

'I believe, sir, she's of the understanding now, it may not have been a simple accident.'

There was a pause. 'And she knows about the involvement of others from the Chamber?'

'Not precise details, no.'

There was a sigh. 'Most acceptable work. You've shaken the ground under their feet just like I wanted. It will be very clear to them we're deathly serious. Well done. I think we can presume our little threat from this band of has-beens and kids is over. Don't you think?'

The Director angled the lens down towards the desk. He feared a close-up on his face would give away the fact that, despite everything he said, he wasn't entirely sure.

The yellow and black police tape flapped across the end of the street. Lights spun on the tops of emergency vehicles as neighbours huddled in stunned silence.

Hunter put his arm around Brodie's shoulder.

'We could have died,' whispered Brodie.

'I know, B. I know.' He squeezed her arm. 'But we're safe. We're all safe. We got out in time.'

Brodie ran her fingers through her hair and pressed her hands against her face to drive out the smell of burning. She didn't think it would ever go away. 'He's lost everything,' she mumbled.

Hunter followed her gaze across the line of the police tape. Brodie's granddad stood in the rubble of his former home. He clutched a metal biscuit tin to his chest.

'Not everything,' whispered Hunter. 'He still has you. And whatever's in that box.'

'My mum's things,' said Brodie. 'Me and a metal box full of papers. It's all he has.'

Hunter lowered his head.

'I'm so sorry.' She was choking on tears, the words clogging in her throat.

'Why are *you* sorry?'

'Because you staying with us before we all went back to Station X was supposed to make things easier.'

'It still did,' he said quietly. 'And anyway, if you hadn't worked out what they meant by sending that dragon, we could have all been inside when the house went up.'

'It was a code,' Brodie said slowly. 'The time – 19.14. The year of the fire in Louvain. The number – 408. The number of Voynich's manuscript Level Five are so sure we should leave alone. And the pendragon. Dragon without wings. Ruler of them all.' She swallowed. 'Level Five of the Black Chamber did this and they meant us to know it was them.'

Brodie heard the vehicle approaching before she saw it.

'What the Danish pastry's that?' blurted Hunter, as

Granddad moved to stand beside them, the metal tin still tight to his chest.

A Volkswagen van was crawling up the hill. It was sprayed bright red and orange and had an extendable concertina roof raised high in the air like a chef's paper hat. Yellow curtains, edged with fluffy white pompoms, bounced against the windows, and along the side of the van, painted in garish green and violet, were a series of Russian dolls with huge maniacal grins stamped on their faces.

The van spluttered to a halt behind a police car. Each of the four huge exhaust pipes, tailing from the back, belched out thick black clouds of acrid smoke reeking of chip fat.

'I guess it's our rescue vehicle,' offered Granddad, taking hold of Brodie's hand.

Another rancid cloud of chip fat spewed out and the van shuddered. The extendable lid flopped forward like a deflated balloon before snapping back into place with a bang.

At the window, the pompom-edged curtains jerked to the side as a face appeared at the glass. Tusia was more weathered since Brodie had last seen her. Her auburn hair tied in place with a floppy red ribbon; her face earnest, lined with concern. 'We came as fast as we could.'

The van backfired once more and this time the expandable roof collapsed entirely.

'What the peaches and cream is this thing?' asked Hunter, covering his nose to cut out the smell.

'The Matroyska,' Tusia said defensively, opening the door and jumping down to stand beside them. 'It runs entirely on vegetable fat so it doesn't damage the environment.'

'It's damaging me,' spluttered Hunter, coughing into his hands.

'You'd better get used to it,' said Tusia. 'My parents have donated the Matroyska for us to get around in. And by the look of things, we need to get away from here as fast as we can.'

A door on the far side of the Matroyska clicked open and Mr Smithies emerged, his face twitching into a nervous smile. 'Hop in,' he said, gesturing the three of them on board.

Tandi Tandari and Oscar Ingham helped Mr Bray towards his seat.

'You sure you're OK, Brodie?' asked Robbie Friedman, who was seated at the back.

She didn't answer.

'Step on it, then,' said Tusia, looking over at Smithies. 'I thought you said we had to get everyone away as soon as we could.'

The engine chugged into life.

'Where are we going?' said Hunter.

'Not Station X,' said Smithies.

'So where?'

Smithies slammed the Matroyska into reverse. 'X means ten, yes? In Roman numerals. Station X was the tenth wireless intercept station in the war. And there were others. Lots of others.'

'So where are we going?'

'The ninth station,' said Smithies. 'We're off to Station IX.'

It took them about two hours to get to Station IX. Smithies backed the Matroyska up carefully behind some overgrown bushes in an obvious attempt to keep the vehicle hidden. Tusia helped him cover the van with branches. 'What is this place?' she said, peering through the half-light.

'A secret operations factory used in World War Two,' said Smithies.

'But it's a mansion.'

'Lots of the places used during the war were. The government was able to take over these great country homes and use them for the war service. This place was known as the Frythe. It was an exclusive hotel but the intelligence service took it over. They began to develop weapons here.'

'Weapons?'

'Chemical and biological weapons in various huts and cabins in the grounds.'

'So while Station X was working as a code-cracking centre, Station IX was working as a laboratory trying to come up with ways to kill the enemy.' Hunter was negotiating clambering over the bushes.

'Exactly.'

'So why are we here?' said Brodie tentatively.

'A hideout,' said Smithies, leading the way across the gravelled drive. 'Come on.'

Brodie hurried after him.

'After such a direct attack from Level Five we need to keep hidden. This place has been empty for over two years. After the war it was bought by GlaxoSmithKline.'

'Who?' interrupted Hunter.

Tusia scowled. 'One of the largest healthcare organisations in the world. Make vaccines, toothpaste, all sorts. They're multinational, Hunter. Into making money.'

'Oh.'

'They owned the Frythe,' went on Smithies, 'but sold it in 2010 to be developed. And lucky for us, it's been empty ever since. There's plans to restore it to its former glory. But for now, it's a place to hide.'

Brodie looked up at the huge mansion. It did little to make her feel better. The windows were boarded, the paint chipped and water pipes leant away from the walls as if they were trying to escape. Ivy clung to nearly every surface, making it look like the creeping vine was trying to hold the building together and stop it crumbling. Huge chimneys strained up to the darkening sky and the steps leading up to the doorway were barely visible through the overgrown grass choked around the edges. But if Brodie narrowed her eyes she thought she could imagine how it might have been once. A posh country hotel before war and industry changed it forever.

'Come on,' said Smithies, leading the way up the front steps to the door. 'Inside!'

'And how are we going to do that exactly?' asked Hunter, taking note of the huge padlock on the door.

Sicknote moved through the group and took the padlock in his hand. Then he delved into his pyjama pocket and produced a key.

'You have a key for an abandoned countryside mansion?' exclaimed Hunter. 'How the egg on toast did you get yourself one of those?'

Even in the growing gloom it was possible to see Sicknote was reddening a little.

13

'GlaxoSmithKline,' said Tusia, suddenly understanding. 'The most well-known healthcare company in the world. I'm guessing Mr Ingham has some inside connections.'

Sicknote twisted the key in the lock. He mumbled something about how of course it was sensible to keep abreast of all the latest medical advances and how connections with a healthcare company was hardly something to be snooty about. Brodie didn't hear it all. She was trying to take in the view inside.

'It's like *Great Expectations*,' she said slowly.

'You what?' Hunter was confused again.

'A story by Dickens. There's a house like this. Totally untouched.' She looked around her. Cobwebs stretched from every surface, softening every edge. Dust carpeted the floor. Everything smelt damp. But an incredible staircase curled its way upwards as if trying to escape the neglect the rest of the house had suffered.

Smithies led the way through the hall to a double doorway to the left. It wasn't locked but rot in the wood had bowed the door, making it difficult to move. Smithies yanked it open and there was a cracking noise like the sound of gunfire. It echoed round the hallway and a startled pigeon flapped its way frantically towards them from a nest it had built in the open fireplace. There were a few moth-eaten sofas positioned around

14

the room, a table littered with papers, and water dripped from the ceiling, puddling on the floor.

'Nice,' said Smithies awkwardly. 'This will do us perfectly.'

Perfect wasn't a word Brodie would have used about Station IX.

'I think it's like camping,' said Tusia cheerily.

'I hate camping,' moaned Hunter.

They'd set up a sort of base in the main room as a quick look round the rest of the ground floor of the building told them the mansion was pretty much uninhabitable. No running water, no electricity and certainly no heating. In fact, even in the room they chose, vines and creepers had shattered much of the glass in the windows, so despite the boarding, cold air rushed in. Tandi attempted to build a fire in the grate after Tusia carefully moved the pigeon's nest outside, but the chimney was so blocked the room filled with thick black smoke and they had to open the front doorway to clear the fog. The fire abandoned, they huddled in blankets brought in from the Matroyska and munched their way through biscuits and crisps Smithies had packed.

'So what do we do now?' said Hunter.

Smithies moved away so he didn't meet his gaze.

'We just sit here till the food runs out?' Hunter added with more than a glint of panic in his eye.

No one seemed very sure how to answer him.

'Sir, I'm sorry to interrupt.' Kerrith Vernan stood in the doorway. She was gripping the door handle so her newly polished nails looked like claws. 'I'm afraid we have a problem.'

The Director leant forward on his leather chair. 'Problem?' This wasn't a word he liked to use.

Kerrith's fingers tightened on the handle. 'With the warning that was sent, sir.'

'Go on.' His jaw was rigid.

'It's about the dragon.'

Friedman and Hunter stood on the steps of the Frythe and stamped their feet against the cold. The rest were inside sleeping.

'Did you let your parents know you were safe?' Friedman asked. 'You don't want them to worry.'

'I rang them,' mumbled Hunter. 'Told them I was fine.'

'And are you fine? You must have been shaken too.'

Hunter bit his lip. 'I'm worried about B,' he said. 'She's flaky, like overcooked pastry, you know. She needs a focus. A story. Something to get her teeth into.'

Friedman stamped his feet again. 'I know just the thing.'

'Please. I don't understand. I did what I was told and . . .'

The guard wasn't in the mood for conversation. 'And I'm just doing the same, mate.'

'But I was following orders and . . .'

The guard pushed the man into the tiny cell, opened the sliding grille and peered through the frame. 'Director's not happy with yer, mate. What can I say? He needs to make you disappear.'

'But I was following orders! Doing what I was told!'

The guard was losing patience. He scowled and slid the grille back into position. There. That was better. Now he could no longer hear anything the prisoner was saying.

He turned the key in the lock and then he walked away.

'This isn't a good idea, Robbie.'

Friedman was holding a book in his hand. 'She needs something. We can't just keep hiding here and not do anything.'

Smithies had his glasses on his forehead. He was concentrating hard. 'But we can't go on with the

17

code after what they've done, can we? Isn't it better we just tell them everything's over? That's what Level Five want.'

'You want us to give up?'

'I want us to be safe.'

'And you think I don't want that? For all of them. For Brodie.'

Smithies took his glasses down from his face and rubbed the lenses on his shirt. He pointed at the book Friedman held. 'But all this will just renew her commitment to the code. It will make her think we believe we should go on.'

'And isn't that what you believe? Despite the danger?'

Smithies said nothing.

'Come on, Jon. If you really thought it was over you'd send them all off, get Fabyan to pay the bank for the house sale, sort somewhere for Brodie and Mr Bray to live and it would all be finished. Instead, you've got us all holed up here. Waiting. What are we waiting for?'

Smithies reset his glasses on his nose. 'We're waiting to be sure,' he said slowly.

'Sure of what?'

'Sure it's safe to go back out there,' he said. 'But it *is* over, Robbie. You know that and I know that.' His shoulders lowered as he walked away. 'I just can't bring myself to tell them yet.'

The Enigma Variations

Brodie stood in front of the bay windows. She'd turned the boarding into a sort of notice-board. Papers were pinned everywhere like ragged curtains.

'OK,' said Friedman, rubbing his hands together and throwing a wink in Hunter's direction. 'You've had two days, Brodie. Forty-eight hours to work. Are you done?'

Brodie grinned. 'Team Veritas recap and introduction to Elgar all ready for you,' she said.

Smithies winced and folded his arms.

'Where's Tusia?' said Tandi.

'Exploring,' groaned Brodie. 'But she said I could start. I can go over things with her later.'

'Fine,' said Friedman. 'OK, Brodie. You've got five minutes.' He clicked a switch on his stopwatch. 'You'll be marked for interesting facts.' He pointed to Hunter, who was holding a piece of chalk poised ready to keep a tally chart on a section of floorboard he'd cleared of dust. 'Off you go. Tell us the story of why we're here.'

Brodie took a deep breath. For just a second she let her hand rest on the locket she wore around her neck. 'MS 408.'

'Which is?'

'An unreadable manuscript we think's written in code.'

'Found where?'

'In Europe. Mondragone Castle in Italy. Hidden in a chest.'

'By?'

'A book collector called Voynich and his friend Van der Essen. Some Belgian professor who travelled with him.'

'And the Professor? Why's he important?'

'Because we think he may've found another book in the castle which was never made public. A code-book to MS 408.'

Hunter marked tallies on the floor. 'And why do we think he found a code-book?'

'Because when there was a fire at the library he worked at, he took one of the books stored there. One book only and hid it in a metal box in a garden.'

Mr Bray tapped the lid of his own metal box resting beside him. 'Even in the middle of a disaster, some important things can be saved,' he said.

Brodie smiled encouragingly before she added, 'But the book from Louvain has never been found.'

'And other attempts to read MS 408?' asked Friedman.

'Have failed because there's no code-book,' said Brodie. 'And because the government doesn't want people to look at MS 408. They've put a D notice on the document.'

'Which means?'

'Which means, "don't touch". Basically.' Her voice trembled. 'It means, leave it alone.'

Friedman glanced down at the stopwatch. 'But we're looking because . . . ?'

'Because Van der Essen left a note with his solicitors to be passed on to a team of code-crackers. The note was a puzzle and we called it the Firebird Code. And when we'd solved it, it led us to the Royal Pavilion in Brighton and to a silver box.'

'Which was?'

'Full of ash,' confirmed Brodie. 'So we thought. Well, it was full of ash. But it wasn't just that. It was a music box. And it played an Elgar tune. So we think the composer Elgar might be important to this whole

21

puzzle. That he might be linked to MS 408.'

'Brilliant,' said Hunter. He added a few more tallies to the floorboard chart.

'So,' said Friedman. 'Elgar's our solution and our lead. The end of the Firebird Code and the beginning to a new search. The music box Van der Essen wanted us to find must be important. Elgar must be important. So, Edward Elgar. What can you tell us about him?'

Brodie looked down to the biography Friedman had given her two days ago.

'Two minutes twenty, BB,' said Hunter, leaning over Friedman's side and reading from the stopwatch. 'Come on!'

'Edward Elgar was born in 1857,' Brodie said, counting off the facts on her fingers. 'He was obsessed with codes. He even named his house "CRAEG LEA" which is an anagram of ELGAR and his initials and his wife and daughter's.' Brodie pointed to a sketch Tusia had made for her pinned to the boarding across the window. 'His daughter was called Carice. That's a mixture of Caroline and Alice, his wife's names. So a coded name. And details. He was into details. Once he wrote in his music that he wanted a clarinet to play "silently" for several bars.'

'Silently,' laughed Hunter. 'OK. What the pickled onion was the point of that?'

22

'Warm-up,' said Brodie. 'Preparation. He knew the clarinet had a big solo coming up and he wanted the clarinet and the player to be warmed up.'

'I like his style,' said Sicknote, fiddling with the travel bands he wore around his wrists. 'It's good to be prepared.'

'Yep. It was all about the detail and all about the code. He even hid codes in his music,' Brodie said, glancing at Friedman for encouragement.

'One and a half minutes,' he urged.

'One day he was daydreaming at his piano,' Brodie ploughed on. 'Playing this melody and his wife overheard.'

'Wives overhear everything,' mumbled Sicknote.

'She liked it so she asked him to play it again. He did, but this time he changed the melody slightly each time he played it. Said each version of the tune matched one of their fourteen friends.'

'So each friend was sort of coded in music?' asked Tandi.

'Exactly. And more than that, he hid something called a theme inside the music.'

'What the bacon sandwich does that mean?'

'The theme's like the message of the music,' Brodie explained, glancing again at her notes. 'People know Elgar wanted the music to have a message because he wrote about that. But no one knows what the overall message was. It's an "enigma".'

'Enigma?' blurted Hunter. 'What's one of them?' His hand was poised above the tally chart.

'A puzzle or code. The piece of music Elgar wrote about his friends is called the *Enigma Variations*.'

'So it's fourteen different versions of a coded message about people he knew?' said Hunter, enjoying the number reference.

'Pretty much.'

'But we don't know what the overall message of the code is?'

'No one does,' said Brodie. 'But maybe the answer's linked with MS 408?'

'Because of the link through the Firebird Code and the music box,' Tandi said.

'So looking at Elgar's music could lead to a code-book for MS 408?' said Hunter.

Brodie ran her hand over the wooden elephant statue brought from Station X and now fastened to the windowsill like a lucky mascot. Her hand slowed as if pierced by the point of the tusk. 'The Firebird Code must mean there's a link. We have to follow it. That's what code-crackers do. Follow links.'

'Anything else?' pressed Friedman. 'You've got thirty seconds.'

Sir Edward Elgar

↳ knighted at Buckingham Palace 5th July 1904

'silent' clarinet = warm up

Caroline Alice - his wife

Caroline + Alice = Carice

↳ his daughter's name

born 2nd June 1857

*theme = message of the music

E. ELGAR
C (aroline)
A (lice)

→ CRAEG LEA

- Played a melody 14 times
- Each version matches one friend
  ⇓
- Also hid a <u>theme</u>   Enigma

ENIGMA VARIATIONS

. died 23rd February 1934 - said his ghost would be heard whistling on the Malvern Hills, which he loved

his music would still be "out there" →

Brodie glanced at the notes. 'OK. Elgar died in 1934. He reckoned people would hear his ghost whistling when he was gone. Up in the Malvern Hills because he loved them so much when he was alive. He said his music would still be out there.'

'Fabulous,' said Friedman. 'Absolutely fabulous.' He winked again at Hunter. 'Five fact-filled minutes.' He looked down at Hunter's chart. 'Well done, Brodie. I declare you the winner of the very last packet of prawn-flavoured crisps.'

Smithies stood up and moved to the front of the room. His face was blotchy. Pink around the cheeks. He rested his hand on the head of the Jumbo Rush Elephant. 'You did great, Brodie. Really great. But . . .'

'Don't do it, Jon.' Friedman's voice was cracking.

'I'm sorry, Robbie. We can't just sit here and pretend any more.'

'Pretend what?' The packet of crisps crackled in Brodie's hand.

'Pretend everything's all right and we're still trying to break the code. We have to face facts. All of us.' He shuffled his feet on the floor and several of the tally marks smudged and disappeared. 'In all your recap and your details you ignored the one essential point, Brodie. Level Five have tried to kill you. Deliberately and purposefully, tried to destroy you and Hunter and your granddad. And no matter how loud the call of the code and no matter how long we hide ourselves here pretending we're still a team, we have to face facts now.' His feet moved again and this time the tally chart was rubbed clean. 'Our attempts to solve the code have to end now. The risks are too great.'

Brodie opened her mouth to argue. She had no idea what she would say, but this didn't matter because there was suddenly a rumbling noise from above their heads.

It began to snow. At least that's what Brodie thought was happening. Actually great flakes of plaster were falling from the ceiling. There was a straining noise as if the whole of the mansion was like a bow being pulled back to fire an arrow.

Then the ceiling caved in.

As the dust and clouds of plaster cleared it was possible to see why.

Tusia was lying spread-eagled, swathed in debris on a sofa in the corner, wooden struts and ceiling tiles surrounding her as if she was a bird who'd made a nest. Her arms were outstretched and in each hand she held huge squares of cardboard which looked like badly formed wings.

'Whoops,' she groaned. And the sofa heaved beneath

her and collapsed so she fell even lower towards the floor.

When the dust settled it was possible to see that, despite falling through the ceiling, Tusia was smiling.

'Look what I found,' she said. 'Sir Edward Elgar.'

Tusia hadn't actually found Sir Edward Elgar in the upstairs rooms of Station IX. She'd found copies of his music. Two huge records with the entire recordings of the *Enigma Variations*.

'Incredible, don't you think?' Tusia said again, sweeping clods of plaster from her hair.

Brodie privately thought it was more incredible Tusia hadn't died crashing through the ceiling but Tusia seem totally unfazed by the fall, as if she'd been sitting on the sofa all along. 'So come on then. How're we going to play them?'

'Erm, Toots, a little awkward,' Hunter said, taking a large clump of plaster from the top of her head.

'Awkward? Why?'

Brodie could hardly put the words together so they made sense. 'Smithies says we have to admit defeat. Go back to the real world and forget about the code.'

Even from under her coating of plaster dust, Brodie could tell Tusia blazed red with anger. 'But no one was hurt!'

'Not this time,' said Smithies. 'But we've got to face facts. Level Five have got serious now. This isn't a game.'

'We never thought it was,' said Hunter, rubbing at his ankle which Brodie remembered had been injured in his fall in the Pavilion.

'I don't want this to end any more than you do,' Smithies said. 'My wife thinks I'm on tax office business and I can't be gone forever. But if we go back to Station X and carry on with our search we'll be in danger. And I can't do that to you all. I just can't.'

Tusia shook the remaining plaster from her shoulders.

Brodie wanted to argue. To say he was wrong. But she remembered the smell of the fire and the sound of the explosion and . . .

'Let's at least listen to the code,' said Tusia quietly.

'What?'

'Let's listen. To Elgar's music. And then we'll do as you say. But,' she handed the records over to Brodie's granddad, 'we should finish with Elgar's song, don't you think?'

Brodie turned to face her granddad.

'I'll do what I can,' he said.

* * *

The Director was pacing round the room. Kerrith looked down at the ground. He was cross. She was embarrassed.

'We're doing all we can to organise a news blackout. Kill the story before it starts.'

'Sir?'

'Heads will roll for this.'

Kerrith rubbed her neck.

'But there's no sign of them?'

'None, sir.'

The Director stopped his pacing. 'Good.' He thrust his hands deep into his pockets. 'Good. That's good, then.'

'And so . . . ?'

The Director considered the question. He lifted his hands up to his face, pressing his fingers together as if he was praying. 'I think we can relax, Miss Vernan. But to be safe, I'd like to track them. Find out where they are. I need men on the ground. Out there looking. Just to be sure. But they'd have to be incredibly stupid or incredibly brave to continue to look for answers after what we've put them through.'

'Sir.'

'But for now, I guess we can say mission accomplished. Job done.' He laced his fingers through each other. 'As long as the story of the explosion dies, then all is well.'

'I've got it working,' called Mr Bray suddenly from the corner of the room. Sheathed in grime was a long wooden unit. According to Mr Bray, this had been a state-of-the-art music centre in its time, housing a radio and record-player.

'Nice one, Gramps,' said Hunter. 'Knew you'd do it.'

Sicknote gulped again on his inhaler.

'So come on then. Where're these records?'

Tusia handed them over, and Mr Bray slid one from the cardboard sleeve and sat the huge thick black disc on the turntable.

Tandi picked up the record sleeve. 'There's information, look. Explanations of what we'll hear. Just for old time's sake, you should all make notes, don't you think?'

Brodie took the album cover and wiped it with her sleeve. Then she took the notebook and pen Tandi offered. She scanned the writing. 'OK. Fourteen pieces, right? For different friends of Elgar. Each friend's marked with initials.' She skim-read to the bottom of the sleeve. 'Except for Variation XIII. That's just called "Romanza" and labelled with three stars. No one knows who that variation's for, right?'

'No one knows,' confirmed Smithies.

Brodie still couldn't get her head round this idea. A famous composer hiding the identity of someone in a really famous piece of music. It must be an incredibly important secret he was hiding if he didn't let anyone know who the music was for.

Mr Bray lowered the needle down on to the grooved track and there was a scratching noise and then a gentle crackle.

The melody began. It had a haunting feel. As the sound lifted to touch the cobwebs draping the room, Brodie felt she was being carried back in time.

The first variation was dedicated to Elgar's wife, Caroline Alice. Brodie smiled at the photograph in the notes beside the description. The third variation was faster and by the time the seventh variation had begun the music was quite loud. The notes said the seventh variation was named after an architect friend of Elgar's called Troyte. The picture showed a serious-faced man with a moustache very like the one Brodie knew Elgar had. Brodie noticed Tusia scribbling frantically on her notes and in desperation she scrawled the words 'nice moustache' just to show willing. It wasn't until Variation IX that Brodie lowered her pen and really listened.

The notes explained the variation was for Elgar's greatest friend, his music publisher Jaeger. Elgar had called it 'Nimrod'. The picture showed another serious face, although Brodie thought there was a kindness in his eyes.

For a moment the whole mansion was silent.

The sound of violins playing was so gentle, it was barely more than a breath on the air. Then, as if drawing strength from the listeners who waited, the music rose, like a wave in the sea, mounting and rising, pulling water to join with it and surge towards the shore. The music soared and notes of the Firebird filled the air.

It took a while for Brodie to realise she was crying.

The album notes lay on her knees. A photograph of a woman looked up at her but she barely registered the face. The strains of 'Nimrod' were still ringing in her ears. It was the song of the Firebird Box.

Mr Bray slid the record back into the sleeve. No one spoke for a while. It didn't seem appropriate.

Finally, Tusia broke the silence. 'Did you like the dog section?' she asked.

Brodie couldn't hide her surprise. 'The dog section?'

'Variation XI,' said Tusia. 'Dedicated to George Robertson Sinclair, but the notes say it was really written to show Sinclair's bulldog Dan.'

Hunter took the album notes from Tusia's hand.

33

Variations on an Original Theme for orchestra — ("Enigma") Op. 36

1898-1899

Elgar →

This piece is dedicated "to my friends pictured within":

*Each version conveys the person's personality.

I - "C.A.E."

Caroline Alice - Elgar's wife

II - "H.D.S.-P."

·His friend Hew David Steuart-Powell ·A pianist

III - "R.B.T."

Richard Baxter Townshend, author

IV - "W.M.B." ← the shortest variation

William Meath Baker - squire of Hasfield, Gloucestershire

V - "R.P.A."

Richard Penrose Arnold, son of poet Matthew Arnold

VI - "Ysobel"

Isabel Fitton, one of Elgar's viola pupils

VII - "Troyte"
Arthur Troyte Griffith - architect Nice moustache

VIII - "W.N."
Winifred Norbury, Elgar's friend

IX - "Nimrod"
   Augustus J. Jaeger - music editor + Elgar's close
                                                    friend
Nimrod = somebody in the Bible
Variation = story of something that happened to
                                              Elgar + Jaeger?

X - "Dorabella"
Dora Penny - friend.

XI - "G.R.S."
George Robertson Sinclair - organist
   First few bars about his bulldog Dan!!

XII - "B.G.N."
cellist Basil G. Nevinson

XIII - "***"   ?

XIV - "E.D.U."
   Elgar himself!

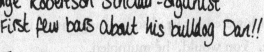

'Elgar was obviously a dumpling short of a hotpot. I mean, I liked the music and everything, but writing sections for dogs is just barking mad.'

Tusia scowled.

'And what about the good bit? You know. Variation IX, written for his best friend Jaeger. You know. The Firebird music.'

'What about it?' Brodie said defensively.

'Well, why did he call that section "Nimrod", when that's not his name?'

'You honestly don't know?' asked Friedman.

'No. It's just fruity, if you ask me.'

Brodie sensed a flicker of compassion sweep across Friedman's face, but she decided not to mention it. 'Anyway, back to Variation XIII,' she said deliberately, 'the one he never explained as belonging to anyone. What'd you think of that?'

'It's a bit over the top,' said Tusia. 'I think it's too soppy.'

Hunter lowered his head so his fringe hung in front of his face. 'You would,' he mumbled.

Smithies stood by the boarded window, his arms folded. 'So, you've heard the *Enigma Variations*. Now what exactly are we to make of them?'

Brodie folded over her notes to hide the phrase about the nice moustache then looked forward earnestly.

'There's two enigmas to the piece really,' Smithies continued, once Sicknote had taken a rather elaborate gulp of his tablets. 'Firstly, there's who is the mystery person hidden by Variation XIII.'

'And the second?' asked Tusia.

'The second's the puzzle of the overall piece. Elgar said there was another theme running across the music. Elgar said the hidden message was the piece's "dark saying" . . . and maybe it was a saying about a code-book . . .' His voice tailed away. 'And if we were going on with this,' he was finding it hard to speak, 'if they hadn't done what they'd done, then—'

Suddenly the air crackled and fizzed and there was a blast of noise from the radiogram. Mr Bray had switched the controls to activate the radio. Sicknote began to groan and rub at his temples, muttering about the imminent onset of a migraine, but Tandi hissed to shut him up. 'Shhhh. It's the news,' she yelped.

The air fizzed again and then a woman's voice in a broad Scottish accent filled the room.

Brodie strained to hear. An increase in road tax. Changes in employment law. Nothing to get excited about. But then . . . 'Shh . . . She's talking about the explosion,' she spluttered.

It was true the woman was talking about an explosion

in a house in the village of Eastdean. Brodie could hardly breathe.

'Reports suggested initially the explosion was suspicious. An ornamental firelighter found at the scene was believed to have been part of an arson plot but the involvement of the decorative dragon has now been ruled out by authorities investigating at the scene. Witness reports claiming to see a ministry car leaving the scene moments before have also been heavily denied. Official spokesmen now claim the explosion was the result of a gas leak.'

Friedman's eyes were wide. 'This is brilliant! Perfect news!'

'What?' Brodie couldn't believe what she was hearing. 'They're saying it was a gas explosion and we know it was Level Five. How's that brilliant?'

Friedman was standing now. He was gesturing at Mr Bray to turn off the radio. The old man nodded and flicked the switch. 'Brodie.' Friedman was speaking softly as if he was talking to a much younger child. 'Of course it wasn't an accident. You know that. We all know that. But this is good. Seriously. This is brilliant news.'

'Why?'

'The dragon and the code and the explosion were all down to Level Five. But they always cover their actions by claiming there was an "accident". That's

38

how they work. Covering what they do. But don't you see? There *were* suspicions. Someone, somewhere slipped up. Made mistakes.'

'What mistakes?'

'The car and the dragon!'

'What?'

'Someone found the dragon. Someone saw a ministry car! People were suspicious and now the story's on the national news. This is big, Brodie, and someone's going to get into big trouble for it.'

'And this is brilliant for us how exactly?'

'It's *national* news, Brodie. They'd never want this much attention. And that gives us time.'

'You think?'

'Of course. They won't risk anything as public for a while. And that has to work for us.'

'So we carry on?'

'Of course.' He looked over at Smithies. 'You have to see that, Jon. Level Five will be twitchy now. Their cover could have been blown and they'll do everything to keep what they do a secret. This could all work in our favour.'

Smithies was rubbing the lenses of his glasses.

'Jon. Come on. You have to admit it. This is our chance to go on. We can go back to Station X.'

Smithies' hands stilled.

'Jon, please say something.'

The air felt charged like just before a storm. Smithies took a deep breath. His eyes sparkled. 'I think we can go back to Station X,' he said.

Kerrith Vernan waited patiently outside the office.

The receptionist looked up from her desk. 'The Director will see you now.'

Kerrith didn't knock as she entered the office. The heels of her boots pressed deep into the carpet. The Director looked up to face her. 'Miss Vernan. Take a seat. Take a seat.'

Kerrith sat upright in the chair in front of him.

'We find ourselves in a bit of a bind, Miss Vernan.' The Director's voice was unnaturally light and airy. 'Seems the team at Station X have waged a little battle against us, and, for the moment at least, it appears they may have won the advantage. We have to be careful, Miss Vernan. Our little warning stunt a few days ago seems to have backfired.'

He ran his thumb across his eyebrow as if smoothing the thoughts in his brain.

'You don't think the explosion will have scared them off, then?'

'It would have done, if incompetents hadn't left a trail. Smithies' team will be laughing at us, Miss

Vernan. They know we'll be weakened by the reports on the news.'

The Director lifted a small, leather-bound folder, tied closed with red ribbon, from the desk. 'You remember this document?' he asked.

He'd shown her the same folder on a previous visit to his office.

'It makes sorry reading, I can tell you. The story of all those who dabbled with MS 408 and came off worse. Dr Levitov, Newbold, Bray.' His smile was broad, as if this part of his story brought him enjoyment. 'More direct action may not be possible for a while, but it doesn't mean we can't continue to attack them. Weaken them where it hurts. I want you and your team to focus on a name which is mentioned in this dossier.'

'Sir?'

'Friedman.'

'The man who made that error in the nineties?'

'The very same. Friedman's brushed dangerously with the code before. In 1992 he was burnt badly in his quest.' There was a note of relish in his voice. 'But it seems he wasn't keen to learn from misadventure.' He twisted the silver cuff link at his wrist. 'I believe Veritas may have drawn him into their little scheme. A foolish move on their behalf. As from now, Robbie

Friedman's fair game. You use all means you can, and I mean all, to bring him down. You take him piece by piece and see to it he's destroyed.'

Kerrith couldn't help but lick her lips.

'Do that and even if they're brave enough to think their little adventure isn't over, Station X will fall like a pack of cards. There's more than one way to bring someone down, Miss Vernan. Our tactics may have changed but it doesn't mean the war is over.'

Variation Thirteen

The advantages of having an American billionaire on your side (even if he was still out of the country sorting paperwork) was, firstly, he could compensate for money lost in a house sale when the building had been blown up and, secondly, increasing security at Station X wasn't a problem.

'Who the chocolate muffin are all these people?' said Hunter as the Matroyska pulled back up the drive to Bletchley Park Mansion.

'Guards,' said Smithies. 'You don't have to worry about them.'

'I'm not worried,' said Hunter. 'I'm just thinking about the queue for lunch.'

Brodie could see Hunter was focusing his gaze on a well-built guard who had a tattoo of a sword on his rather bulging bicep.

'They're here to keep you safe,' laughed Tandi, 'not eat your food. And their cover story is they're working on the museum. A revamp. Timely, I think, as it's now under new ownership. And them being here has another advantage.'

'Oh?'

'Means with the museum staffed by those keeping us safe, we as teachers can concentrate on your lessons.'

'There'll still be lessons?' groaned Tusia, a little too loudly. 'We have Elgar's Enigma code to crack.'

'And I think we all learnt last time, ignoring learning's not the way to ensure secrets are broken.'

Tusia flushed so brightly her face almost matched the scarlet bow in her hair.

'Let's get Mr Bray inside and sorted with some new clothes and a room to stay. Brodie, Hunter, I think you'll find Fabyan has sent you new clothes too to replace those you lost in the explosion. And a few books. He knew what you'd really need.'

Brodie beamed.

'A few hours to settle back into Station X and then meet in Hut 11.'

'So,' said Smithies, who Brodie noticed seemed to be

looking a lot less strained than he had done at Station IX. 'It's about time we started tackling the Enigma.' The light through the window of Hut 11 seemed to make his eyes sparkle. 'We need to know why we've been left a music box which plays Elgar's "Nimrod" as a clue to reading the most mysterious manuscript in the world.'

'That about covers it,' said Tusia.

'Miss Tandari, do you want to remind us what we're dealing with?'

'We've three problems to solve,' she said. 'Firstly, the overall message of the *Enigma Variations*, which has confused people for years. Secondly, the identity of who the thirteenth variation was written for, again a puzzle that's had the best minds guessing. And then, when we've solved those two things we might be clearer about why we've been left a music box.'

Brodie jotted down the three problems in her logbook. She rather wished there was only one to deal with.

'Now I suggest if any of these puzzles is easier to solve, it'll be puzzle number two. Who the thirteenth friend was in the Variations. So,' Tandi rubbed her hands together and her bracelets clinked, 'we start there.'

Brodie bit the end of her pen.

'Someone was hidden in the code of the music. Hidden for a reason. To keep a secret. A secret Elgar took to the grave with him.'

Brodie felt a surge of excitement. Surely people had asked Elgar who the mystery person was. Surely he'd felt tempted to tell them. She couldn't imagine modern famous people keeping a secret as big. So it was obviously a secret worth keeping. Something very important. Brodie felt her heartbeat quicken. Finding out secrets was what being at Station X was all about and it suddenly felt really great to be back.

'OK,' cut in Smithies. 'There's three main candidates for the secret identity. It's obviously a woman, as the piece is called "Romanza" which means Romance. So it has to be someone Elgar was in love with.'

'But Elgar was married,' said Brodie. 'Caroline Alice. I read all about her.'

'And gave a very good introduction to her,' encouraged Hunter, obviously remembering their game at Station IX and Brodie's quick lesson about Elgar's love of coded names.

'Yes.' Smithies held up his hands to stop them. 'Caroline Alice Elgar's one candidate.'

'She obviously loved him loads,' said Brodie, remembering more of what she'd read. 'The book said Caroline Alice was the love of Elgar's life. Apparently,

3 Problems to Solve...

2. The identity of who the 13th Variation was written for.

1. The overall message of the variations.

a hidden theme that is, in Elgar's words, "not played"

and a "dark saying"

* Could be a symbol or literary theme

Some people think the overall message is Shakespeare's 66th Sonnet and the word 'Enigma' stands for the real name of the <u>Dark Lady</u> of the Sonnets.

Here the "dark saying" is a pun on the nursery rhyme Sing a Song of Sixpence: "Four and twenty blackbirds (dark) baked in a pie (π)."

3. Why have we been left a music box?

Another suggested theme is π (as in maths). The first 4 notes of the variations are the scale degrees 3-1-4-2, which correspond to an approximation of π. →?!

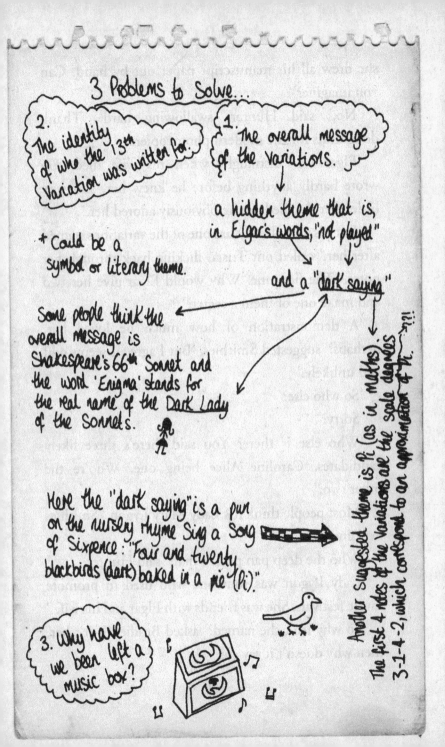

she drew all his manuscript paper out by hand. Can you imagine?'

'No,' said Hunter, swallowing hard. 'Thank doughnuts for the modern photocopier.'

'Elgar was distraught when his wife died. He wrote hardly anything before he knew her, and very little after she died. So he obviously adored her.'

'But his wife already has one of the variations named after her,' called out Tusia, flicking back through her notes. 'The first one. Why would Elgar give her two and make one of them a secret?'

'A demonstration of how much he loved her, perhaps?' suggested Smithies. 'But I agree it seems odd and unlikely.'

'So who else?'

'Sorry?'

'Who else is there? You said there's three likely candidates. Caroline Alice being one. Who're the other two?'

'Most people think it's Lady Mary Lygon,' Smithies explained.

'Who the deep pan pizza's that?' said Hunter.

'Lady Lygon was someone who used to promote music festivals. She was friends with Elgar and his wife.'

'So why isn't she named?' asked Brodie. 'If it's her, then why doesn't it say so?'

'The story is, Lady Lygon was travelling to Australia and Elgar wrote to ask if he could use her initials but she didn't have time to write back. So he used the code of three stars instead.'

Brodie chewed her fingernail. There was something wrong with that suggestion and she was trying to work out what it was. She thought back to Station IX when they'd listened to Elgar's music and an idea began to form like a bubble made of soapsuds. 'That doesn't make sense because of the dog bit.'

'Excuse me?'

'The dog bit. Variation XI.' Brodie was aware everyone was waiting for her to explain. 'If Elgar wrote about a dog and gave it the initials of his friend Sinclair then it doesn't make sense he couldn't use Lady Lygon's initials, even if she didn't give permission. I mean, what could she be offended about? It's a beautiful piece of music after all.'

'Yeah, using your initials to write a piece really about a dog makes more sense to get upset about. B's got a point. And anyway . . .' Hunter paused. 'It's not very code-like, is it?'

'Code-like?'

'Well, you know. It's a bit over the top giving the piece of music a secret name when you're saying it's only because who it was written for didn't bother to reply and say he could use her name. It's just disorganised. Not mysterious. And surely something called *Enigma Variations* has got to be all about the mystery . . . not a mess-up with an unanswered letter.'

Brodie was impressed. 'Yeah, we've got to remember about *hiding* things. That's what connected Van der Essen's book to MS 408. Them being *hidden*. Elgar must've been *hiding* something else or why bother with the code at all?'

'Which leads us to candidate number three,' said Smithies. 'Now here's someone it perhaps makes more sense to hide.' He had a glint in his eye. 'But you know we have to be careful about "perhaps".'

Brodie leant forward eagerly.

'Helen Weaver was an early friend of Elgar's. A *special* friend. Before he met his wife Caroline Alice. Historians skirt over this time in his life. Elgar adored his wife and so talking about another woman he loved before wasn't really the thing to do.'

'People have a habit of ignoring parts of their history which don't fit the view others have of them,' said Miss Tandari quietly. 'But things that are important have a way of working their way out in what we say or do, or the music we make.' She seemed to be lost in her own thoughts. 'It's hard to ignore our past, however hard we try.'

Friedman shuffled awkwardly beside her and looked down at the ground.

Brodie vaguely remembered reading about a Helen Weaver in the book Friedman had given her. She scrabbled in her bag and pulled the book out. She turned to the index and scanned the list of entries. 'Here. Helen Weaver. Here we are.' She read to herself then lifted her eyes from the page. 'They were engaged!'

'Engaged?'

'Yep. Engaged to be married. Helen and Elgar spent two wonderful weeks together in Leipzig and then according to this,' went on Brodie, keenly scanning the pages of the book, 'after two weeks away, Helen left him.' Brodie waited to let her words register. 'She ran off to New Zealand.'

Sicknote pulled hard at the chain connecting his mug to the radiator and leant forward so he could hear more clearly. Even Tusia sat forward in her chair.

'I don't think it's actually possible to run to New Zealand from England, BB.'

Brodie scowled. 'No. She didn't run. She sailed. Across the sea.'

Tusia flicked through her notes. 'It sounded like the sea.'

'You what?'

'Variation XIII. I thought the music sounded like the sea.'

Smithies looked so proud he was fit to burst. 'See, Oscar. Yet again they prove how brilliant they are.' He turned through his own notes in front of him. 'It sounded like the sea and that's deliberate. Elgar actually hid a tiny piece played by a solo clarinet written by another musician called Felix Mendelssohn in the middle of Variation XIII. Mendelssohn's piece was all about a journey across a sea.'

'So you think Helen Weaver's the most likely candidate to be the mystery person?' said Brodie. 'Because Elgar loved her once and she travelled over the sea to New Zealand.'

'It sounds like her contribution to Elgar's life was before much of his music,' said Granddad. 'Maybe he wanted to acknowledge the time they shared. Just because something happened a long time ago, doesn't mean it's not important. Maybe's there a reason Helen was still important to him.'

'Or perhaps there's a secret they shared?' suggested Hunter. 'I mean, going off to New Zealand seems pretty drastic, don't you think?'

'Even if you aren't aware of the damage you could do to the planet with all that travel,' added Tusia quietly. 'I mean, it's a bit extreme. Wonder what drove her to New Zealand of all places.'

'Hold on,' said Hunter quietly. 'Isn't it too easy? People have been struggling over who Three Stars is for years. It can't be that simple.'

'What about a secret right under your very nose? The very best type,' laughed Brodie, quoting Smithies when he'd explained how the Code and Cipher School would work inside the museum.

'Maybe you're right,' said Smithies. 'Perhaps it's Helen Weaver, his lost love. It makes sense historians forgot to think about Elgar's past and focused only on the friends he had in his present. An easy but dangerous mistake. But we mustn't ignore that Lady Lygon was away overseas when Elgar supposedly asked permission to use her initials, so that could explain the sea reference hidden in the piece. So *maybe* it's her. And of course it *could* be his wife just because Elgar loved her so much he wanted to include her twice.' Smithies flexed his fingers. 'What I need you to do is give it more thought. Three women. Three possibilities. We have to narrow it down if we're going to move on.'

'We need to find a link which can't be argued out of,' said Miss Tandari. 'Something about one of these three women which makes so much sense their argument drowns out all the others. Only if we find

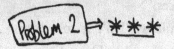

Problem 2 → ✱✱✱

- Caroline Alice → already has Variation I.

- Lady Mary Lygon → most people think ✱✱✱ is her.
  ↳ friends with Elgar + Caroline
  → didn't reply to Elgar about using her initials
  so he used ✱✱✱ ?

  ✱ She was on her way...
  to Australia

  ⇓
  BUT not using her initials doesn't
  make sense → Dan the bulldog!

Also not very mysterious → no hiding

- Helen Weaver
  ↳ engaged to Elgar!
  but she left him and went by boat to New Zealand

In ✱✱✱ Elgar included a solo clarinet
quote from Felix Mendelssohn's concert
overture <u>Calm Seas and Prosperous Voyage</u>

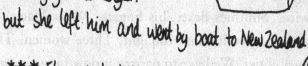

} link to Helen's journey abroad?

We need to find a
link that can't be
argued with!

that sort of link will we know who's hiding behind the three stars.'

Nothing too hard then, thought Brodie. Nothing too hard at all.

'Are you sure this is legal?'

'Of course this isn't legal.' Kerrith frowned at the man beside her, drawing her lips into a thin pursed line. 'But it *is* our orders.'

She was outside the flat, with a locksmith knelt in front of her, trying to pick the lock.

Kerrith looked at her watch. 'Will this take you much longer?'

The locksmith sniffed and wiped his nose on his sleeve. 'It'll take just as long as it takes,' he said, a golden tooth glinting in his lopsided grin, before turning once more to the lock.

Seven minutes later the door opened. Kerrith narrowed her lips again and then folded a wodge of notes carefully into the locksmith's hands. 'You tell no one. Absolutely no one. You understand?'

The locksmith flashed his toothy smile again and pocketed the cash.

Kerrith wiped her hands together disdainfully then pushed open the door.

The flat wasn't large. Curtains hung closed at the

windows so the whole space shone with a soft sepia glow. It was sparse, barely decorated – a few nondescript paintings on the walls – no ornaments, no TV, no computer. The bedroom uncluttered. A made bed covered with a simple duvet. Empty wardrobes. No mirrors. The kitchen bare too, the cupboards empty except for a few packets of Cup a Soup and an unopened packet of digestive biscuits. The oven looked unused.

Kerrith ran her fingernail across the work surface. Nothing. The place told her nothing.

Suddenly a voice broke the silence. 'Ma'am. Look at this.'

Kerrith hurried out into the hallway.

A spring-loaded ladder suspended from an open hatchway led to a loft space above.

'This better be good, Funnell,' Kerrith called as she climbed tentatively up the rungs, the heels of her shoes catching precariously on the metal.

'Oh, it is, ma'am. It is.'

When Kerrith reached the loft space it was impossible not to gasp.

The area opened out into a makeshift office. A large oak desk sat under a Velux window. Across the desk were scattered pictures and sketches, notebooks and folders. Stacked beside the desk were box files meticulously labelled on the spines, and hanging from and tacked to every beam and strut of the void were photographs and notes.

Kerrith folded her arms. 'It's good, Funnell. Bring it all in.'

'Ma'am?'

'I said, bring it all in. Every scrap of notes and writings. Box it all up and bring it back to the Chamber.'

'Everything, ma'am?'

Kerrith turned again to the ladder. 'Every single thing.'

'I'm going for his wife,' said Hunter. 'Nice and simple. Two songs because he loved her.'

'I'm going for Lady Lygon,' said Tusia. 'Some silly slip-up because he forgot to get permission to use her name and everyone's been driven mad ever since thinking there's a secret conspiracy. And you?'

'I'll have to take Helen Weaver, then.' Brodie grinned. 'The lost love. It makes the best story.'

'So,' said Hunter, kicking off his shoes and dabbling his toes in the water of the lake. 'How you gonna narrow it down?'

Brodie sat up from where she'd been lying on the grass and scowled at him. 'Me?'

'Yep, you, BB. My argument's sorted. Undying love

for his wife and all that. Until you show me otherwise, I'm going with that idea.' And he leant back on the grass with his hands behind his head and closed his eyes.

Brodie wasn't impressed. But it was a challenge. And challenges were her thing and so part of her leapt up and seized the challenge tight.

It was a shame then, after all her enthusiasm, she couldn't find much in the history books about Helen Weaver.

'It's got to be something to do with why she went away,' said Brodie, helping herself to a slice of toast at breakfast.

'Why?' said Hunter, now on to his seventh slice.

'There must be a reason she needed to go halfway round the world after she broke up with him.'

'Probably just cos Elgar met my girl Caroline Alice and there was no competition,' Hunter spluttered, wiping marmalade from his T-shirt. 'What?'

'You're really just so uncivilised,' moaned Tusia.

'That's what Caroline Alice's parents said about Elgar,' said Brodie. 'They thought she was marrying beneath them.'

'Cheek!' said Hunter, reaching for his eighth slice. 'Poor bloke.'

'Poor bloke to have Helen Weaver walk out on him's

what I say. But why go as far as New Zealand?' Brodie sighed. 'The books say she was recovering from TB but New Zealand would hardly be the place to go to get better.'

'Why?'

'It's so far away! Would you want to go all that way if you were really ill? Bouncing around in a boat sailing halfway across the world. If she wanted to go abroad, she could have gone somewhere closer. Like Europe.'

'You OK, B?'

'She travelled before, didn't she? Before she left him. They were together for two wonderful weeks somewhere.' She put the toast down. 'Where was that?'

'Leipzig.'

Tusia glared at Hunter. 'Cover your mouth.'

'What?'

'Cover your mouth.'

'What, all the time? That's a bit drastic, Toots, even for you.'

'I mean when you sneeze.'

Hunter rolled his eyes. 'I didn't sneeze. I said *Leipzig*. It's in Germany. It's where Helen and Elgar spent their blissful two weeks.'

'Maybe that's it, then,' said Brodie.

'Leipzig?'

59

Tusia frowned again.

'Maybe it's where they went *together* over the sea, not where she went when she left him that's important. What do we know about Leipzig?'

The silence which greeted her question suggested the answer was not very much.

'I don't know why we're doing this,' groaned Tusia, dragging the encyclopaedia from the library. 'It's only you who thinks the mystery woman is Helen Weaver.'

Brodie opened the encyclopaedia and propped it on the grass. 'It's called teamwork. It's important. Remember.' She was sure Tusia was making a face but she ignored it. 'OK, Leipzig. What's so special about you?' Brodie flicked through the pages till she found the right section.

There was a large picture of the town crest stamped on the top of the page. A shield with a yellow griffin, stretched and looking rather angry. Brodie made a quick sketch in her logbook. Miss Tandari said they had to work like bloodhounds, collect every scrap of information, and that's what she was going to do. 'OK. So why would Elgar bring Helen here?' she said, scanning the notes on the town.

Tusia ran her fingertip across the text. 'Seems there's

a good musical history in Leipzig. It's got a musical conservatoire.'

'What's one of them?' asked Hunter.

'Like a music school. Bit posh.'

Brodie scanned the page. 'It was set up by Felix Mendelssohn. He was—'

Hunter had sat up straight, hand raised. 'Who?'

Brodie read the name again. 'Felix Mendelssohn. Why?'

'I never forget a name.' Hunter got to his knees.

'And this name's important, why?' Brodie was trying to follow where this was going.

'Variation XIII!'

'Yes, that *is* the problem we're working on,' groaned Tusia. 'The identity of the person Elgar wrote Variation XIII for. Keep up, Hunter.'

'It's you who's not keeping up,' he growled, snatching for Brodie's notebook. 'The sea bit. The hidden music in Variation XIII. The clarinet solo. Remember who wrote that?'

Brodie grabbed her notes back and turned to the page. 'Felix Mendelssohn,' she said quietly.

Tusia flicked through the encyclopaedia. 'There's loads of statues of this guy, look. All over the town. Felix Mendelssohn must've been very important to Leipzig.'

Brodie looked down at the photos. 'So now he's important to us,' she said. 'Because he's the link we needed to make it all make sense. To turn a "maybe" into a "nearly certain".'

Hunter rocked back on his knees and gestured for her to explain.

'Helen Weaver is the person hidden by the three stars. It's the links, look. Elgar loved her. But lost her. After they'd been to Leipzig. Something she found out about him sent her halfway round the world. But I reckon Elgar still loved her. He couldn't miss her out if he was writing music about his friends. So he hid her in code. And just to make sure, he put a piece of music in her variation written by Mendelssohn, the guy who was so important to the place Elgar had been to with Helen. And Elgar chose a bit of music written by him all about the sea to connect with Helen travelling to New Zealand. It's all there. All hidden in the music. And he needed to hide it because of how he felt about her. I think Helen Weaver is the one,' she concluded with satisfaction.

'Brilliant,' said Hunter. 'Annoying, because I wanted it to be his poor wife. But brilliant.'

'And Lady Lygon was just a convenient red herring,' said Tusia reluctantly. 'But you're right. The thing about hiding and the connection with Leipzig means

Leipzig

Town Crest ↓

"Leipzig" means "settlement where the Linden trees stand"

· 200Km South of Berlin

· Once a "major centre of learning and culture"

publishing
music

· University founded 1409

· German National Library based here, founded 1912

· City employed "Light Guards" – used to light 700 lanterns across the town
"Light is knowledge"!

· Felix Mendelssohn was named Conductor of the Leipzig Gewandhaus Orchestra
· He concentrated on developing the musical life of Leipzig
· In 1843 he founded a major music school – the Leipzig Conservatory
· Died aged 38 in Leipzig.

Helen Weaver does make the most sense.'

'And makes it the most interesting,' added Hunter. 'You can bet a chocolate cupcake they were hiding something bigger than that they'd once been in love.'

Tandi pushed the newspaper across the table. Sicknote's mug clinked against the chain connecting it to the radiator. 'There's been more takings,' said Tandi.

'Where?'

'Bristol this time.'

Smithies was standing by the window watching as Hunter, Brodie and Tusia collected the pile of books they'd been reading and made their way back towards the door to the mansion.

'So?' Sicknote was speaking as he rummaged in his pyjama pocket.

'We don't panic,' said Smithies.

'And we just wait?' Sicknote spluttered as he slugged down two gulps from his inhaler.

'Perhaps we should make use of our connections, Robbie. Just to be sure.'

Friedman turned away from the window. 'I'll go tonight.'

'So, we've managed to solve the mystery identity behind Variation XIII,' mumbled Tusia, a drawing pin clenched tightly between her lips. 'I reckon that's a pretty good start.'

It was amazing, thought Brodie, how solving a piece of the puzzle could make you feel so good even when you weren't entirely sure how the solution fitted with the other pieces.

Tusia banged her head on the crystal suspended from the ceiling and a pattern of shattered rainbows danced across the ceiling.

'You all right, up there?' Brodie asked nervously, looking up at her friend, who'd insisted on standing on a chair on top of a chest of drawers in order to rearrange the posters on the wall.

Tusia wobbled a little. 'You know I'm fine with heights,' she mumbled. Brodie knew this was true. The first time she'd met Tusia she'd been perched on the mansion roof, hanging tightly to the weather vane. 'Here, pass me that poster,' she said, waving her arm vaguely behind her.

Brodie lifted up the updated version of the International Chess League and passed it up to her. Most of the names listed on the chart were, in Brodie's opinion, unpronounceable, but they seemed to mean something to her friend. A vast web of interconnecting names and links. And it was the links and the lines between them and how they all joined in some vast game she didn't quite understand which made her think Tusia's poster was strangely beautiful.

Hunter hurried from the Apple, Pear and Plum Store, his arms laden with sweets. He stopped when he saw a figure in the shadows.

Friedman stepped out of the dark.

'What you trying to do to me?' Hunter groaned. 'Give me a heart attack?'

Friedman looked down at the towering pile of sweets and chocolate. 'No,' he mumbled. 'Looks like you've got that covered.'

Hunter shrugged. 'Yeah, well. A man's gotta eat.'

'You doing OK?' Friedman said quietly. 'Since the explosion, I mean?'

'Sure. It's all good now we're back here.'

'And Brodie?'

'B's fine. Seriously. You don't need to worry.'

Hunter thought for a moment he saw something like a laugh twitch in Friedman's eyes, but then it was gone.

'I need to go away for a few days,' he said. 'Something I need to do. You'll keep an eye on things, right?'

Hunter's arms were beginning to ache. 'Sure. But Smithies and the others? They'll still be here, won't they?'

'I know. But you're a good friend, Hunter. To the other two, and I just want to be sure, you know?'

'Things will be OK. Now we're back here at Station X, things will be totally fine. You don't need to worry.'

Friedman smiled awkwardly and then he stepped back into the shadows.

The Dark Sayings from the Past

Brodie woke early. Tusia was busy exercising, so Brodie resisted the urge to snuggle back under the covers, and instead reached for the copy of MS 408. She longed for the pages to speak to her, to tell her their secrets, but staring at them long and hard didn't seem to be enough. She snapped the book shut.

The excitement of days earlier when they'd seemed to discover the secret identity of Variation XIII had paled a little and Brodie felt frustrated. There was still so much they needed to know. There was the 'dark saying' or the overall theme of the *Enigma Variations*, whatever that was. And the link to the Firebird Box, if there really was one. Then of course, there were the 240 pages of MS 408 which were still unreadable however hard she looked at them.

Brodie stared up at the chess team league table and narrowed her eyes in concentration. Maybe they should think more about Helen Weaver. If Elgar went to all the trouble of hiding her in code, and she ran away to the other side of the world, then what did she have to hide? What would women in the eighteen hundreds hide? It couldn't be that she loved another man, surely? She'd have told Elgar and he'd hardly have written about her in code. She was ill. They knew that. The books said tuberculosis. But that wouldn't be worth hiding because lots of people in the eighteen hundreds had TB. It was hardly something you hid. Brodie pulled the covers up tight under her nose and traced her finger along the satin edging of the blanket. The weather was too warm for blankets really. Tusia seemed to be able to sleep with no covers on the bed, but Brodie liked her blankets. She liked being secure. Being covered.

The edge of her nail caught on the satin trim and as it did a connection fired in her brain. Cover! Maybe having TB was just a cover. A cover for another illness it *was* important to hide. Or, and Brodie could hardly breathe as she processed the thought, maybe not an illness, but a medical condition. A medical condition even now women might try and hide.

Brodie jumped up from the bed. Tusia flexed her body into a particularly strenuous shoulder stand. 'If you don't mind, Brodie. Calm energy only. Any tension affects my aura.'

'Having a baby,' blurted Brodie, allowing the blanket to fall at her feet. 'Do you reckon Helen Weaver was having a baby and that's why she ran away?'

Tusia lowered her body to the mat with a thud.

'People now often have children when they're not married. But then, in the eighteen hundreds, it would've been terrible. You'd certainly have to hide. I mean, I know New Zealand would be a bit extreme but even so. It makes sense. Helen was going to have a baby so she ran away.'

'Now hold on a moment,' said Tusia, taking a towel and dabbing at her forehead. 'That's what Smithies would call too big a leap.'

Brodie wasn't listening. 'There must be something about Helen Weaver's family we've missed. We need to get to the library.'

Tusia wrapped a caftan around her, but Brodie, having retrieved her shoes, simply hurried out of the room, leading the way towards the mansion.

Hunter was sitting by the lake munching his way through a stack of chocolate digestives. 'Hey, nice nightie, B,' he called, through a mouthful of biscuit.

'She reckons Helen Weaver had a baby and that's the link to the secret Elgar was hiding,' Tusia explained as she hurried to keep up. 'She's possessed.'

'Yeah, well.' Hunter grabbed the tube of biscuits and joined the run. 'Elgar's baby. That's a secret you'd hide.'

It turned out, however, not to be a secret they could prove.

'I was so sure,' moaned Brodie, banging her forehead half-heartedly on the table. 'It makes perfect sense.'

'To you it does,' said Tusia, trying to restack the books they'd taken from the shelves. 'But we can't make leaps without proof.' She closed the largest book. 'Helen married when she got to New Zealand. Someone who worked in a bank. And they had two sons. Nothing here suggests either of them was Elgar's.'

'It was such a good idea, though,' moaned Brodie. 'A secret really worth hiding.'

Tusia lifted the closed book from the pile and slotted it back on the shelf.

Hunter looked down at the still-open encyclopaedia. 'Bit sad this,' he said quietly. 'One of the sons, Kenneth, was killed in the war. Apparently he and his brother came to London and met Elgar. But the dates don't match. Neither can be Elgar's son. They're too young. And this picture of Kenneth doesn't make him look like Elgar anyway.'

'What, cos he hasn't got a weird moustache,' said

71

Tusia, leaning over to look. She narrowed her eyes a little.

Brodie lifted her head from the table. 'What?'

'I don't know. It's probably nothing. But . . .'

'But what?'

Tusia looked embarrassed. 'Look, I'm all for individual looks and everything, but Helen's son. He's got an odd-shaped nose, don't you think? I mean, distinctive looking.'

Brodie stretched across and peered in closer. 'Kind of crooked looking.'

'Crooked and . . .' Tusia chose her next word carefully. 'Familiar.'

'Familiar?'

'I've seen this shape of nose before,' Tusia muttered. 'It's ridiculous. I mean, not the nose shape, but the link if there is one. But it could be the link we need.'

Brodie was standing now. 'How familiar? Who?'

'And it's not just the nose,' went on Tusia. 'It's the eyes. Something about the eyes.' She hurried towards the door, still clutching the open book.

'Erm, where you going? Toots?'

Tusia didn't wait to explain.

Brodie and Hunter followed her like rats following a piper, until they came to Hut 11. Tusia pushed open

the door, flicked on the lights, and ran to the display
board at the back.

She'd stopped in front of a picture which had been
tacked up months before. 'It's him,' she said softly.

With her finger, Tusia sketched the outline of a
crooked nose.

'Potato skins and onions, I don't believe it.' Hunter
lowered his final chunk of biscuit from his lips. 'The
likeness is incredible.'

Brodie looked down again at the picture of Helen
Weaver's son. 'It can't be coincidence,' she said. 'Two
people can't look so alike. Unless . . .'

Tusia finished the sentence for her. 'Unless they're
related,' she said. 'Helen Weaver's son Kenneth, and
this man.'

'Brothers, you think?'

Tusia's face seemed to light up.

'Unbelievable,' Brodie mumbled. 'Helen Weaver. A
woman who's engaged to Elgar and then goes on to be
mother to this man.'

The three of them stood back and stared at the
photograph.

And with smiling eyes, and a somewhat crooked
nose, Professor Leo Van der Essen, the writer of the
Firebird Code, smiled back at them.

* * *

73

Friedman poured extra salt into his portion of chips and grabbed a wooden fork from the container on the counter. He cradled the paper cone and then, catching his reflection in the silver of the deep fat fryer lid, he pulled his hat down tighter across his head.

He walked out of the shop and stopped by the bin.

'So?' The man standing beside him took a large bite from a battered sausage, then placed the sausage into the paper cone on a bed of mushy peas. Friedman had known Les for years. As a cleaner at the Black Chamber, he was his source for inside information. He'd been his link to Smithies and the one who'd persuaded his old friend to meet him in the Greasy Spoon café when he'd discovered Van der Essen's Firebird Code. He was the only link with the inside he and Smithies could trust.

Les frowned. 'It ain't looking good. They don't seem to be moving on. There've been two raids in the last week, and the missing persons list is growing. Kerrith's still taking part in covert surveillance.' He broke off to eat more of the sausage. 'They've realised there's little they can do to close Station X down. And they're nervy. After the fiasco with the explosion. But . . .' He waited to build the tension. Friedman prodded the chips with the fork. 'They're on to you, mate.' He sniffed and gulped the rest of the sausage in one.

'What d'you mean?'

'She's had box loads of clobber delivered to her office. No idea what it all is. But I get the sense they're gonna make it personal, mate. They're digging deep.'

Friedman moved the fork across the chips as if he were stirring them.

'Look at what they've done in the past. They'll want to weaken your team whichever way they can.' He sniffed again and dipped a pickled gherkin into the mushy peas before putting the packet down on the bonnet of a nearby parked car. 'Look, I found this.'

He handed over a sheet of paper listing all the names of those at Bletchley.

'And this too.' He took from his pocket a small grainy photograph of three children standing together in front of what appeared to be a garden shed.

Friedman's heart lurched. He recognised himself and a younger Smithies. And he recognised her. Alex. Brodie's mum. And he knew who'd taken the photograph.

'I'd lie low for a while, mate,' continued Les, returning to his chips and mushy peas after wiping a rather obvious fat stain from the bonnet of the car with his sleeve. 'That Kerrith's a piece of work. She's not letting go of things at Station X.'

'But there's heightened security. The best money can buy.'

Les rubbed his greasy fingers together. 'There's some things you just can't protect yourself against though, ain't there? The truth for one, I mean.'

Friedman ran his finger along the inside of his collar. Suddenly he had no appetite left for finishing his chips.

Smithies called an extra meeting, after allowing time for Brodie to change out of her nightie, and Tusia's discovery was shared with the team. Brodie was sad Friedman wasn't back to hear what they'd found out. She was somehow sure he'd be particularly proud. Of course they couldn't be entirely certain of the link, but the physical evidence seemed so real everyone decided it was too important to ignore.

Brodie felt good. A bit like someone at a fairground banging a hammer again and again, hoping to make a weight shoot up and ring a bell. Maybe they were getting nearer. Bit by bit, the truth was getting closer. It was strange then, after feeling so excited by the discovery, the feeling began to fade and was replaced by a nagging worry.

She tried to clear her head by going for a walk beside the lake. Hunter had gone to the Apple, Pear and Plum Store to stock up on tuck supplies. Tusia was supervising this time. Brodie left her order for flying saucer sweets and Polos with them, then made her way round the edge of the lake to watch the fountain, spluttering and belching water in great looping arcs across the sky.

She'd sat in the same spot a few months ago trying to make sense of the Firebird Code. It seemed odd she'd felt depressed then because the Study Group wasn't making progress and today she felt bad because they were.

The sun was climbing in the sky before she noticed Granddad walking along the path to join her. 'Can I?' he said, gesturing down at the ground.

She shuffled to make room for him.

'No. I really mean, can I? Do you think I'll get down there?'

It wasn't the getting down that'd be a problem, she knew. It'd be the getting up.

He sat and tapped her knee. 'You OK?' he said.

The wind made ripples on the lake, making her shiver.

'I'm family, Brodie. You don't have to hide things from me.'

She tugged a blade of grass from the ground and twisted it round her finger like a ring.

'Come on. Tell your granddad all about it. That's

why I'm here. I mean, that and the fact the house I'd just sold has been blown up. Seriously. What's wrong?'

'I've been thinking about Helen Weaver and Van der Essen. We're all excited because of the connection. The fact they might be related could be a vital piece of the puzzle. It might lead us to an answer.'

'So?'

Brodie tried to sort the muddle in her head. She held tight to the locket. 'I wish I knew more. Not just about the code. But about me,' she said.

'You don't feel connected. Is that it?'

'Yes. No. I don't know.'

'Because you're connected to me.' His eyes seemed very sad. 'Let me fill in the gaps. What d'you want to know?'

She wondered how she could squeeze so much wondering into words to say out loud. 'I just think about my mum and . . . I don't know anything about her. Not really. Not important stuff.'

'What d'you want to know?'

'What she loved?' she said quietly.

'You.'

She tried to laugh. 'Well, what did she hate?'

'Not having answers.'

Brodie steeled herself for the next question. 'Why did she go away and leave me?'

Her grandfather's eyes darkened.

'What was she finding out? What was so important she left me behind?'

'She wanted you to be safe.'

Brodie's hand slid from the locket. 'Granddad,' she said and her voice was merely a whisper. 'There's something else.'

He looked across at the water.

'Whenever I've asked you before you've always found a reason not to answer.'

He pushed furrows into the grass.

'Granddad?'

He shook his head, and awkwardly, he pushed himself to stand, wobbling a little in the light of the sun.

'Granddad, please. You don't even know what I'm going to ask.'

'I know, Brodie,' he said firmly. 'You're going to ask me about your father.'

The question died on her lips.

He looked across at the lake and the waters creased and rippled towards the shore. 'I'm sorry, Brodie. It's just not the time.'

'When, then? When will it be time? If everything we do's about making connections with the past, when will you let me know?'

He didn't answer her as he walked away.

Brodie sat by the lake until the sun was at its highest point in the sky. When she stood up, Friedman was standing behind her.

'You're back. There's so much to tell you and . . .' Her voice stopped in her throat.

Friedman's eyes were shadowed. It looked like he hadn't slept for days.

'You OK?' she said quietly.

He kicked at the ground with his toe. 'Brodie, there's something . . .' He didn't finish his sentence.

Smithies had emerged from the mansion. He glanced at Friedman and Brodie couldn't make sense of his look.

Friedman kicked at the ground again. 'I should go.'

Smithies nodded, then he turned to Brodie and steered her away from the lake.

'Was he OK? Friedman, I mean?'

Smithies seemed to be thinking about how best to answer. 'Amazing thing the mind,' he said authoritatively.

'The mind?' She had no idea where this conversation was going.

'We have, amongst us here,' went on Smithies, 'some of the most incredible minds in the country and yet, it has to be said, some of the most delicate.'

'Hunter's always telling us how many code-crackers go a little mad.'

'Yes, about this issue,' Smithies continued. 'I think your friend Hunter may well be right. He seems so steady. So sure. I guess because his skill, his gift, is dealing with numbers, something for which I feel he believes there's a fair degree of certainty.'

Brodie weighed the idea in her head.

'You, on the other hand. Your strength's story and when the story's a sad one, or a confusing one, then your sense of inner balance gets a little shaken.'

'I guess.'

'I've been watching you,' he said, and his voice was soft. 'I know the explosion and finding out what you did about Level Five and their suspected involvement in your mother's death must have shaken you. But I want to warn you to focus on the present, Brodie. The past helps us with solving clues, but you have to take care.'

'But thinking about Elgar's past made us realise Helen Weaver was the person hidden by Variation XIII. You said we shouldn't ignore the past.'

'Very true,' he said, almost reluctantly. 'But it's a balancing act, like walking a tightrope.'

'It's that dangerous?'

'Sometimes it is, Brodie. Sometimes it really is.

Stray too far from the now into the before and after, and you risk danger. I'd like to take you with me, if you'd be so kind. I've cleared it with your granddad. A small jaunt from the Station. Only a brief visit. Don't worry now, I've asked the kitchen to save us both generous servings of the lasagne.' He clapped his hands together. 'I'd like you to come and meet my wife.'

The burly man with the sword tattoo on his arm cleared the security checks at the gate for them. Brodie felt reassured he was there logging everyone in and out. She was sure no one would argue with *him* if he told them to leave.

They travelled in the Matroyska, the pompoms edging the yellow curtains bouncing against Brodie's shoulders as Smithies drove. At last they stopped round the corner from a line of houses all painted just the same. All the gardens had pots of tamed and carefully manicured flowers. Lace curtains hung at every window. It was, thought Brodie, a very ordinary street.

Smithies glanced down at his watch before stepping out of the van and moving round to open Brodie's door. 'Now please follow my lead with the conversation,' he said. 'No codes, no Elgar, and certainly no Station X or IX.' He tucked his shirt more tightly into his trousers. 'I may talk a lot about the interest rate and tax dodges, but don't let it put you off.'

Brodie felt more than a little nervous.

'It'll be fine,' he said almost confidently. 'Just smile a lot. She'll love you.'

The front door opened and a small rotund woman, wearing a very nice floral pinny and bright yellow Marigold gloves, made her way down the passage to meet them.

'Sarah,' Smithies said in a gentle voice like the one he'd used with Brodie. 'We have a visitor.'

The woman blushed and leant in close to her husband. He whispered something which made her brighten slightly before he added, 'Maybe we could have a tray of tea and biscuits.'

'Supper's at six, tonight,' she said, but the way Smithies looked at her made Brodie think he already knew this. Mrs Smithies reached into the pocket of her pinny and drew out a folded sheet of newsprint which Brodie recognised as the TV pages from the paper. 'We have to be done by seven,' she said nervously. Brodie saw sections of the TV listings had been highlighted in thick yellow pen.

'We will,' he said calmly. 'Brodie's only visiting.'

Mrs Smithies hurried off to the kitchen. Brodie

could hear the clinking of biscuit tins and the boiling of the kettle.

'I wanted to show you something,' Smithies said, glancing briefly towards the door. 'Follow me.'

Brodie walked behind him as he led the way to an upstairs room decorated as a nursery. The walls were pink, edged in lilac, and in the corner was an ornate wooden crib, draped in lace and canopies.

'You have a child?' It seemed a ridiculous question as Smithies and his wife were surely too old to be new parents and she'd never heard him mention any children.

'We had a daughter. Corris. She died when she was very young of something called meningitis. It was tragic and unexpected, and made much worse because Sarah and I'd waited so long for children. We thought for a while we couldn't have them, and then Corris was our precious gift. And then we lost her. My wife never recovered, Brodie. The loss so great she never really emerged from the darkness of that time.'

Brodie turned away from the crib. She couldn't bear to look any more.

'There's no word for it,' Smithies said quietly. 'If you lose a husband or wife then you're a widow or widower. If you lose your parents, then the word's orphan.' He looked away awkwardly. 'But there's no word for if you lose a child. It's not supposed to happen. My wife was a brilliant woman. Had a wonderful future ahead of her. But her mind was ruined by our loss.' He flinched in an effort to compose himself. 'I still love her, of course. But she's not the woman she was. I still believe she'll come back to me. But sometimes waiting exhausts me. What I do, what I'm involved in . . . I can never share with her. But somehow the puzzles and the codes keep me sane – whereas they've taken so many others to the edge of madness. Somehow drowning in the codes and the search blots things out. That's why I love them. For me MS 408's a gift. It helps me strive for something new.' Brodie understood a little of what he meant. 'But Sarah. For her it's different.'

'She knows nothing about Bletchley?'

'She thinks I work in a tax office. Easier that way.'

'Why'd you bring me here?'

'So you can see what can happen. When you're trapped in loss and grief. People cope in different ways.' His eyes narrowed as if wondering if he should go on. 'We've never talked about Oscar,' he said at last. 'His unwillingness to even think about dressing smartly for the day. Or Robbie's need to be alone. Even Tandi and her need to prove herself as a teacher here. But they're all ways of dealing with the pain.'

He allowed time for his words to filter into her mind.

'I know you wonder about your father, Brodie, and about what really happened to your mother, but you have to be careful not to get stuck in your wondering. Your granddad will have his reasons for his secrets, just like I keep secrets to protect my wife. You just have to trust him.'

After a while they left the nursery and Smithies shut the door. Brodie knew not to say any more.

They joined Mrs Smithies for tea and biscuits and she chatted about the weather, and in an odd sort of way, Brodie felt safe. When she stood to leave, the woman hugged her and smiled appreciatively at her husband.

'I'll be back later,' Smithies said, 'in time for supper.'

As they walked back to the Matroyska, Smithies slowed his pace. 'I'd appreciate it if this little visit remains just between us, Brodie. I don't feel the others at Station X need to know.'

'Of course not, sir,' she said, clambering into the seat beside him. 'But, sir. There's just one thing.'

'Go on.'

'Do you have two suppers every day?'

He patted his stomach straining under the confines of his patterned blue shirt. 'I most certainly do,

Brodie. I didn't say secrets were risk free. Just sometimes necessary.'

Smithies shut the door behind him. 'Well?'

Friedman ran his finger inside the line of his collar. He drew a crumpled piece of newspaper from his pocket. 'More raids. York this time.'

Smithies read the newspaper cutting, then lifted his glasses and rested them on his forehead. 'OK. We knew they'd change tactics. Knew Level Five would try and be clever. They've always taken in anyone who looked at MS 408. We know that. It's why everything we've ever done has had to be in secret.'

'But these are night-time raids, Smithies. To people's homes.'

'But we're safe here. The best security protection money can buy. A lot of money.'

Friedman lowered his head.

'There's something else?'

'Les said Kerrith was digging. Wanting to make things personal. If she . . .'

Smithies rested his hand on Friedman's shoulder. 'It will be OK.'

'And what if it's not. What if . . . ?'

Smithies began to pace. 'So what do you suggest?'

'The truth maybe?'

Smithies said nothing.

'She knows about Alex and the Chamber. I just wonder if . . . whether . . . you know . . . whether now's the time.'

Smithies took a deep breath. 'Brodie knows things were complicated. She knows perhaps there's more to say. But do you want to be the one to tell her? Do you really?'

Friedman ran his fingers in deep furrows through his hair.

'She knows all she needs to. And you telling her anything else will destroy her. It will destroy all we're trying to do.'

Friedman clutched at the key around his throat. 'But I could explain . . .'

'You could never explain what happened, Robbie. Never.'

'But I think the Chamber's closing in, Jon. We could be running out of time.'

Smithies took his glasses and twisted them between his fingers. 'So what d'you suggest we do?'

'Leave Station X for a while.'

'Run away?'

'No!' Friedman tugged at his hair. 'Not running away, just keeping ahead of the game. Keeping them guessing.'

'And you think moving away from a place with all this security and going somewhere else is best? For the kids? For the search?'

'I just think perhaps we should keep moving. Jon, please . . .' Friedman hung his head.

Smithies took a deep breath. 'OK. We tell the kids we're following a lead. But nothing else, you understand.'

'Jon . . .'

'Nothing else, Robbie.' He thought for a moment. 'And to be safe, we make use of disinformation. You know what I mean?'

Friedman nodded.

'I'd ask you all,' said Smithies, the next morning over breakfast, 'to go and pack a case of clothes.'

'Are we going home?' blurted Hunter, his voice doing little to hide his concern.

'No. Not home, Hunter.'

'Oh, thank the prawn-flavoured crisps for that,' he quipped.

'No. I'd like you to pack enough clothes for a week. We'll be travelling.'

'To where?'

'Little Malvern.'

'Little where?'

89

'Malvern.'

'Well, who the fluffy marshmallow lives there?'

'Lots of people, I believe, Hunter. Although we're only particularly interested in one of them. And he no longer lives there as he's dead.'

Tusia frowned.

'Little Malvern was the home of one of Britain's most famous composers,' he teased. 'Edward Elgar. So, go and pack your cases for we're off once more in the Matroyska.' He smiled as if determined to cheer himself. 'Elgar's birthplace, here we come.'

Friedman sat by the window of the café, watching the trains. It felt good to be alone. He needed this. Just for a while. He had some thinking to do.

'More coffee?' said Gordon, pot raised in his hand.

Friedman pushed his mug across the table. 'Thanks.'

'Off somewhere good?' Gordon asked as he poured.

Friedman patted the piece of paper on the table beside the mug. The route from Bletchley was marked in thick red pen across the map. 'Should be an adventure,' he said. Then he downed the rest of the drink and made for the door.

5

Nimrod's Song

'Elgar's birthplace museum,' announced Smithies as the Matroyska shuddered to a halt, after a rather hairy journey over the Malvern Hills.

'Now, it's a schoolday,' Miss Tandari said, 'so we need to be as subtle as we can.'

Sicknote sneezed, making a sound like a juggernaut, and Brodie wondered if subtlety would ever really be their strong point.

'Our aim,' Miss Tandari went on, 'is to find out more about the link between Van der Essen and Elgar.'

'And we need to be discreet,' added Friedman, glancing quickly around.

'The man's getting paranoid,' whispered Hunter. 'Seriously. Who's going to be watching us in Little Malvern?'

* * *

The car pulled in close to the kerb. Discarded chip papers crumpled under the tyre. Two suited men stepped out. Neither of them was happy.

'What on earth does she expect us to find here?' said the taller of the two men as he sidestepped a squashed pickled gherkin.

'Connections,' muttered the other. 'It's all about connections. MS 408 and those cronies at Station X. That's what she wants. Links in a chain.'

'A chain on which to hang them all,' laughed the other.

Brodie led the way towards Elgar's cottage. The long garden was filled with heavy cream roses. There was a white wooden front door under an arched porch and four lattice-paned windows.

'It's like a picture off a chocolate-box lid,' said Hunter, knowingly.

'We should split up,' said Smithies. 'Some of us take the Elgar Centre and the Carice Elgar room.' Friedman and all the younger members of the group joined Smithies and made their way into the main part of the museum in the cottage.

They paid at the entrance, where a bicycle, apparently used by Elgar, was propped in the porchway. Then a small, rather shrivelled-looking guide, with an unfortunate stoop, thrust guide books in their hands and suggested that as it wasn't long until closing time they ought to make their way through to Elgar's study which, after all, was the most interesting room in the house.

As they walked they heard the piano.

Rounding the corner, Brodie saw a tall skinny boy seated at the keyboard, his fingers dancing across the keys.

It was beautiful. It was the Firebird music. 'Nimrod'.

Brodie waited for a moment, air catching in her throat until the boy turned to face them.

He lifted his hands.

'Oh, don't stop playing,' Brodie pleaded. She felt the colour blush to the roots of her hair.

'It's fine,' he said, jumping up. 'I was finished anyways and I have to get to work.'

Brodie thought he didn't look old enough for a paper round, let alone a real job.

He bounded over to the wizened guide and hugged her. Brodie was worried she'd snap, but she simply smiled encouragingly. 'Same time tomorrow?' she said, in a giggly voice which sounded as if it should be being used by someone several decades younger.

'Totally.' He hurried down the stairs without turning.

'Who's that?' said Friedman.

The old woman appeared not to hear.

'That boy,' Friedman said again, this time a little more sharply.

'*That boy* is Sheldon Wentworth.' She waited for a moment as if this information should've been enough. 'He lives next door in the Plough Inn. He works there mostly.'

'So he's not at school?' Tusia looked intrigued.

The old lady leant forward, scared perhaps she'd be overheard. 'Sheldon's a bit special, if you know what I mean.'

They didn't really know what she meant, but decided not to push things.

'He's a fan of Elgar, then?' went on Smithies.

'He understands his passion. After all, there's a lot to be a fan of.' She seemed to remember then, what she was there to do, and started showing them things Elgar used to own, like an old gramophone, a battered set of golf clubs and some tatty cycling maps.

'You wouldn't happen to have anything here to do with Helen Weaver, would you?' Smithies said hopefully.

The old woman wrinkled her nose. 'No! Edward

Elgar was devoted to his wife and keeping any memorabilia here, to do with the woman who abandoned him, would be totally inappropriate.'

Smithies looked down to the floor. It was getting late and the air was stuffy. 'Let's get back to the Matroyska,' he whispered.

They made their way over to the camper van where Miss Tandari, Sicknote and Granddad were waiting.

'Anything?' asked Sicknote.

'Nothing,' groaned Smithies. 'I'm not sure coming all this way's going to be worth it.'

Miss Tandari tried to look supportive. 'Well, we've had more success,' she said. 'We've found us somewhere to stay.'

'Is it far?' asked Hunter. 'I'm going to die of starvation if we don't eat soon.'

'Right next door,' she said brightly, pointing down the lane. 'And it's called the Plough.'

Mrs Wentworth, the duty manager, showed them all to their rooms and it became clear very quickly she was Sheldon's mother. They worked this out, not because of her name badge, but because of the way she shouted at the boy in words Brodie would have blushed to repeat while she insisted he hurry up with the drinks order the group had placed.

They'd been shown through to a back room which Mrs Wentworth said they could use for their evening meal. Granddad sat in a large, lumpy armchair by the fire and the rest of the group spread themselves around and gave their meal orders. Sheldon, and a waitress called Kitty, hurried backwards and forwards delivering drinks.

'So, your son, then?' ventured Smithies, when the boy had brought the final portions of cheesy chips and pasties. 'He's a bit of a music fan, then?'

'He's lots of things,' Mrs Wentworth said, balancing the tray against her hip. 'Most of them annoying.'

'We saw him at work next door.'

'He ain't working next door. He just wastes his time there when he could be helping out here and bringing in the money.'

Smithies ran his finger around the top of his beer glass, causing it to hum. 'They suggested next door, he's rather an exceptional boy.'

'That's one word for him,' she snapped. 'They called him gifted.' She blurted this word as if it were the most awful of swear-words. 'It's a nightmare. His father cleared off and I don't have the time to deal with him. Not with everything here. He makes a right nuisance of himself at school. Got thrown out of two of them, he has, for not doing as he's told. Bit of a rule breaker.

They put up with him next door. Gives me a break, I guess. They let him play the piano. Waste of space them great big things, if you ask me.' She wiped her face with a tea towel. 'You want ketchup?' She returned fleetingly with a large plastic squeezy bottle of red sauce before rushing back to the kitchen to continue her shouting.

Brodie felt sad. She couldn't understand why Sheldon's mum would want to stop him playing the piano. He was brilliant at it. And he obviously loved it so much. She couldn't imagine how she'd feel if anyone tried to stop her reading.

Suddenly she realised they were all alone again and that Smithies was speaking.

'So, we got a very frosty reception in the main house when we mentioned Helen Weaver. What'd you lot discover?'

'Nothing new,' said Sicknote. 'There's a few pictures over in the Elgar Centre of people who inspired him, but nothing to show a link to Van der Essen.'

Brodie heard a door closing and noticed Sheldon had returned to wipe down the tables.

'Van der Essen,' he said, leaning forward and taking Hunter's plate which had been emptied entirely. 'I've heard of him. Some Belgian bloke. Came to visit Elgar once.'

Smithies lowered his fork to his plate. An awkward silence hung in the air. Smithies glanced across the room at Friedman. 'You've heard of Van der Essen?' he said, directing his gaze now at Sheldon.

'Yeah. There's something over in the house about this Belgian guy and Elgar's long-time friend, Dora Penny. Some meeting they had.'

'Dora who?'

'Dora Penny. I know. It's a bonkers name. But loads of people have heard about Dora Penny.'

'They have?' Smithies' voice was very quiet.

'Sure. She's Dora "Bella". Dora Penny was her real name.'

This answer didn't make things any clearer.

'From Variation X,' added Sheldon.

Brodie had little memory of the tenth variation from the record as it had followed the 'Nimrod' variation which had made her cry.

'And do you know what this meeting between Elgar and Dora and Van der Essen was about, then?' pressed Miss Tandari.

'Suppose it was about the cipher.'

'The cipher?' Brodie could tell Tandi was trying to hide the excitement in her voice. 'You mean the puzzles in his music? The mysteries of the *Enigma Variations*? We're very interested in them.'

'Everyone's interested in them. Anyone who likes puzzles, I mean. The great mystery of the story inside the music and the secret about the unnamed friend.'

Brodie tried not to look too smug. She was sure no one would tell him they believed they'd solved at least the second thing he'd mentioned.

'I'm not knocking an interest in them,' Sheldon added. 'But the real puzzle Elgar left behind, the one people forget and the one really worth spending time on, is the Dorabella Cipher.'

Painful expectation hung on the air.

'An unreadable message left all in code. I reckon if you find one of them then you've got to work out what it says.'

Brodie looked round the room. Everyone seemed to be wearing the sort of look she'd only really seen once before at a funeral, when no one knew quite what to say for the best and was so worried they'd say the wrong thing, they said nothing at all and furrowed their brows into deep thoughtful creases. She could feel the tension; heavy, like just before a storm breaks.

'He's our way in,' said Friedman after Sheldon had at last left the room.

'Our what?'

'He's our way of finding out more.'

'But he's an outsider.'

This seemed to make Friedman bristle. 'Haven't we all been one of them? I reckon the boy might have answers. He knows loads about Elgar. He knew about a cipher. I reckon we ask him to help us.'

'How can we, without letting him know why we're interested?' said Miss Tandari.

'We can't,' said Friedman, glancing towards the window. 'It's a risk, I know.'

'But he's just a boy. Working in a kitchen.'

'Who knows things we don't. We haven't got all the time in the world. I say we need all the help we can get.'

'But the kid's a rule breaker, his own mum said so,' pleaded Sicknote.

'And that's just what we need!' said Friedman. 'Someone prepared to break the rules to break the code.'

6

A Friend called Dorabella

'OK. I can't really believe we're doing this,' said
Smithies, shutting the door to the back room and
leaning for a moment against it. 'But one thing we've
learnt in the last few months is if we want to get
answers then we need to take risks.' He smoothed
his tie once more against his belly. 'You seem a likeable
lad, Sheldon.'

'I've been excluded from school! My father walked
out and my mother can't stand me!'

'Seems clear to me, you've been misunderstood. You
obviously have amazing musical talent and perhaps
that's not being put to the best use.' Smithies looked to
Friedman for confirmation. 'I must explain the
information I'm going to share with you is highly
classified. I'd ask you repeat nothing I say to anyone.'

'How do you know you can trust me?'

'We don't.' He coughed nervously into his hand. 'We're all involved in a project. A secret-breaking project. The school thing's a bit of a front. Anyway, our efforts have served us quite well so far, and we believe we've found a link between a code we were working on and Elgar. We want to make you a proposition. We have a bit of a musical secret. Something to do with Elgar we're sure would fascinate you. And you seem like the type of person who's up for a challenge.' Brodie was sure he glanced in the direction of the kitchen. 'We'd like to offer you a deal. Bring us anything you can on Elgar, Van der Essen and Dorabella and we'll let you in on an incredible mystery.'

'There's nothing here. We're wasting our time.'

The man with the pointed shoes turned his back on the chip shop.

'She told us to keep an eye on things.'

'It was a meeting with a cleaner. Someone must have heard something.'

'Well, nothing worth knowing.'

The taller of the two kicked a discarded chip wrapping. 'Any other leads?'

The other man didn't answer.

They walked in silence back to the car. As they

pulled away from the kerb, one of the men was suddenly aware of a buzzing noise coming from his jacket pocket. He slid his mobile from its case. The screen flashed red. 'Brilliant.' He grinned. 'He has something for us.'

It was dark. Brodie was cold. They'd been sitting in the back room of the Plough for hours. It seemed clear to everyone, Sheldon wasn't going to come.

'We set a test,' said Smithies, 'like the test we gave to you, and we have to face the fact, he's failed. If it was easy, then none of us would be here. We can't blame the boy. He's just not interested, that's all.'

The door clicked open. 'Oh, I'm interested,' said a voice.

Light flooded into the room from the corridor. Sheldon stood framed in the light. 'Here,' he said quietly. 'I think these are the things you're wanting to see.'

He unwrapped a small bundle and passed to Brodie a battered photograph in a scuffed walnut frame.

The photograph showed Elgar, complete with his generous moustache, standing with Van der Essen, recognisable because of his crooked nose and unruly hair. In the middle of the two men stood a young woman who was grinning. The caption below read, 'Sir

Edward Elgar with his close friend Dora Penny with visiting Belgian Professor Leo Van der Essen. 1913.'

'Brilliant,' said Friedman. 'Tell us all you know about this photo.'

Sheldon began to explain. 'Elgar liked having people to visit. Liked having his photo taken too. Even had his photo taken on his death-bed.'

'Seriously?' said Tusia.

'He really did. But this photo's weird.'

'What, weirder than a picture of a bloke just about to die?' said Hunter.

'Sort of.' Sheldon was relishing the chance to share. 'Weird thing about this photo is he thought he was dying at the time. Said so in his diaries. He was always being ill and moaning, so the odd thing's not really the photo but that he dragged himself out of bed to meet this visitor. And that he wanted a photo taken.'

'And we know this from his diaries?' said Friedman.

'Yep. He must've had very important business with the Professor to get him out of his sick bed.'

Sicknote muttered something about how difficult it was to be a martyr to your health and how every day was a challenge.

Brodie cast a knowing glance in Hunter's direction. 'He'd make an effort to see Helen Weaver's son though, wouldn't he? However ill he was.'

'Course. The history books say Elgar met both Helen's sons and there he is, bold as a bagel, with Van der Essen. Surely we're right about Van der Essen being Helen's son.'

Brodie peered closer. The connection was there, frozen on film. Elgar and the son of a girl he'd loved years before. A man who'd gone on to write the Firebird Code.

'Helen Weaver?' said Sheldon. 'The girl who left him? You reckon Van der Essen is Helen's son.'

Brodie looked across the room at Smithies. 'Yep. And we reckon Helen Weaver was the unnamed friend in the *Enigma Variations*.'

Sheldon looked surprised. 'Really?'

'We'll go over that all later,' said Friedman, obviously anxious to get on. 'We need you to tell us if you've any idea what the meeting was about.'

'No idea at all. Important enough to photograph and stick in a frame, so I guess it was something big.'

Brodie considered Sheldon's argument. Was it bigger than meeting up with the son of a long-lost love? Couldn't it have been just that? But why was there someone else in the photo? The third person. Why include her?

'This woman,' said Brodie. 'She's the one you called Dorabella? From the *Enigma Variations*? Do you know why she's there? I mean, here at this meeting?'

Sheldon raised his eyebrows. 'Dora was a family friend. She was around a lot. But why she's in this particular photo, I'm not sure.'

'But she was important enough for Elgar to write one of his variations for. So Elgar cared for her?'

'Elgar had lots of friends. But she must have been special because he wrote the Dorabella Cipher for her.'

Excitement fizzed in Brodie's blood.

'About that,' said Smithies, keeping his voice light in an obvious attempt not to sound too keen. 'You said you might be able to tell us about this cipher?'

'Elgar wrote Dora a note completely in code,' explained Sheldon. 'I don't think anyone's ever been able to read it. Do you want to see it?'

'Should you serve fried onions with a burger? Is Rocky Road ice cream better than vanilla?' spluttered Hunter. '*Of course* we'd like to see it.'

Sheldon took out another frame from the half-unwrapped bundle. On the framed piece of paper were three short lines of writing. A series of linked semicircular squiggles in place of letters. It was signed at the bottom, with a date which looked like 1497.

Tusia began to make a quick sketch of the cipher.

'Story goes,' went on Sheldon, passing the framed letter around, 'Elgar sent this to Dora in July 1897.'

'But it says 1497,' cut in Hunter.

'I guess it's part of the cipher,' suggested Sheldon. 'It wasn't sent secretly. Just tucked inside a letter from Elgar's wife to Dora's stepmother. But Elgar wrote "for Miss Penny" on the back so we know it was for Dora.'

'And people have tried to work out what the cipher says?' asked Miss Tandari.

'Yep. Even Dora couldn't. She asked Elgar to tell her, but he just said she, of all people, should've known. He died without telling anyone at all the secret of whatever he'd said with those eighty-seven symbols.'

'Eighty-eight symbols actually,' said Hunter. 'If you count the weird dot next to the fifth shape in the third row. That looks pretty deliberate to me.'

'OK, eighty-eight. If you want to be precise.'

'Do you think Van der Essen knew about the coded

message?' asked Brodie, thinking back to the photograph of the three of them. 'Maybe he knew how to read the squiggles. If the three of them met. Maybe he was in on the secret.'

'Yeah. Van der Essen loved puzzles,' added Tusia. 'Elgar could've told him how the weird writing worked.'

'Or,' said Sicknote pragmatically, 'he could've said absolutely nothing about it. Van der Essen could've just popped round for a cuppa tea, had a slice of cake and had his photo taken, caught Elgar up to date with how his poor old mum, Helen Weaver, was and then left.'

Hunter frowned. 'Are you sure there's no other clues?'

'I've found something else weird,' said Sheldon.

'What, more notes written in loops and semicircles?' asked Brodie.

'Not in the same squiggles, no. But I've found notes.'

'Excuse me?'

'Musical notes. I mean notes *in* notes. It's the last thing I've brought. Here.'

He took a folded letter from the bundle and passed it round. The letter was dated 1901, again addressed to Dora. It began in normal writing but then Elgar had sketched the lines of a musical stave and finished the letter with musical notes.

Whether you are as nice as

or only as unideal as

'Elgar was kinda complicated,' said Sheldon. 'He sort of mixed up music and letters of the alphabet like no one else ever did. If things happened to him he wrote about them in words *and* music. He was in Cornwall once and wrote a piece of music and put the word "Tintagel" over it. That's the place in Cornwall. When he wrote music about the crucifixion he had Jesus's words written over the music but he never wanted them to be sung. It's like for him musical notes and letters could be swapped around to mean the same thing. He mixed up words and musical notes in his head. When he wrote to Dora, it seemed OK to swap musical notes for words.'

'So do you think Van der Essen knew he did that? Wrote other things instead of the alphabet, I mean. Squiggles and musical notes? Maybe Van der Essen made sense of the code even if Dora didn't?'

'Perhaps,' said Smithies, his forehead narrowing into lines. 'But why'd we presume that? You know we have to be careful about making assumptions.'

'We're not presuming. We're just using what we

know,' said Tusia defensively. 'Van der Essen was into codes. We know that. He wrote the Firebird Code. Elgar was into codes. We know that. He wrote the Dorabella Cipher. Maybe, and it's only a maybe, the two men talked. Maybe, Van der Essen told Elgar his plan to write a code and Elgar explained his funny squiggles to Van der Essen.'

Hunter folded his arms. 'Doesn't work.'

'What do you mean? Doesn't work?'

'It doesn't work, Toots. That theory. It doesn't make sense.'

'Why?' Tusia snapped.

'The dates. Elgar met Van der Essen in 1913. It says so under the photo. But Van der Essen didn't have to hide the book *we* think's the code-book for MS 408 until during World War One and that was later. 1914.'

'But,' said Tusia, following Hunter's lead, 'if he found a code-book for MS 408 in Mondragone Castle he'd have found it by the time he met Elgar. Van der Essen went to the castle with Voynich in 1912. So, maybe he had the code-book but didn't need to hide it or write a code to protect it yet. Maybe it's just that when he visited here, Van der Essen picked up ideas he could use in his code when he needed to.'

'Makes sense,' interrupted Brodie. 'Yes it does! Look, it gives Van der Essen time to find the special box to hide the code-book in. And to know about the Dorabella Cipher and get to steer the finders of the Firebird Code towards it.'

Hunter took it up, beginning to pace. 'OK. So from the beginning . . . Van der Essen and Voynich find two books. One in code. One to be used to read the code. That's in 1912. In 1913 Van der Essen meets his mum's ex-boyfriend, Elgar. They chat. They have their photo taken with Dora and Elgar explains his coded writing to Van der Essen. The Professor likes the idea. War's getting close so he makes plans to hide his code-book. He writes a puzzle which leads us to Elgar and hides a music box which plays some of Elgar's music.'

'The music box is like a back-up plan,' said Brodie. 'Another clue in case the code-book inside was damaged. So we'd still get to Elgar and maybe whatever they talked about when they had that photo taken.'

Miss Tandari rubbed her eyes. 'It could just have been a box though. Given by Elgar as a pressie, or just bought by Van der Essen to hide the code-book in. Remember, it was in the middle of the war. Van der Essen wouldn't have had long to choose something as a hiding-place. Maybe that's all it was. Somewhere convenient.'

A heaviness spread across the room. Tusia's brow was knitted tight in concentration. 'But the box was moved, remember. The box full of ash was dug up and hidden in the Royal Pavilion. Even when whatever was inside the box had burnt, the box was still important enough to hide and write a code about.'

Brodie's head was thumping. 'So there *is* a link between Elgar and Van der Essen. It's connecting Dorabella that's the problem. Dora Penny and her funny squiggled code? Why her? How does she fit in with all of this?'

Friedman lowered his voice. 'Supposing we go with the idea Elgar explained his squiggled code to Van der Essen? Maybe he gave the music box to Van der Essen. The Professor hid it and that was supposed to lead the finders to the Dorabella Cipher. Perhaps even with the codebook destroyed there's something in the Dorabella Cipher to help with the reading of MS 408.'

Granddad folded his arms. 'Bit of a giant leap, isn't it? Saying the Firebird Code must lead us to the Dorabella Cipher.'

'It *would* be a leap if there wasn't the photo of the link,' urged Smithies. 'Van der Essen and Elgar and Dorabella. *The three of them together.* We'll keep going round in circles unless we go forward with the idea they might be connected.'

Sheldon stepped forward and raised his hands. 'I think it's time,' he said forcefully.

'For what?' said Brodie.

'Time you let me try and make sense of what you lot are talking about. You've been going on and on about Van der Essen and Dorabella and Elgar. And I've listened and I've tried to keep up. Really I have. But the only way I'm going to have a clue what you're talking about is if you let me know what it is.'

'What *what* is?' said Hunter.

'This Firebird you keep going on about. I've done my bit and I've brought you the cipher and the photos and the musical letters. Now I think it's your turn. You'd better tell me about the secret you promised to share.'

'OK,' said Miss Tandari. 'We'll show you.'

The office was small and stuffy. TV monitors showed the mansion from every angle. It was getting dark.

'Here.' The man reached below the desk. He slid a crumpled map towards the two men who waited on the other side. 'It's clearly marked.'

The route stood out in thick red pen. It wound over hills and through towns. It was easy to read.

'You've done very well,' said the second man. He took a wad of folded notes from his inside pocket.

'I'm not interested in your money,' the man behind the desk said.

The two men looked confused.

'This is about something else.'

The two men thought it best not to argue. He wasn't the sort of man you argued with. They took the map, folded it carefully and walked to the car.

There was something comforting about seeing the Firebird Box again. Brodie felt connected. To the Firebird and to those around the room.

Miss Tandari put the box on the table.

Friedman stepped forward and loosened the chain around his neck. Then, almost reluctantly, he handed Smithies the small golden key.

'This box,' explained Smithies, 'is from Van der Essen, the Belgian professor.' Sheldon's eyes widened. 'And it led us here. Listen.'

He used the key to release the secret compartment. Then he pushed the folded piece of paper he carried in his wallet through the jaws of the musical box and turned the handle. The music played.

Sheldon lifted his head and swayed a little. 'Nimrod.'

Smithies allowed the dying strains of the music to evaporate on the air. 'We came here looking for connections. And the photo you showed us makes us think we're on to something. We can't be sure but we think there's a link between this music box and the

Dorabella Cipher. If there *is* a link then we need to know what message is hidden inside the Dorabella Cipher and why Van der Essen wanted us to know it.'

Sheldon's eyes narrowed a little. 'Can you play it again?' he said.

Smithies looked surprised but turned the handle.

The air filled with sound again. And then Sheldon smiled.

'It's too dangerous.'

'It's the only way.' Friedman was almost growling at Sicknote.

'It'd be breaking and entering.'

'Well, we can hardly go over there in the daytime, can we?'

Sheldon said there was something about the Firebird tune. Something important. And to explain he'd need to play the piano. And there was a piano in Elgar's house. So it all made sense. But Sicknote wasn't sure.

It took them half an hour to wear him down.

Kitty the waitress earned extra money by doing a nightly clean at the museum. This was their chance. Sheldon would get them inside. He'd explain to Kitty he wanted to play the piano. She'd believe that. As long as she didn't see them, they'd be fine.

Sadly, this didn't really turn out to be an accurate description.

'You can't come in at this time of night.'

Brodie was hiding behind Elgar's bike and a loose spoke was dangerously close to her left nostril.

'You know us musical types,' blagged Sheldon. 'We just *need* to play.'

Kitty said something rude under her breath. 'I've got a need to be undisturbed. Evie's a taskmaster almost as bad as your mum.'

Brodie doubted this was true although the little old guide had been quite particular about things.

'You better not get in my way,' Kitty said.

Clearly, she wasn't happy as she stormed away from the door, her mop and bucket like weapons in her hands.

Sheldon ushered them inside.

Creeping along the passage was a nightmare. Floorboards creaked and groaned and Sheldon resorted to trying to cover the noise with ridiculously loud singing.

'I've got a job to do,' came a yell. 'Keep it down.'

Sheldon steered them quickly into the music room and leant his back against the door. Sweat was beading on his brow. 'Is everyone OK?'

Brodie thought her heart pulsing in her throat wasn't the best of signs but she didn't say anything.

'You can do this quietly, right?' said Sicknote. They'd been over the plan a hundred times.

'Yes,' said Sheldon. 'All you need to do is listen and compare.' He sat down at the piano and lifted the lid. 'The Firebird,' he said softly. 'First you need to hear it again.'

Miss Tandari took the box from her beaded bag, fed the paper through the slit and turned the handle. And in the half-light the Firebird sang.

Sheldon turned round on the piano stool, lifted his hands and rested them gently on the keys. As the notes from the music box began to fade, his fingers moved gently across the piano, joining his own notes with the tune on the air. 'Do you notice?' he whispered, allowing the strains from the music box and those from the piano to merge.

'Do we notice there's eighty-eight piano keys?' whispered Hunter.

'I tend to play them, not count them,' hissed Sheldon.

'Sorry,' said Brodie. 'Counting's his thing.'

'Weird,' said Sheldon. 'It's not important about the number of keys. What else do you notice?'

'How brilliantly you can play?' mouthed Granddad.

117

'That's very kind,' he blushed, 'but listen.' The notes from the Firebird Box rose and just for a moment the notes from the piano separated from the tune before re-forming to make one tune again.

'There's a slight change,' Sheldon whispered. 'A variation. The tune from the music box's classic "Nimrod" by Elgar. But there's a few notes in the middle section which are different. Here, do you see?'

He moved his hands again, playing first the melody from the music box and then his slightly altered version.

'So what *is* the difference between the two pieces?' said Hunter.

'Dorabella,' smiled Sheldon.

'What?' Brodie urged him to explain.

'The difference is the notes from the Dorabella letter. Not the cipher. The *letter*. Literally. Those musical notes Elgar drew at the end of his letter to her I showed you. They're the difference.'

Brodie wasn't following the argument.

'The tune of the music box is "Nimrod" *and*,' he emphasised this word, 'the tiny fragments of music he added in that really strange letter in 1901. Elgar did it all the time in his musical writing. It's called "quoting". It's where the composer puts other bits of music hidden inside the piece.'

'Like Elgar did with the section by Mendelssohn which led us to make the connection about Leipzig, remember,' said Tusia. 'The bit in Helen Weaver's Variation XIII about a sea journey.'

'So you're saying Elgar "quoted" another piece of music in the middle of the melody from the music box?' whispered Hunter.

'Yep. He's "quoting" the musical notes he added to the end of that letter to Dora Penny.'

Brodie could hardly contain her excitement. 'Dorabella is connected to the Firebird Code. So the *Dorabella Cipher* must be important too.'

It was almost more than they could have hoped for. A real connection. Brodie thought she might burst. Then things juddered to a halt.

'We still have no idea how to read Dorabella's cipher though, do we?' said Tusia despondently. 'We've got a connection. The cipher. But how do we read it?'

'We focus on what the shapes in the cipher could stand for,' said Miss Tandari.

'They look like sheep to me,' said Tusia.

'Oh, very useful,' said Sicknote.

'I'm just saying what I see,' whispered back Tusia.

She'd brought the cipher with her and was running her finger over each loop and arch.

'Look, you're the shape and space expert,' said Sicknote, taking the message from her and holding it up to the light. 'Any better ideas than sheep?'

'To read it, I'd have to know what each shape represents.'

'Obviously,' sniffed Hunter.

'I'd need a Rosetta Stone.'

'A what?'

Miss Tandari hurried to explain. 'In 1799, in a place called Rosetta, a huge ancient Egyptian stone was discovered. No one could read the ancient Egyptian hieroglyphs.'

'As meaningful as these sheep shapes, then,' said Tusia with a determined glare in Sicknote's direction.

'But the beauty of the Rosetta Stone,' went on Miss Tandari, 'was it had other writing on it. One in classical Greek and one in a language called demotic. Scholars who worked out the sections of writing all said the same thing.'

'So if you could read the Greek or the demotic,' said Sicknote, 'you could work out what the hieroglyphs meant.'

'Still took them three years to do it though,' said Smithies.

'So what you're saying,' said Brodie, 'is we need to find something where the meaning of the symbols used in the Dorabella Cipher is translated and then we can read the hidden message.'

'Exactly.'

'So we could look for that while we're here.' She gulped down a nervous breath.

'Now hold on a minute.' Sheldon looked drained of most of his colour. 'You came over to listen to the piano. You didn't say anything about looking around the rest of the house.'

'But it's a chance to look around on our own.'

'You're not on your own,' pleaded Sheldon. 'Kitty's here.'

'She's cleaning.'

'She'll see you.'

'Not if you're careful and you keep playing the piano so she thinks you're in here. Just give us time to check out Elgar's office. All the time you're playing we'll know we're safe. What do you think?'

'I think you're mad.' The colour had returned in patches to Sheldon's cheeks. 'But I think I quite like that.'

7

The Rosetta Stone

The car was making quick time along the motorway. The man in the passenger seat ran his finger along the red line marking the route.

'How much longer?' said the driver.

'An hour. Maybe less.'

'And you're absolutely sure they'll be there?'

'It's all here. Recorded on the map.'

'Perfect. And they'll be unprotected and vulnerable?'

'Absolutely. Just how we like them.'

'Perfect.' He switched on the radio and began to sing. Today was turning out to be a good day after all.

'He never said there was an alarm.'

'We never asked,' hissed Sicknote.

'It's fine,' said Hunter, taking charge. 'We just need

not to panic. There's a countdown clock. We've got a minute. We just have to be logical. I reckon with the size of the alarm we go for eight digits. So that gives us a possible choice of a hundred million combinations.'

'What!' It was impossible to be sure who was doing the most yelping.

'Birthday. Elgar's birthday.'

'What? We have one minute; there's a good chance of being discovered by the cleaner; the alarm has a hundred million combinations and you want to talk about Elgar's birthday!' squealed Tusia.

'The digits, you banana. What are the digits for his birthday?'

'Second of June, 1857,' said Granddad, shuffling forward.

Hunter pressed 02061857 into the keypad on Elgar's office door. Nothing.

'OK. His wife. Let's try his wife's birthday!'

'Ninth of October, 1848,' blurted Sicknote.

'How on earth do you remember that?' gasped Tusia.

'He was much younger than his wife,' said Sicknote. 'It stuck in my mind.'

Hunter bashed away at the keypad. Nothing.

'His daughter then. When was her birthday?' He was getting frantic now.

'No one will know that. This is ridiculous.'

The keyboard was flashing. The countdown clock showed ten seconds.

Brodie held her head in her hands. This couldn't be happening! She slid her hands down her face and stared at a concert leaflet framed on the wall in front of her. 'Enigma,' she yelped.

'What?'

'When it was first performed? The *Enigma Variations*?'

'No one's going to know that one,' squealed Hunter.

Brodie stared at the frame. 'Nineteenth of June, 1899,' she blurted. 'It was in London and . . .'

The rest of the sentence was lost as Hunter tapped in the keys. 19061899. There was a gentle hiss. The flashing light on the countdown clock stopped and the internal door swung open. They were inside.

'Nice one, B,' said Hunter.

She tried to grin but her lips were trembling.

The car pulled into the service station. The driver stocked up on crisps and chocolate. It was a long drive, and why the team from Bletchley would find it necessary to be visiting a museum so far away was totally beyond him. Still. He folded the map over on the dashboard. They were nearly there.

* * *

'OK,' said Smithies, looking at his watch. 'We have to be quick and we have to be careful. All the time we can hear Sheldon playing, we're safe. The piano stops and we're in trouble.'

Brodie didn't want to think about that.

'We need a code-book,' said Hunter. 'Something like a Rosetta Stone where Elgar wrote down what he meant by all those sheep shapes. And we looked round the room before. So it's got to be hidden. In his desk maybe.'

Brodie reached forward and tugged at the drawer. 'Locked,' she groaned.

'That's OK,' said Miss Tandari, drawing a hairpin from her hair.

'You're going to actually break into the desk?' said Sicknote, his voice higher now.

'Looks like we are.' Brodie grinned.

Smithies shut the office door, dragged a chair across the room and propped it against the door handle.

'OK,' said Friedman, taking charge. 'I reckon we should rely on no more than about ten minutes of uninterrupted time. I'd think after ten minutes we'll be pushing our luck, however good Sheldon's little concert is. We need to work methodically and put everything back where we found it to cover our tracks.'

Miss Tandari knelt at the desk, her eyes narrowed as

if she was threading a needle. There was a gentle click and the desk drawer slid open.

Smithies stepped forward appreciatively. 'OK. We look for anything and everything that may act as a way of working out what those semicircles and loops in the Dorabella Cipher mean.'

From outside the strains of piano music were lifting and falling.

Miss Tandari worked on her knees, flicking through the papers in the second drawer, passing sheaves of them to Smithies and Friedman who laid them out and scanned them for clues.

'It'd help if we knew precisely what we need,' mumbled Tusia, working through the bottom drawer of the desk.

'A code-book, obviously. But if that's too much to hope for, then any semicircular symbols in anything else he wrote,' said Brodie. 'If we find he's used them somewhere else, we can work out what they mean.'

'And you don't think people will have tried this before us?'

'Yes.' Brodie knew her voice sounded like the one used by a rather snappy schoolteacher. 'People may have looked for a code-book . . . but I think it'll be cleverer than that. The shapes hidden in something else, like the extra notes hidden in the Firebird music.

That's what we need to find.'

There was a crash from just behind her. 'Sorry.' Sicknote bent down to retrieve the pile of books he'd knocked from the desk. From outside, Sheldon's piano playing faltered a little.

'What are all those?' hissed Hunter as he restacked them.

Tusia looked up. 'Maps,' she said.

'Maps?'

'Yes. You know what a map is? Flat pictures of the ground.'

'OK. Keep the custard in your trifle. I just wondered why a composer would have so many maps, that's all.'

'No idea,' said Smithies, who'd moved to help Tusia restack them. 'This isn't a map though, look,' he said, pulling a small thin volume from between the stack. 'It's a diary. Sheldon said Elgar was a diary keeper.'

'Odd to keep a diary in the middle of all your maps, though, don't you think?' said Tusia. 'And weird to have quite so many of the things in the first place.'

'I know why he had so many maps of the place,' said Friedman. 'Didn't he like to cycle round here? Aren't they all maps of the Malvern Hills?'

Tusia scanned through them. 'Yeah. Makes sense. Cycling maps of places nearby he used to cycle to. Maybe not so odd.'

'So maybe,' said Hunter tentatively, 'if the diary's *with* the maps then perhaps this diary's different to others he kept. Have a look.'

Tusia flicked open the pages. 'Nice idea. But doesn't work. This diary's empty. Not written in at all.'

'What year is it?' asked Brodie.

'1897,' said Tusia, handing it over.

Brodie flicked the pages. 'Hold on,' she said. 'There's writing. Look. Just in one month.'

'Oh, I do that all the time,' said Tusia. 'I start a diary in January and never get up to February.'

'That's not what he's done,' said Brodie. 'Elgar hasn't written anything at the beginning of the diary, just in the middle. In June.'

'June 1897?' asked Hunter.

Brodie looked up. 'Why?'

'That's the month before he sent the cipher to Dorabella.'

'You remember the month he sent the cipher?'

'Obviously, BB.'

Brodie looked more carefully. 'There's entries for every day in June. Except one. June sixteenth. He's simply written "went to a place of rest".'

'And there's no more writing except for that month?'

Brodie flicked backwards and forwards through the pages. 'The last entry's on June twenty-sixth.'

Hunter groaned. 'OK, so all very interesting in a boring sort of way. Anyone found anything else?'

'Mostly photos,' said Miss Tandari, whose hair hid most of her face as she worked. 'Sheldon said he liked having his photo taken.'

'Any of his death-bed scene?' pressed Hunter.

Tusia shot a look of disapproval.

'OK! Only asking!'

'Hey, look. Isn't this Dorabella?' said Miss Tandari, passing the photo round.

Friedman held the photo up to the light of his torch. 'Looks like her to me.'

'And here's another one,' said Miss Tandari. 'Elgar and Dorabella again, look, this time with their bikes.'

Friedman put the photo down and rummaged through another stack of papers. 'This lot's just letters written to Elgar,' he said, 'but it could take years for us to find anything of any use.' He held up a bundle tied together with red ribbon. 'We've no idea what's important.'

'Well, *they* look important, with the whole red ribbon thing,' said Tusia. 'Who are they from?'

Friedman opened the first envelope and pulled out the letter tucked inside. 'Jaeger,' he said. 'His music publisher. Remember?'

'The one he wrote "Nimrod" for?'

'His greatest friend,' said Friedman.

'Well, surely he told his "greatest friend" what the semicircles and loops in the code stood for,' said Hunter. 'Must be something in there.' He darted across the room and sat with Friedman, where one by one they removed the letters from the envelopes, scanning through the pages.

'Nothing here except depressing stuff,' Hunter said at last. 'Looks like Elgar didn't believe he was a genius. Jaeger had to keep writing and telling him. Looks to me as if Jaeger kept him going.'

This comment seemed to amuse Friedman. 'We all have someone who keeps us together when we're coming apart,' he said softly.

'Yeah, well, this Jaeger was keeping Elgar together big time,' said Hunter. 'Sounds like the guy might have given up writing music altogether if Jaeger hadn't encouraged him.'

Miss Tandari knelt to help put the letters back into the envelopes. She stopped for a moment and thrust an empty envelope under Hunter's eyes. 'Odd, don't you think? We're looking for odd, aren't we?'

'It's the letters we're interested in, not the envelopes . . .' His voice tailed away. 'Whoa. Wait a currant biscuit.'

'What?'

Hunter held up the envelope. In the top corner, small and looking at first like a franking mark used by the postal service, was a faint circle. 'It's an alphabet wheel,' Miss Tandari said. 'Ingham told you all about them in the code lessons at Station X. Basic tool of code-writing. Look.'

Brodie squinted to see a small drawing of a circle which had been cut into four equal segments.

'Looks like sections of a pie,' said Hunter eagerly.

Around the edge of the circle, like the numbers on a clock face, were letters and numbers. More of each were placed on the two crossed diameter lines.

'But the letters are all jumbled up. Why's that?' asked Tusia.

'Not a toffee of a clue, but I reckon we should take it.'

'We should take the envelope?' said Brodie anxiously.

'We're rummaging through a museum exhibit, BB, in the middle of the night while the cleaner's being distracted by someone playing the piano. I think we've already taken risks, don't you?'

'But we didn't say anything about *taking* stuff. Only finding things.'

Hunter glanced down at his watch. 'I don't think leaving helpful things behind's really an option.

The Letter Wheel
on the envelope from Elgar's desk.

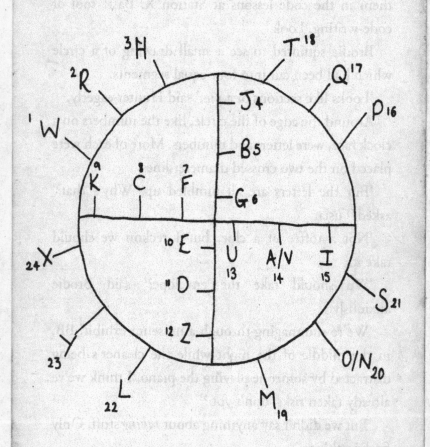

³H
²R
¹W
K₉
C⁸
F⁷
X₂₄
E¹⁰
D¹¹
Z¹²
²³
L₂₂
M₁₉
T¹⁸
Q¹⁷
P₁₆
J₄
B₅
G₆
U₁₃
A/V₁₄
I₁₅
S₂₁
O/N₂₀

How the toffee apple
is this going to help?

Besides, you had no problems taking a precious silver box from the Royal Pavilion.'

'But we'd been led to take that. Van der Essen left it for us.'

'And who's to say Elgar didn't leave this for us to find? We're in too deep now, B.'

'He's right, Brodie,' urged Friedman, taking the envelope and folding it up before pushing it into his inside pocket. 'I reckon the wheel's important.'

Brodie was just about to argue, when she became aware that the piano, which had been playing 'Land of Hope and Glory', had now become incredibly loud. Not only that, but the tune had changed to the 'Death March'.

'Quick,' hissed Smithies. 'Must be a signal.'

There was general pandemonium as letters and notes, photographs and maps were pushed back into drawers and stacked on the desk.

'Take the unfinished diary,' said Hunter.

'What. Are you mad?'

The 'Death March' was getting louder and louder.

'I reckon it's important too,' Hunter yelped, stuffing the diary under his jumper and pushing a map book into the belt of his trousers.

Miss Tandari slammed the final drawer and pushed the hairpin back into the lock.

The sound of the 'Death March' was so loud the windows shuddered in their frames.

'Hurry,' urged Brodie.

'Oh yes, it all works much quicker, BB, when you tell us to be fast,' hissed Hunter.

Miss Tandari jabbed the pin harder and turned. Then she staggered to her feet.

Tusia darted forward for the chair and dragged it free of the door handle. 'Come on!' she blurted.

The car pulled into the car park. The wheels spun on the gravel. The driver left the lights blazing.

'Why here?' he said, stepping out of the car. 'Of all the places they could come, why here?'

'No idea, mate. They're into old things, aren't they? That's what they like.' He was making towards the front door of the museum.

'How do we do this, then? Director said we shouldn't be over the top. Not like last time.'

'Poor Fletcher. I warned him we'd be seen. He wanted to make a show of things with that dragon. I warned him to play it safe.'

'And us? We should play it safe?'

The other man laughed. 'I'm not really in the mood for safe, mate. You?'

'Not really.' He reached over to the back seat of the

car and pulled out what looked like a sports bag.

'Tools?'

'Things to persuade with. If we need them. But I reckon caught here in the middle of the night, they'll come quietly, don't you?'

'I reckon they will.'

They walked together then, towards the museum door. The car lights blazed bright. And it began to rain.

Brodie looked out of the window. 'There's a car there,' she hissed. 'Lights on. We can't get out the door.'

'So what d'you suggest, B? The chimney?'

Brodie tried not to panic. 'Here,' she said. 'This way. It's our only chance.'

'You've got to be kidding me. After the last time we tried to climb from a great height?'

Brodie had pushed open the window. 'It's up to you. Do you really want to wait to be found? Or walk out to be caught?'

Hunter's face showed he was panicking. His eyes were wide.

'We'll be OK,' said Miss Tandari, steering him forward. 'We can do this.'

'Seriously? Because I'm not so sure we can.' He was peering from the window. The drop was two floors. A drainpipe the only route down. It was raining. The pipe wet and slippery.

'Watch how I do it,' said Tusia, swinging her leg over the ledge. 'Hand over hand. Slowly. But not too slowly,' she urged.

Brodie turned to her granddad. 'Can you?' she blurted.

He didn't need words to answer her. He may have been able to ride a scooter and, up until recently, rollerblades, but it was totally clear that climbing down a drainpipe was probably beyond him. 'You go,' he whispered. 'Let me face them.'

'No . . . I . . .'

'Brodie, please,'

'B?'

Brodie stood by her granddad. 'You lot go. We'll find another way! Please!'

Friedman slid over the ledge of the window. For a moment his eyes locked on hers. Then he was gone.

There was a noise. In the hallway. And the sound of the front door opening.

The bag was heavy. It banged against the older man's leg as he walked. He put it down on the floor just inside the doorway. Then he slid the zip open and drew out a baseball bat. 'Ready to do some persuading?' he said.

Brodie stood with her granddad.

The light from a car spilled inside the hall. Brodie took hold of her granddad's hand.

Then a voice called out.

Suddenly an internal door flung open.

'Evie?' Sheldon stood in the hallway. The elderly guide stood framed by the light of her car headlights.

'You were having a concert and you didn't tell me,' the guide moaned. 'Seriously, Sheldon. And I have to hear it from Kitty. Come on, then. Let me hear what you've been working on. I know inspiration can strike at the strangest of times.'

It was unfortunate that the two men who broke into the 'House on the Hill Toy Museum' in the middle of the night were armed with baseball bats. The police were not impressed. It seemed the argument that they were following a lead didn't wash well with the officers.

The men had been made to stand beside the police car while they were handcuffed ready to be driven away.

'What's this?' said the lead officer, taking a piece of paper from one of the men as he clicked the handcuff shut.

In the rain the red line marked on the map had begun to run like blood.

'It's nothing,' said the man. 'It means nothing at all.'

The officer let the map fall. It floated in a puddle for a moment and then, under the weight of the rain, it sank.

Friedman passed a packet of peanuts over the table to Hunter. 'You all right, mate?'

'Oh yeah. I'm totally all right after a completely unnecessary climb from a museum window.'

Miss Tandari patted his arm reassuringly. 'How were we to know it was only Evie's car? We thought we'd been followed. That Level Five were after us.'

Friedman looked over at Smithies. Brodie saw something shift in his eyes. It was almost as if he was trying to tell Smithies something.

Brodie tried to push this thought from her mind.

Seeing her watching, Friedman turned to Brodie. 'You were very brave to stay with your granddad,' he said. 'Braver than all of us.'

'Yeah, well, family's important, isn't it?' she said. 'I couldn't have left him. Not to face Level Five alone.'

He turned away without saying any more.

The Director's chair was facing the window. He had his back to the door. He didn't want to see anyone.

He wasn't a patient man. But he was a reasonable

man. But even the most reasonable of men had their limits.

He spun the chair round to face the desk. Then he pressed the button on the intercom. 'Get me Miss Vernan,' he said.

'Yes, sir.'

'I'm relying on her for results, and I need them quickly,' he said.

He would not face another disappointment like today's disaster. The team at Station X were playing him. And he wasn't in the mood for games.

The next morning, Brodie leant against the side of the Matroyska.

'So,' said Sheldon, hurrying over to join them. 'Last night? Did you find all you need?'

'Maybe,' said Smithies, 'but one thing's for certain. We can't stay here much longer.' He tried to ignore Sheldon's look of disappointment. 'We've taken a huge risk. We need to get back.' He turned to the Matroyska and began to fill the tank with rather dubious-smelling cooking fat Sheldon's mum had donated to make sure they made a quick getaway.

Sheldon lowered his head.

'Hey, Fingers,' called Hunter in an attempt to lighten the mood of saying goodbye. 'Don't look so sad. Take a look at this while Smithies gets us set to leave.' He led the younger group round to the back of the Matroyska and pulled down his unicycle from its precarious position on the cycle rack at the back.

'Wow,' said Sheldon. 'You can ride this thing?'

'Yep. When the thing's in working order.' He glanced across at Brodie. 'There was a time when it was out of action for a while after BB decided to try and crush it.'

'That's hardly fair,' Brodie cut in. 'You ran me over with it, if you remember.'

'Details, details,' laughed Hunter. 'You're always worrying about details.' He rolled the single wheel forward and back. 'So, you want a go, Fingers? Payback for all you did for us last night.'

Sheldon clambered aboard. It was clear to see his skills with a piano didn't transfer to the unicycle. He rolled backwards and forwards once and then, after making a high-pitched scream like a hyena, he landed flat on his back.

Hunter helped him to his feet. 'Look, it's all about balance and speed,' he said, riding literal rings around them. 'B. You want to show him how it's done?'

Brodie was considering her answer when Tusia stepped forward. 'Here, let me have a go,' she said confidently.

Brodie was sure she saw the tiniest glint in Hunter's eye. Tusia clambered on, and with Hunter and Sheldon supporting her she did in fact do quite well.

'I can do it,' she yelled, her eyes wide. 'You can let go.'

'You sure, Toots? It's harder than it looks.'

'I said, let go.'

'*OK* then.' Hunter and Sheldon lifted their arms.

There was a second, maybe more, where she looked comfortable. Even good. Then, with her feet circling madly, the unicycle carried her down the hill, past the end of the Matroyska and behind a bush and out of sight.

A bird screeched up into the air. Leaves exploded in a shower. Then a strangled voice spluttered, 'I'm OK,' before there was an ominous crunch.

'Oh, chocolate wafers,' yelped Hunter. 'If we have to have the thing repaired again I'll never get to ride it.'

They hurried down the hill to where Tusia lay crumpled on the ground, twigs and branches spiked her hair. Next to her the unicycle sat upended, the single tyre turning like a Ferris wheel.

'You OK?' Brodie blurted.

'Thought you were a gonna,' said Sheldon, offering to help her up. Tusia staggered to her feet unaided.

'Oh, I see. Back to your old self,' laughed Hunter.

'Thought for a minute we'd heard your last words.'

Brodie stopped in her tracks.

'Brodie. You look a little weird. I'm going to be OK,' Tusia said reassuringly, 'though it's nice you're worried.' She added a trace of venom to her words and shot a look at Hunter.

'Last words,' said Brodie slowly.

'No, well, don't think they're necessary now,' said Tusia, pulling the longest twig from her hair and discarding it in the bushes. 'I'm sorry to disappoint some of you but I think perhaps I might actually survive.'

'Not yours. His.'

'Oh, come on, BB,' said Hunter. 'You know I was only trying to lighten the mood. I wasn't trying to get anyone hurt. There's no need to be mean.'

'*Elgar*'s last words, not yours,' Brodie groaned. 'I remember now, reading about them.'

'OK,' said Sheldon, failing to hide the puzzlement from his voice.

'Just before he died, Elgar whistled part of a tune he wrote and said, "If you're ever walking in the Malvern Hills and hear that, then don't be frightened. It's only me."'

'A whistling ghost,' said Sheldon. 'Neat.'

'It's not the ghost that's important,' snapped Brodie.

'Well, it kind of is, if you're the dead thing,' said Hunter.

Brodie scowled again.

'The whistling then?' offered Tusia more supportively.

Brodie shook her head. The others looked at her blankly. 'It's the *hills*,' she said at last. Still their faces showed no understanding. She ran to pick up the unicycle, whose wheel turned slowly now. 'Three things Elgar was obsessed with. Music. Puzzles and . . .' She waited. 'Cycling round the Malvern Hills.'

'Rather odd combination,' said Tusia.

'Yes. But it's what he loved. He did it all the time.' Her mind clicked over. 'But he didn't often go alone.'

Hunter went and took the unicycle from her. He was obviously slightly afraid she'd drop it.

'Dorabella,' said Brodie.

'Oh, at last we're back to the cipher,' said Sheldon.

'Yes and no,' said Brodie. 'I think it's all connected.' She clapped her hands together. 'He wanted Dora to read the code. The Rosetta Stone he left for her. The things that'd make sense of the squiggles had to be something she understood. So the code had to be something she'd "get" and what she "got" was cycling.'

'Cycling?'

'Yes. They cycled together. We found that photo of

them with their bikes. Cycling's what they did. She wasn't into puzzles but she was into bikes, and so when Elgar said she of all people should be able to read the cipher, maybe the clue she needed was bikes.'

It was obvious absolutely no one else was following her logic.

'I don't get how it helps,' said Tusia. 'The bike thing. Even if they did have that in common, how's it help?'

'The Rosetta Stone,' blurted Brodie. 'The thing in common.'

'Still not following you.'

Brodie began to pace. 'OK.' She tried to make it simple. 'Centuries ago no one could read hieroglyphics, right? Until they found the Rosetta Stone. Then, people could make sense of the strange Egyptian letters because the message was also written in something they did understand. Greek or demotic. Languages they could read. And so the language Dorabella could read was "biking".'

Tusia raised her hands up in the air. 'Biking. It's a language now?'

'Yes. No. Well, sort of. Biking was a language Dorabella understood. Something she and Elgar both knew and shared.'

'But biking's something you *do*. Not something you *write*, B.'

'Except when you want to record the routes you took. The way you went on the bikes.'

'Maps,' realised Hunter. 'The maps are important?'

'Maybe!' said Brodie. 'They're really written versions of what they did on their bikes.'

Tusia was pacing up and down. 'OK. I'm getting there. But how do the maps help?'

Brodie tried to explain. 'The maps show the hills they cycled over, right? The Malvern Hills. And what shape do hills make when they're drawn on maps?'

'Er?'

'Come on.'

'Loops and arches,' Tusia yelled, her eyes widening with realisation. 'Lines to show contours. Lumps and bumps like the cipher.'

'Exactly!'

'So we need to look at the maps and the shape of the ridges of the hills and somehow link these with the shapes used in the cipher.'

'Yes.' Brodie smiled, bending down and sketching various loops and semicircles in the dusty soil with her finger. 'The hills are shown by lines. The lines make the cipher. We just have to somehow put the two together.' She stood up and wiped her hands clean. 'The cycling maps are our Rosetta Stone.'

8

Over the Hill

Kerrith looked up from her desk.

Spread across the room were the papers and notes from Friedman's flat.

One thing was becoming very clear to her.

The man was obsessed with MS 408.

There were intricate drawings and pictures, sketches and plans. Little of the notes made sense, but it was entirely obvious Friedman was searching incredibly hard for answers.

And one other thing was becoming clear too. Friedman hadn't been searching alone.

Kerrith traced the writing. A neat and careful style in crimson ink. Something bothered her. Something seemed familiar.

She snapped a stick of celery in half and chewed it

disdainfully. She'd spent so many hours on this project, her cardio sessions and Pilates lessons were getting more and more difficult to attend. She was having to resort to greatly restricting her calorie intake and it made her scratchy.

She snapped off a final bite of celery and swallowed, then lifted another notebook from the table. She flicked the pages despondently. More pictures. More sketches. All the same and all leading nowhere.

She flicked the book shut and tossed it to one side of the desk and as she did so a small slither of paper fluttered out. A receipt.

Back in the Plough, they joined tables together to make one long working space and then, using the 'chair against the handle trick' once more, ensured the door couldn't be opened from outside.

'The cycling maps are the key,' said Smithies, spreading the pages flat.

'You see how these shapes match the ones used in the cipher,' said Brodie. She opened the logbook. Across the page was the Dorabella Cipher Tusia had carefully copied.

'But how do we read them?' asked Miss Tandari. 'I see the ridges, like you say, but how do we know what each hill shape means?'

There was a fair degree of mumbling and rejected ideas. Seeing the shape of the hills like the letter shapes in the code was one thing, but making sense of what they said was another.

'Maybe we read round the map,' said Tusia hopefully. 'Take every hill Elgar and Dora cycled together.'

'Brilliant idea, Toots. Priceless,' said Hunter. 'Except how do we know exactly where they cycled?'

'Well, I don't know,' huffed Tusia. 'Did they mark their routes on the maps?'

Brodie peered in closely. 'There's some ink marks but none have letter names next to them. We can't just take the shape of the hills and swap them for letters of the alphabet. We need to find out what routes they cycled and in what order.'

'Maybe they wrote down where they cycled. In some of those letters you'd found?' offered Granddad.

Friedman looked despondent. 'None of the letters were honestly that cheery. All the ones I saw were about trying to get Elgar to lighten up and believe he could write good music.'

'Oh.'

'Yes. Big sugar-coated oh,' said Hunter. 'If the shapes made by the hills are important, how on earth will we ever match the shapes to routes he took? I'm guessing there's no family videos of him careering round the countryside with his friend Dora.'

Tusia didn't look impressed. 'I don't think people from Elgar's time videoed everything they did and put it on YouTube or Facebook.'

'Shame,' said Miss Tandari. 'He could have tweeted every day he took a different route. Then we'd have a record on Twitter of each hill shape he cycled over.'

A thought was forming in Brodie's mind. 'Say that again.'

Miss Tandari squinted a little. 'Which bit? Shame he—'

'No. The bit about him changing it every day,' interrupted Brodie.

Miss Tandari looked confused. 'I just said he could tweet the different route he cycled and that'd be a record—'

'Like a diary,' exploded Tusia.

Miss Tandari looked a little taken back with all the interruptions. 'If you say so.'

'I do say so. It's the diary. It'll make it all fit together,' said Tusia.

'It will?'

Tusia could hardly contain herself. 'You don't keep a diary *with* a whole load of maps unless it *connects* with those maps. It makes sense. Elgar kept diaries about his health. Sheldon told us. I reckon if we look closely at the diary he kept with his maps it'll show the *routes* he took when he was out on his bike.'

Brodie scrabbled through the pile of maps and found the small leather-bound diary. She flicked to the entries for the month of June, the only pages to have any writing.

'Well?' urged Tusia, craning her neck to see. 'Am I right? Does it list the routes they took?'

Brodie read from a block of writing in the first entry, scanning the words then stopping. 'Here,' she said, 'listen: *Weather fair . . . Dora and I cycled towards Hanley Swan.*'

Tusia peered at the map and traced the shape of the hills with her finger. 'Here, look. Here it is. This must be the route they took. Perfect.'

'I *knew* the diary was important,' said Hunter.

'Why? Because it's got numbers in, and numbers are your thing?' asked Brodie.

'Maybe. It's just it bothered me there were twenty-six entries in the diary.'

'What's odd about that? I told you, it's usual to give up keeping a diary,' cut in Tusia.

'But not to start and stop in the middle of the year,' said Hunter. 'The month of June always connected the diary to the cipher. June was just before Elgar sent Dorabella the cipher. Now you're saying it's important because it lists his cycling routes. I reckon that'll give us the shapes we need for the code. And,' he was drawing himself up tall now, 'twenty-six's important too.'

'Why?' said Granddad.

'Number of letters in the English alphabet,' said Hunter.

'Go on,' said Smithies slowly, as if scared anything he said may break a spell.

'OK. We're guessing Elgar wrote his message to Dorabella using weird curved shapes to match the route lines made by hills on his cycling maps.' He flicked his fringe away from his eyes before he continued. 'So now the next stage,' said Hunter, 'is to use the hills on the map to help us find a letter of the alphabet for each shape.'

'And that's why the number twenty-six's important?' pressed Brodie.

Hunter positively beamed. 'Look,' he said, holding the diary open as the pages fluttered. 'He made twenty-six entries. He wrote twenty-six times about the cycling routes he and Dora made. Our job's to find those twenty-six routes on the map. One route for each diary entry.'

'So you're suggesting there's one diary entry for each letter of the alphabet,' said Miss Tandari.

The diary pages stilled. 'It's worth a try!' said Hunter. 'The language of cycling. Each letter might equal one series of lumps and bumps on the map. Perfect!'

Brodie grabbed the diary. 'OK. So how do we do this? Organise it, I mean? Do you reckon we write down the first route and say the shape that makes must be the letter A . . . and the second entry and shape must be the letter B? Do you think it's that simple?'

Granddad spluttered a little. 'Simple. That's not the word I'd use.'

'But simple about the ordering of the letters, I mean. Twenty-six entries. Twenty-six letters. Do we just work through them in order?'

Tusia's eyes were widening. 'What about the wheel?'

'The bike wheel?' said Hunter.

'No! The alphabet wheel.'

Friedman rummaged in his pocket. 'This thing?' he said, holding up the envelope he'd taken from the museum, with the circular print at the top corner like a franking mark, and numbers and letters written side by side across segments of the circle.

Tusia took the envelope and put it on the table so everyone could see. 'A wheel shape, see?' she said. 'And the letters of the alphabet have been marked on and numbered. Letter A's number fourteen. So I reckon we have to take the fourteenth entry in the diary, find that shape on the map and make that the letter A. Now if that is the way it works it *is* simple.'

Brodie could feel her shoulders tightening. 'And why are we doing this?' she said. 'Using the wheel, I mean, and not just writing down the shapes in the order they're listed in the diary?'

'Wheel,' beamed Tusia. 'The wheel shape. If this coded language is the language of cycling then I think using the wheel to arrange the letters has to be part of it. Don't you?'

'I guess,' Brodie said doubtfully.

'Oh, come on,' said Tusia. 'It's all a guess, isn't it? All of it. But a guess using the very best links we can find. A code about cycling and shapes on a map and a code wheel to arrange the letters. That's got to be part of the connection. We can't miss it out.'

Brodie had to agree it made a sort of sense. Why else would Elgar have kept the envelope and not the letter inside? So, taking a clean page from the logbook, she drew the wheel out large for all to see, adding the letters around the edge.

'So we take each entry from the diary in turn, and find his route for that day,' said Hunter.

'Keep going,' said Miss Tandari.

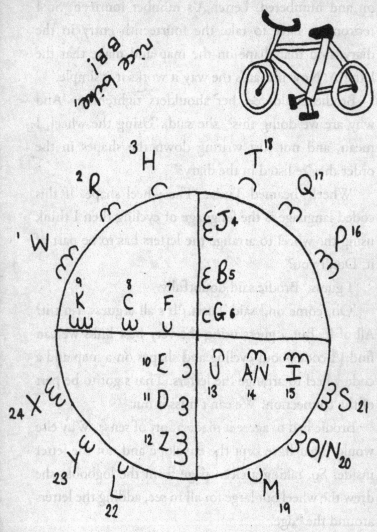

'And we find the shape of the hills he cycled and match it to that number letter on the wheel. Let's take the route for day one in the diary.' Hunter called out the direction of the route to Hanley Swan and Tusia traced the journey with her finger across the map. 'What shape does that make on the map?' he asked.

'A three-humped shape on the slant, like this,' she said.

'So, if this is the first shape, then using the alphabet wheel from the envelope this shape stands for the letter W.'

'Why?' asked Hunter.

'Because according to this alphabet wheel, the letter W is next to the number one. First route equals first letter, equals W. Get it?'

Miss Tandari gestured to Brodie, who added a three-humped shape next to the letter W.

'I think I get it,' said Sicknote quietly. 'Which route did he cycle next?'

Hunter turned to the next page in the diary, scanned the entry, then read out the route.

'*Weather inclement . . . Dora and I did not get as far but cycled towards Brickbarns Farm.*'

Tusia traced her finger across the map. Again the hills inclined up towards the top of the map, but this time there were only two of them.

'You think this is the shape for the second letter on the wheel?' asked Granddad.

'I guess,' said Hunter. 'And according to the wheel, route number two should stand for the letter R. Let's add it and see.'

It was a painstaking and laborious task. Brodie twisted the end of her plaited ponytail around her finger like a noose as she worked. Each route was found on the map, the shapes of the contours traced and the symbol moved to the alphabet wheel.

There was a lot of discussion about what to do on day sixteen's entry. Elgar had simply written

Weather not suitable for cycling . . . day of rest.

After lots of deliberating, Hunter suggested they wrote this phrase next to the letter P on the alphabet wheel as this was marked as the sixteenth letter. No one seemed entirely sure this was the best idea, but no one could think of anything better.

There were also two places where Elgar seemed to have cycled the same route.

'So that squiggle must share two letters,' said Brodie authoritatively.

Smithies pushed his glasses up on to his forehead again. The air in the room was heavy. It was growing late; the light coming in from the window was fading. Sicknote gulped from his inhaler and rubbed his forehead as Brodie looked down at both of her watches and then wistfully at her granddad as she worked out how long they'd been working.

Just then the door began to rattle.

Smithies began scooping the pages and papers away as a voice called from outside, 'It's only me.'

Tusia removed the chair from the door to let Sheldon in.

'Well then, how've you been doing?'

Smithies stretched and patted the table. His voice was a little wobbly as he spoke, as if he wasn't entirely sure he wanted to share the idea aloud. 'I think,' he said quietly, 'we've done it.'

Brodie couldn't sleep. The bed was uncomfortable. Tusia snored.

Brodie got up and crept along the corridor.

At home she found reading would relax her. But she'd finished all the books she'd packed. She figured going downstairs and working on the code would be a good use of her time. There was no reason now why she couldn't take the letters they'd made from the shapes and fit them into the Dorabella Cipher and try and see what it said.

It became clear though, she wasn't the only one awake.

Smithies and Friedman were in the back room. The light was low and they were speaking in hushed voices. Brodie waited on the stairs, sitting down carefully and drawing her knees up against her chest so she couldn't be seen.

'We don't know it's connected.' It was Smithies speaking.

'Oh, come on. Two men. In suits. Breaking into a museum in the middle of the night. A museum I'd left clues for.' Friedman's voice sounded edgy. 'The news said they had baseball bats.'

'You mustn't be paranoid.'

'Paranoid?' He was spluttering now. 'After what they did! You don't think they're capable of tracking and watching us?'

'Of course they're capable. I'm just not sure we should jump to conclusions.' Footsteps made it sound like he was pacing. 'If they followed your clue then we tricked them. So that's good. They have nothing on us, Robbie. Nothing to prove we're looking at MS 408. Nothing they can use against us.'

'But it means there *is* a leak in security. Someone passed that clue on.'

'I know. But we can't tell the kids. We do nothing

to unsettle them. Understand? Nothing.' There was a pause. 'We take this step by step and we watch our backs. Always. Am I clear?'

Friedman didn't sound like he was reassured. Smithies was talking again but Brodie couldn't be certain what he said. Something about Sheldon now. She shuffled forward on the stairs.

'It just adds to the risk, that's all.' It was Friedman speaking.

'He'll be better off than he is here, and the others like him. I think it'll be a good move.'

'Oh, come on, Jon. The others have secret-breaking in their blood. What do we really know about him? And you said we should watch our backs!'

Smithies sniffed. 'Don't you think we should just go with talent when we see it? Haven't we paid a high enough price for being selective about those we let join us?'

There was a murmuring Brodie couldn't quite make out. She grasped tightly to the locket she wore around her neck. It calmed her slightly.

'We can't go over this ground again.' Friedman was speaking; this time his voice was hushed and harder to hear. 'We did what we did and Alex paid the price. It was an error. I told you I wanted to explain.'

Brodie's throat tightened. It seemed impossible to

159

draw enough air into her lungs. She shuffled forward on the step, her heart beating so loudly she was sure they'd hear.

Suddenly there was a shuffling noise like an animal stirring. The pub cat, who'd been resting by the fire, twitched her tail and pricked her ears, instantly alert.

'What is it, girl?' It was Smithies again.

The cat stood and walked towards the foot of the stairs. Brodie swallowed and closed her eyes, in a vain attempt to make herself invisible.

Friedman followed the cat out into the passage. 'Brodie?'

She opened one eye.

'How long you been there?'

'Long enough to hear you talk about my mum.' She surprised herself with how harsh her voice sounded.

Friedman stepped out into the passage and steered her into the room to join them.

'What did you mean when you said Alex paid the price?' She lifted her head to stare at Smithies. 'What error?'

'Childhood stuff, Brodie. From long ago. A game, Brodie, nothing more.'

'And it had something to do with why my mum died?'

'No! I promise you. It was years and years ago. When Robbie and I were kids with your mum.' He looked across at Friedman. 'There was someone else then. At Bletchley. Someone we could have included in our fun. And we made a mistake. We left him out.'

'And how did my mum pay for that exactly?'

'Brodie,' Friedman pleaded. 'We made a mistake as children. People make mistakes. But nothing we did had any effect on your mum.'

'But you said . . .'

'Your mother's death was a waste of a precious life. A tragedy. But we were talking about long before that. You must believe us.'

Brodie was unsure how to answer.

Smithies linked his arm across her shoulder. 'We've said before, Brodie. The best way to serve your mother's memory is to solve the code.' He looked older suddenly and weighed down with sadness. 'That's what she would have wanted. Now, as you're up, why don't you join us? We were just about to tackle Dorabella using the alphabet wheel.'

Brodie sat down with them. But the uncomfortable feeling in the pit of her stomach didn't go away.

The next morning at breakfast Miss Tandari pulled up a chair next to Brodie. 'You look tired,' she said.

Brodie rubbed her eyes. 'I'm OK. But I'm a bit scared.'

'Scared?'

'I heard talking last night. Friedman thinks we're being watched. They don't know I heard them. Well, not that bit, anyway.'

Miss Tandari rocked her fork backwards and forwards on the table.

'If we're being watched, are we safe here?' Brodie persisted.

The fork stopped moving. 'I'm not sure, Brodie. If Level Five are really watching us here then that can't be good. But it's important we don't tell the others.'

'You want me to keep a secret from my friends?'

Miss Tandari's eyes darkened. 'I want you to help protect them.' She said nothing more for a moment and then her voice sounded almost urgent. 'Things will feel better if we just focus on the cipher and get that read.'

The Dorabella Cipher refused to give up her secrets.

By the time the others emerged for breakfast, Brodie's head was thumping and her eyes itched with tiredness. 'It's nonsense. Total nonsense,' she groaned.

Tusia didn't seem thrilled by this observation.

'If you swap each coded squiggle for a letter from the

wheel,' Brodie continued to explain, 'you just get rubbish. However you break up the letters, they just don't make words.'

Hunter helped himself to a bowlful of cereal and splashed milk all over it. 'Well, perhaps it's in another language, not English.'

Everyone looked up.

'We've been through this at Station X,' said Tusia. 'Russian's my limit and there's no way any of that's in Russian,' she said, gesturing at the open logbook and Brodie's scrawling notes and jottings.

'It's not French,' Brodie added. 'At least I don't think it is.'

'Perhaps it's German,' said her granddad. 'What? You're surprised I know German?' He was smiling despite himself. 'How do you think I got chosen to work at Station X in the war?'

Brodie was embarrassed to admit she hadn't really thought about it. Her granddad lowered a spoon to the table. 'Let me see, then.'

Brodie passed up the logbook where she'd substituted every squiggle in the cipher for a letter from the alphabet wheel.

Her granddad pondered the paper studiously, running his tongue across his chipped front tooth. 'No.'

'No, what?'

'It's not German.' He lowered the logbook to the table and resumed munching his cereal.

'Great,' said Tusia, grumpily. 'We spend ages looking at cycling maps, substitute eighty-seven squiggles for letters and then we can't read it.'

'Eighty-eight,' said Hunter.

'What?'

'There's eighty-eight squiggles,' he said. 'We agreed you have to count the dot.'

'And your point's *what* exactly?'

'I'm just being precise.'

Sicknote stood up, twisting the end of his necktie belt around his wrist.

'You all right, Oscar?' asked Smithies. 'You look a bit pale.'

Sicknote reached into his pyjama pocket and pulled out a container of tablets and shook them. 'Migraine coming. Seeing stars.'

Tusia rolled her eyes. His words bounced in Brodie's head as she thought longingly of how good it had felt when they'd solved the puzzle of who Elgar had hidden under his code of three stars. She flicked absent-mindedly through the logbook, the images blurring as the pages turned. All their notes and writings. All their guesses and rejections. It seemed so maddening they'd hit another brick wall.

'What the lemon meringue's that?' yelped Hunter, slowing her hand.

'What's what?'

'That picture of a chicken.'

Brodie scowled. 'It's not a chicken, thank you very much.'

'Looks like one, B.'

'It's a phoenix.' She peered down at her own artwork. 'Not the best I've ever drawn but it's clearly not a chicken. I drew it when we were working on the Firebird Code. Made notes about phoenix songs and stuff.' She looked down at the page. 'And . . .' Sicknote's words still rolled in her head, 'stars.'

'Excuse me. I can see now it's not a chicken, B, but it looks nothing like a star.'

'Eighty-eight,' Brodie mumbled.

'Yep. Eighty-eight. Number of symbols in the Dorabella Cipher,' said Hunter.

'It's an incredibly important number,' blurted Brodie.

'OK,' said Hunter. 'Doubt it's as important as 3.14, which is the value of pi, which of course is my favourite number of all time . . . but if you say it's important then—'

'Shhhh!' Brodie was standing now, her hands raised

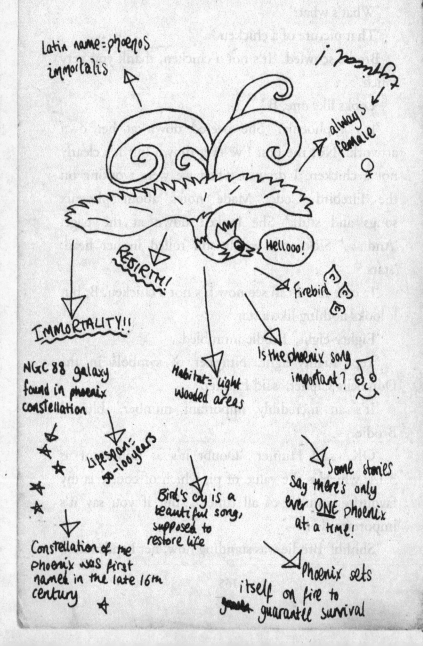

to stop them talking. 'There's a spiral galaxy located 160 million light years away from Earth.'

'Is there, darling?' asked Granddad, obviously a little unsettled by Brodie's sudden outburst. 'We were kind of concentrating on Elgar and the here and now, to be honest.'

Brodie was determined to continue. 'The spiral galaxy,' she said. 'It's located somewhere special.'

'I think we're agreed that all of space's rather special, Brodie,' said Miss Tandari.

'Yeah, I know. This spiral galaxy has a number. The number eighty-eight. And NGC 88 is in a special constellation. It's got a special name.' She wasn't to be deterred.

'And this special name's what?' asked Smithies.

'The phoenix constellation.'

'Phoenix?'

'Yes,' said Brodie. 'The Firebird.' She felt a wave of excitement swell round the table. 'Look. I made notes about it when I made my "chicken" drawing.' She passed the logbook to Tusia. 'See. The phoenix constellation. It includes galaxy NGC 88.'

'So,' continued Smithies, catching the thread of her thought. 'Perhaps the number eighty-eight's important. A link between the Firebird Code and the Dorabella Cipher.'

Hunter stood up now, flicking his fringe away from his eyes. 'It is,' he said softly.

'It is?'

'Of course eighty-eight was important to Elgar,' said Hunter. 'We've already talked about it.'

Brodie was desperately trying to remember what they'd said.

Hunter smiled. 'Eighty-eight's the number of keys on a piano.'

It hadn't been easy to get Sheldon from the kitchen. His mother, wearing a green striped apron streaked with what Brodie hoped was ketchup but looked remarkably like blood, stood with her arms folded in the doorway. Her glare could have burst balloons.

'Right,' said Smithies. 'Now we're getting closer to solving this puzzle, but we think we need your help. Again.'

'Fire away,' Sheldon said. 'What do you have in mind this time? More breaking and entering? Stilt walking?'

'Funny you should mention that, Fingers,' cut in Hunter, 'because I do have some stilts in the—'

Smithies didn't allow him to finish. 'Look, here's what we've got already. A code using eighty-eight symbols, each of which requires a letter. Eighty-eight letters in total from which we can't make any sense at all. Now, a musician chooses the notes he wants to combine to make a tune.'

'Yep, that's kind of important to the whole music idea,' said Sheldon. 'The notes you choose, I mean.'

'And,' went on Smithies boldly, 'the notes you leave out, surely. The rests and pauses you have are what make the melody. The way you vary your selection of notes like Elgar did with the *Enigma Variations* is the way you tell your story. You don't play every one of the eighty-eight keys on the piano. You have to leave some out. Now Elgar hid a person in the *Enigma Variations*. We believe it was Helen Weaver. She led us to Van der Essen and in turn to Dorabella. Just supposing Elgar wanted to hide another *person* from us.'

'In another piece of music?' said Sheldon.

'No. Not this time. This time in code.'

'In the Dorabella Cipher, you mean. You reckon there's a *person* hiding there?'

'The name of the person maybe. We thought there might be a message but we can't make sense of all of the letters we've got, so let's go with what we know Elgar's done before. He's hidden people in his work.'

'He hid Mendelssohn in the *Enigma Variations*, didn't he? That snippet of music he "quoted" by the composer from Leipzig. Finding him led us to Helen Weaver,' said Tusia.

'Exactly.' Smithies was beaming. 'So we know what Elgar's done in the past is hide *people*, not necessarily *messages*.'

'He did it too with the name of his house,' blurted Brodie. 'Remember? CRAEG LEA . . . the name of his house which hid the initials of all his family along with the name Elgar.'

'Perfect,' said Smithies, practically bouncing from foot to foot. 'Totally perfect.' He glanced over at Sicknote. 'You getting how good they are at this, Oscar?' he asked.

Sicknote looked impressed despite his migraine.

'So suppose in amongst all these squiggles and lumps and bumps, Elgar's simply hiding the name of a person for us to find?'

'Well, they'd be a person with one hugely ginormous name,' said Hunter. 'A name with eighty-eight letters. That might be even worse than my name to deal with!'

Smithies shook his head. 'That's what I'm getting at. I don't think we need all these letters and squiggles. I think we only need some of them. I think the person's hidden somewhere among all these shapes but some of the lumps and bumps are just there to make it hard.'

'They've certainly managed that,' said Tusia.

1 2 3 4 5 6 7 8 9 10 11 12 13 14 15 16 17 18 19 20 21

22 23 24 25 26 27 28 29 30 31 32 33 34 35 36 37 38 39 40 41 42 43

44 45 46 47 48 49 50 51 52 53 54 55 56 57 58 59 60 61 62

63 64 65 66 67 68 69 70 71 72 73 74 75 76 77 78

79 80 81 82 83 84 85 86 87 88

'It's disinformation. Like with the Firebird Code and the word Excalibur.' Brodie could see a tiny spark of understanding shimmering in Hunter's eye. 'We didn't need the word Excalibur. We needed the words hidden behind it. Inside it really.'

'So,' said Smithies. 'Which *person* is Elgar hiding in the Dorabella code? Which notes *from* the eighty-eight squiggles of the Dorabella Cipher do we have to select to get the secret? Well?'

Sheldon looked round. 'You expect *me* to know that?' he said nervously.

'Yes. We do.' Smithies was trying ever so hard to keep the anxiety from his voice. 'How do we know which of the eighty-eight notes are important? How do we find the key?'

Brodie watched and, almost as if prompted by the need for answers, Friedman fingered the chain around his neck again.

'The Firebird Box,' yelped Brodie. She could hardly form the words. 'What about the Firebird Box was so important, apart from leading us to Elgar?'

'Well, it contained the variation. The alteration in the melody. Those notes which were in the letter to Dorabella.'

'It's those notes, then,' said Brodie firmly. 'They're the important ones. So important they're worked into the music-box tune and written out on paper for Dora Penny.'

'So what numbers are those notes, then?' asked Hunter.

'What do you mean, what numbers are they?' asked Sheldon.

'The notes from the letter. What numbers, out of the eighty-eight possibles, are those notes on the piano keyboard?'

Sheldon's eyes widened. 'Oh. I see.' He turned quickly and then shouted over his shoulder, 'Wait here!'

After a few seconds of silence, Miss Tandari asked nervously, 'You don't think he's gone to get a piano, do you?'

Brodie felt a bead of sweat prickle on her brow.

When Sheldon returned though, he was carrying a can of shaving foam.

'What the potato in a jacket are you doing with that?' asked Hunter.

'Trust me,' said Sheldon. Brodie tried not to remind herself the person she was supposed to be trusting had been excluded from two schools, and instead watched as he shook the can vigorously and then demanded the table was cleared of all the notes and papers.

Then, without any explanation, Sheldon sprayed a

thick layer of foam across the entire top of the table.

'Is he a currant short of an Eccles cake or what?' hissed Hunter.

'You want to know what numbers the notes are,' said Sheldon defensively, 'then I'll show you.' He traced with his finger, separating the foam into rectangular sections. 'See?' he said.

'No. Not really,' said Hunter. 'In fact, not at all.'

'I do. I do,' yelped Tusia. 'You're making a keyboard, right?'

Sheldon wiped his foamy fingers on his trousers. 'An eighty-eight note keyboard. I'm improvising! The mark of a great musician. Anyway.' He stood up straight. 'Here we go. This is where the notes from the music-box variation and the letter to Dora are on the keyboard. Get ready to write them down.'

Hunter grabbed the rather foamy logbook.

'There,' said Sheldon, the imprint of his fingers from his silent tune, marked on the shaving foam keys. 'Got them?'

'Not really,' said Hunter.

'Well, you just count. That's your bit.'

'OK. OK.'

Hunter thrust the logbook in Brodie's direction and counted out the marks his fingers had made on the eighty-eight foamy keys on the table. 'There are two 42s, five 47s, one 49, six 50s, two 52s, two 54s, one 55 and a rest of course.' He paused. 'Sounds like my ideal Chinese takeaway order.'

Smithies frowned. 'We need to concentrate,' he said.

'Fine. I was just saying.'

'So,' said Smithies. 'Let's look at the cipher.'

Miss Tandari had taken the logbook and was busy numbering each squiggle in the Dorabella Cipher from 1 to 88.

'What shapes you got?'

Miss Tandari looked along the list, writing down first the squiggle under the number 42 and then the squiggle under number 47 until she'd written down a shape for every number Sheldon had called out.

Tusia held up the alphabet wheel. For every shape from the cipher Miss Tandari selected, Tusia found the letter on the wheel.

'So,' said Smithies, practically jumping in his excitement. 'What letters have you got?'

Miss Tandari read them out. 'Two Rs, six Os or Ns, six As or Vs, two Ss, two Hs, one L and there's a rest.'

'Place of rest,' said Hunter. 'We agreed that'd equal a letter P.'

'OK,' said Miss Tandari, taking the paper now and holding it so most of the group could see. It was impossible to place the work down on the table as,

Whether you are as nice as

B flat ⎱
D   ⎰ together   50
                         42
G ⎱
C (top) ⎰   47
                         52
B flat ⎱
D   ⎰   50
                         42
– Rest

G, B flat, D   47, 50, 54
G, B flat, E flat   47, 50, 55
G, B flat, D   47, 50, 54

I told you number
88 was important.

Stop writing
on my notes
Hunter!!

Or only as unideal as

B flat   50
G   47
C (top)   52
A   49

88 piano keys

despite rapid evaporation, lots of the foam was still clinging to the surface. 'What do those letters make?'

There was an awkward silence.

'Remember,' said Brodie cautiously, 'Elgar was the king of anagrams. There must be a name in there he wanted Dorabella to know which he either told Van der Essen or the Professor worked out for himself.'

'Who was he trying to hide?' asked Tusia.

'Anyone?' begged Smithies. 'Anyone got any idea at all?'

They stared at the letters, selected from the eighty-eight symbols, and Brodie tried with all her might to make them shuffle into sense.

At last Hunter leant back in his chair. All eyes turned to face him. 'Well?' Smithies could barely breathe the word. 'Can you read it?'

Hunter's grin was wide. 'Yes I can. I really can.'

The Message Elgar Left Behind

'Where shall I put it?' The delivery man stood in the doorway, his arms laden down with two large boxes.

Kerrith looked up from her desk and swept a stray strand of hair behind her ears.

'Erm. Hello? It's rather heavy, miss.'

Kerrith narrowed her lips into a thin grin. 'I'm sure it is,' she said slowly, then waved in the direction of the window. 'Put it over there and be careful not to step on anything.' She gestured towards fragments, notes and papers which littered the floor like crazy paving.

The man picked his way through the paperwork and put the boxes down under the window.

'And you're sure that's everything?'

He straightened his back. 'Everything from the

basement labelled "Bray".' He waited for a moment in the doorway.

Kerrith looked up at him like he were a rather irritating fly she'd failed to swat. 'Well?'

He coughed quietly.

She smiled then, rocking back on her deep leather chair, as if suddenly getting the punch line of a very long joke. 'Ahh. I see you're waiting for a tip. Well, here it is.' She pressed the tops of her fingers together. 'Next time this department send you for paperwork on the express orders of the Director, make sure it's brought here quickly.'

He moved his lips ready to speak.

'That will be all,' she said and then she turned back to the papers on her desk.

A faint whiff of shaving foam lifted from the table.

Hunter pushed the logbook forward and surveyed the room. 'Here,' he said. 'The person hidden by the code.'

Across the paper in capital letters large and clear was written:

ORPHAN HANS SAVONAROLA

'I know who Savonarola was,' said Smithies.

Sicknote shuffled forward in his chair, taking the lead. 'An Italian. A priest. A leader in Florence

42 47 49   50   52   54   55

$\sqrt{}\,2 \times 42$ ✓
$\sqrt{}\,5 \times 47$ ✓
? $\sqrt{}\,1 \times 49$?
rest← $\sqrt{}\,6 \times 50$
× 2×52 ✓
$\sqrt{}\,2 \times 54$ ✓
$\sqrt{}\,1 \times 55$ ✓

I knew the symbols weren't sheep!!

R = ⌒
O/N = ϖ
S = ϖ
H = ∩
L = ∪
A/V = ⌒
P = rest

O R P H A N   H A N S

S A V O N A R O L A

during the late 1490s.'

'1497?' asked Hunter. 'The date at the end of the Dorabella Cipher was 1497.'

'So it was. So it was.' Suddenly aware all eyes around the table were on him, Sicknote continued. 'Savonarola was a leader during that time. Quite a famous one.'

'Because he was a good leader?' asked Tusia.

Sicknote's eyes widened. 'Ah, now there's an interesting question. Is it possible to separate people into those who are simply good or bad?'

No one answered.

'Savonarola was an *earnest* man. He believed totally in all he did and he believed Florence was the city of his destiny. He developed very strong ideas about what was right and wrong, and he saw it as his job to make sure only righteous things survived. He destroyed everything that didn't fit in with his view of life.'

'Destroyed?'

Sicknote nodded. 'He objected to music and art and games. He destroyed paintings and sculptures and musical instruments, even dresses and hats and ancient poems. He even objected to chess, Tusia, and had chess pieces destroyed.'

Brodie glanced over at her friend who was reddening a little in an attempt to contain her anger.

Sicknote hesitated and chose his next words carefully. 'He destroyed people too.'

'He killed them?' asked Tusia, gulping nervously.

'He had them executed if they didn't support his views or live a life he thought was worthy.'

Hunter looked down at the code. 'So, do you think the words "Orphan" and "Hans" are actually Savonarola?'

Miss Tandari looked down too. 'I don't think so,' she offered. 'I've heard of him and I remember his first name was Girolamo.'

'So who does "Orphan" and "Hans" refer to, then?' asked Brodie, trying her best to keep up.

'Someone who died because of what Savonarola did?' suggested Granddad.

'Perhaps.'

'Someone who died in 1497,' pressed Hunter, referring back once more to the date.

'Most likely.'

'And why was that date so important to Savonarola?' asked Tusia.

'Because,' said Miss Tandari, moving forward to rest her arms against the slightly steaming table, 'it was the year of something that's been recorded in history as the Bonfire of the Vanities.'

'Go on,' urged Sheldon.

Sicknote took up the story again. 'In February of that year, on the Shrove Tuesday festival, a huge bonfire was organised in the centre of Florence. Young boys were sent around the houses to collect things for the fire. All the things I've mentioned. Books, mirrors, clothes. The bonfire burnt for many days. Savonarola himself was seen dragging paintings into the flames.'

'So that's the connection, then?' suggested Tusia.

'Sorry?' Sicknote leant forward in question.

'The fire? It's what really links them. Both the codes we've looked at. The Firebird Code and the Dorabella Cipher.'

'I suppose it is,' agreed Granddad.

'And you think Hans, whoever he was, died because of the fire Savonarola built?' asked Tusia.

'Seems logical,' said Sicknote.

'But how does all this stuff about bonfires and Savonarola fit with Van der Essen and the book he had which we think was a code-book for MS 408?' asked Brodie, hardly bearing to form the words. 'I can't see the link.'

Smithies scratched his head. 'Let's see. We thought Van der Essen found something in 1912 in Mondragone Castle that was a code-book for MS 408. That's the theory we've been working on. Then in 1913, Van der

Essen meets with Elgar, a man who's connected to his mother. Perhaps a man he trusts. We've worked on the basis he told Elgar what he'd found and then agreed to leave a coded message in the music box which would lead us to a cipher Elgar wrote and then eventually to the missing code-book?'

'That's what we thought made sense of the meeting,' said Tusia. 'But Elgar hid names. We know that. That's why we think there's names hidden in the Dorabella Cipher.'

'But why "Orphan Hans Savonarola"?' said Brodie. 'It may be the name of the person Van der Essen passed the code-book on to? The person who had the code-book for MS 408?'

'It can't be, can it?' said Hunter. 'What about the date? The link to the Bonfire of the Vanities. 1497. The date at the bottom of the cipher. Van der Essen can't have passed the code-book to this Hans guy, unless of course he could travel back in time. Whoever Hans was, all this suggests he lived four hundred years before Van der Essen!'

'Well, the code must talk about someone who had the book then, in the past,' said Miss Tandari. 'Not the person who Van der Essen passed it on to.'

'Well, that's not good,' yelped Tusia. 'If that *is* what it means, that really isn't good. I mean, supposing this

Hans really did have the code-book in 1497 and what Van der Essen really discovered in Mondragone Castle was *that*. There's a chance, then, Van der Essen never had the code-book in the first place. Maybe what he hid in Louvain was just the name of the person who *had* the book to make sense of MS 408.'

'Sort of makes sense,' said Miss Tandari. There was a silence while everyone digested this. 'It'd explain why Voynich never talked about finding two books. Van der Essen simply found the name of the person who'd *had* the code-book, not the code-book itself. And the Firebird Code and the Dorabella Cipher were all an elaborate way of hiding the identity of that person.'

Smithies pushed his glasses up on to his forehead again. He looked suddenly older, his eyes lined by thick black shadow. 'We know what Elgar and Van der Essen wanted us to know,' said Smithies sadly. 'That someone called Hans had the book which could be used to read MS 408.'

'I still don't get what's wrong with that,' said Brodie keenly. 'Why isn't that good, Tusia? We've solved the Firebird Code and now Elgar's Dorabella code and they lead us to Hans. What's the great big problem?'

Smithies shook his head. 'You're forgetting the fire. It's the thing which links them, isn't it? That joins the two codes. And not only that, but it's the source of ultimate destruction.' His voice was softer now. There were no other sounds in the room. 'We thought Van der Essen's Firebird Box would contain the missing book. And we were wrong.'

Brodie remembered the pain of holding the ash-filled box.

'And now look what Elgar's Dorabella Cipher's led to? Just a name and a reminder of fire. This Hans that Elgar captured and stored forever in the code, may very well have once held the book which would let us read MS 408. But the message of Dorabella is about more than Hans.'

'It's about Savonarola,' said Sicknote.

'And 1497,' said Hunter.

For a moment no one else spoke as the penny dropped. Brodie tried to swallow but her throat was too tight.

'The translation of Voynich's manuscript may have existed once,' said Smithies. 'And Hans may have had it. Elgar never did. Van der Essen never did. Their job was just to tell us who'd had it in the past. But . . .' He didn't finish his sentence.

It was Tusia who eventually voiced the words Brodie couldn't bear to hear. 'Elgar's code is just telling us the book's gone? The translation was destroyed in the Bonfire of the Vanities by Savonarola in 1497?'

The cell door swung open. The policeman wasn't happy. 'Charges dropped,' he moaned. 'You're free to go.'

The two men walked together out of the police station. A car was waiting for them. The darkened window rolled down slowly. A hand appeared. It offered the men a small slip of paper with a location and a time printed on it. Then the window rolled closed and the car pulled away.

They stood together beside the Matroyska. Sheldon kicked at the ground, lifting dust in thick grey clouds, but no one said a word to stop him. 'It's sort of a pain you've come to a dead end. Smithies's been chatting to my mum and he'd convinced her to let me come and join you.' He kicked more sharply this time and Sicknote spluttered loudly and reached for his surgical mask. 'It's so totally typical,' Sheldon went on. 'I find a way out of something and things go bad. Seems there's really no escape from this place,' he sighed. 'What will you lot do now?'

'Go back to Station X. Pack up our things, I guess,' said Tusia.

'It's sort of ironic,' said Brodie. 'We thought it was finished last time, because of the ash from the fire. Now it really is.'

'We thought it was all over. It is now,' said Hunter playfully. No one laughed.

'Whatever book was supposed to be used to read MS 408 is gone,' said Friedman. 'It means the language of MS 408 can never be shared.'

Brodie looked at him carefully. There was a haunted look about him. 'But I just don't understand,' she said, 'why they went to all that trouble. Elgar and Van der Essen mixing up their complicated codes to lead us to . . . what? A book which got burnt five hundred years ago. It's like some terrible sick joke.'

Sheldon stilled his feet and the dust fell like gentle rain. 'It's been great, though,' he said at last. 'A sort of adventure with you all. I mean, I know it hasn't ended well. But I've had a great time.' He seemed to choose his next words carefully. 'It was sort of like having friends.'

Brodie hugged him then. It was awkward. She caught her nose against his shoulder and it hurt quite a bit. Her eyes watered, but it was because she was sad about leaving. Not because of the pain in her nose.

They climbed into the Matroyska and Brodie pulled the yellow curtains away from the window so she could wave. Then she leant her head against the window and tried to close her eyes. Sleep just wouldn't come though.

While they were approaching the motorway Brodie became aware of a distracting shape in the wing mirror. She looked over her shoulder and tried to see out of the back window.

Some way behind them, a cyclist was weaving across the road. It was difficult to see who, if anyone, was steering the bicycle as balanced on the handlebars was a very large suitcase tied up with rope. On top of this was an old-fashioned piano-accordion.

'What the rhubarb crumble's that?' mumbled Hunter, craning his neck to see more clearly.

The Matroyska slowed to a halt as the bike wove towards them, braking sharply, causing the bellows in the accordion to fill with air and blast out a note like a foghorn.

'Sheldon?' asked Brodie, as they craned their necks through the window to see more clearly. 'Is that you?'

Sheldon lifted his head above the suitcase and grinned. The accordion deflated with a squeaky sigh.

'What on earth are you doing?' asked Smithies, clambering down from the driver's seat.

Sheldon was obviously finding it hard to breathe and his words, when they came, pumped out in short blasts making him sound like the piano-accordion. 'Elgar's bike,' he said. 'Stolen it. Can't go back.' He collapsed there, lowering his head on top of the tied-up suitcase.

'You stole Elgar's bike?' ventured Smithies.

'Borrowed.' He could still hardly breathe. 'Doesn't need it. Dead, you see.'

Miss Tandari clambered from the Matroyska and handed over a bottle of water, which instead of drinking, Sheldon threw all over himself. 'Great,' he said. 'Much better. Thanks.'

'He really is a wafer short of an ice-cream sundae,' Hunter said.

Obviously refreshed by the water, although dripping slightly from the end of his nose, Sheldon began to explain. 'Look, I realise I haven't known you lot long, but I get you're disappointed. I mean the whole thing with the Dorabella Cipher was a bit of a shame.'

'And he's also a master of the understatement,' whispered back Brodie.

'So I got to thinking when I saw you leave.' He reached into his trouser pocket and pulled out a string of now rather soggy tickets. 'A concert,' he said, 'might cheer us up.'

'A concert?'

A drop of water splashed from his nose on to the dusty ground.

'Royal Albert Hall. This evening. A celebration of

Elgar. He may have stopped your quest, so at least let him cheer you up with some music before you go your separate ways.'

Miss Tandari reached out and took the soggy line of tickets from him. 'Where did you get these?'

'Oh, the museum gets sent them. Freebies, you know. Evie stacks them away.'

'You stole these as well as the bike?' Miss Tandari was obviously doing her best to try and look serious.

'Not exactly. The museum never paid me for my work. My mum had a bit of an issue with that, you may have noticed. No one else was going to use them. It's all OK. Honest. My mum's fine with it.'

'Your mum's fine with it?' Brodie found it hard to imagine there was anything Mrs Wentworth was really fine with.

'Well, sort of. I didn't explain to her your quest was over. That you'd reached a dead end. Last thing she knew was you'd offered to take me off her hands. Covering a few tickets to keep me out of trouble is, as far as she's concerned, a small price to pay.'

'But you know it can't last. We've got nothing more to go on. Our puzzle's over even if it's still in pieces.'

'Hey. I just want one last bit of fun with my friends. What's the problem with that?'

Smithies looked up at the windows of the Matroyska,

searching for approval from those still on board.

'But where exactly do you intend us to stay in London after the concert?' asked Miss Tandari.

Sheldon straightened himself against the handlebars of the borrowed bike. 'Simple,' he said, pulling a small businesscard out of his other pocket and shaking it to remove some of the excess water. 'The Plough's got a sister branch called the Carthorse just outside Victoria. I'll explain everything and we'll be set for a night or two. What do you say?'

Smithies looked up again at the windows and Friedman nodded encouragingly.

Brodie was suddenly aware everyone was smiling. And beside her Miss Tandari handed out cubes of chocolate. Maybe things weren't quite so terrible after all.

'It won't be much,' said Sheldon, loading his cases and bags on to the Matroyska and attaching the bicycle to the rack used by the unicycle, 'but at least it will be going out in style.'

The men waited outside the railway station.

The car pulled close to the kerb and the engine died.

'So?'

'They're not coming straight back.'

'Any ideas where they're going?'

The driver nodded. He took a piece of paper from the dashboard and passed it over. The light from the lamppost illuminated the marking on his arm as he pulled his hand away.

The concert was good. But it was hard, somehow, not to feel angry with Elgar for hiding such a disappointment in his code. It took an ice cream in the interval to lighten the mood.

For the second half, Brodie took a seat next to Friedman. She followed the pieces in the programme notes and was interested that the last sections of music to be played were from the 1920s, written after Elgar's wife died. The title was 'The Arthur Music'. The notes explained that during King Arthur's lonely death, his friends marched mistily past him like Elgar's own friends had done in the *Enigma Variations*. Brodie saw that Sheldon, seated at the front of the box, was wiping tears from his eyes.

Beside her, Friedman fidgeted in his seat.

'You OK?' she whispered eventually.

'Not sure.' He passed her a pair of opera-glasses. 'Take a look.'

Brodie peered through the glasses at the stage area, but Friedman pulled her arm. 'Not there. The audience, look. That box in the grand circle.'

Brodie trained the opera-glasses in the way Friedman directed and then twisted the lenses to realign the focus.

What she saw made her stomach tighten.

Two men in dark suits sat alone in a box designed for many more people. They were paying intense attention. But not to the concert.

'They're watching us,' whispered Brodie.

'I know.'

'But why?'

Friedman's face showed there could only be one possible answer.

'Level Five?' said Brodie. 'You think they've followed us here?'

'They're on to us, Brodie. Tracking every move. This proves it.'

'But we haven't done anything wrong.'

Friedman didn't answer her. He simply reached for the thick velvet curtain hanging at the back of the box.

'What you doing?'

'Checking?'

'Checking what?'

'How closely they'll follow.'

Brodie watched the curtain swing to, and then without a word to anyone, she followed Friedman out of the box.

'We can't be sure they're from the Chamber, can

we?' she hissed as Friedman jogged along the passageway. 'We'll soon find out.'

Friedman led the way. The sound of the concert was muffled by the heavy tread of the carpet. He ran past the signs on the wall labelled 'Choir East' and to a wide flight of stairs leading upwards. Brodie ran quickly to keep up. At the top of the stairs the passageway opened again on to a wide curling corridor. 'Here' said Friedman, pulling Brodie to the side. 'We mustn't be seen.'

To their right was a lift. Brodie's heart was beating in her throat. The corridor was quiet, but the air was so thick she could barely swallow.

Suddenly, the lift door slid open. Two men stepped out. Men in dark grey suits.

Friedman lifted his finger to his lips and pressed tight. Brodie knew she couldn't make a sound. She pressed her back against the wall. As long as she was still; as long as she was silent; they wouldn't see.

The men stepped out of the lift. They looked down the corridor. One was mumbling, a pair of opera-glasses swinging in his hand.

Brodie wasn't sure what made him drop them. The glasses rocked for a moment back and forth on the carpet. The man lowered his head dejectedly and bent down. And it was from this crouched position, his head low to the ground looking up, that he saw them.

Friedman grabbed Brodie's hand. He tugged her out into the passage and he ran, kicking at the opera-glasses as he ploughed past the two men. Brodie heard the sound of breaking glass as the lenses shattered.

Friedman dragged her onwards. Her feet pounded the floor as her heart thumped against her ribs. They ran past signs to a restaurant and a bar, as all the time the sound of the concert made the building throb.

'In here,' Friedman yelled. Brodie looked up at the sign. 'Elgar's Restaurant'. It seemed ironic.

A solitary waitress stood at a table inside the door. She was cleaning a glass with a thick white cloth. 'I'm sorry. You can't be in here. I'm afraid . . .'

Brodie didn't hear the rest of what she said.

Friedman dragged her between the line of tables, and behind her she heard the sound of falling crockery. Plates laid for tomorrow's service sliding from the tables as the men careered behind them, pushing tables out of their way.

Brodie's throat was burning. Air clogged her mouth, and her lungs strained to pull in more.

'You have to keep moving, Brodie. You have to . . .'

He was yanking her onwards, through the restaurant like the path of a maze. And behind them the men kept running.

'Here!' Friedman pulled her through a doorway and turned sharp left. He thumped the buttons on the lift call. The lights flickered faintly. 'Come on! Come on!'

There was a whirring sound. A shifting of levers. The sound of footsteps heavy in the restaurant. Shouting.

'Come on! Come on!' The lights flashed above the doorway. There was a gentle hiss.

But the men were out of the restaurant. Steps away.

The lift doors opened. Friedman pulled her inside.

The first man reached towards the lift.

The doors shuddered. His hand slipped.

As the doors closed and the lift began to descend Brodie saw clearly the point of his shoes. They looked like child-catcher shoes.

Friedman paced inside the lift as it descended. 'I knew we were being watched. I knew it.'

'But I don't understand why,' Brodie yelped. 'They can't prove we're looking at MS 408. What can they have on us?'

Friedman pressed his hands against the lift doors. He didn't answer her.

The lift shuddered to a halt. Friedman kept his finger pressed on the 'door closed' button.

'What are you doing? We need to get out of here. Tell the others we're being followed.'

'Brodie, do you trust me?'

'Of course.'

'And you believe I'd never do anything to hurt anyone.'

'We need to get out of here, Friedman. To get away.'

Still he held his hand against the button. 'Brodie.' His face was pained as if he could hardly speak.

'What?'

'I need you to know, your mother was my greatest friend.'

'OK. OK.' She didn't know what to say to him. 'The key. From Belgium. I get it. You were friends.'

'She was my best friend, Brodie. I need you to know that.'

Brodie lowered her head. She couldn't look at him. He was scaring her.

He took a deep breath and took his hand off the button. The doors juddered open. He grabbed her hand and he ran towards a doorway. An opening to the world outside.

The London air was cool against her cheeks.

And the concert was over.

People spilled out of the doors into the night. A mass of people seeping out on to the street. They were safe. There was no chance anyone could find them amongst this crowd. Whoever was following them would be lost in the throng.

'You OK?' he said, when he turned to face her.

She had no idea how to answer him.

They hurried through the people and across the road. Panting, he sank down to the grass. She sat beside him, shivering in the cold. 'Why is Level Five watching us even here,' she said at last, 'if Van der Essen and now Elgar were just messing with us?' She looked up at the memorial statue of Prince Albert. For a moment it was as if he was laughing at her. Below an intricate canopy of stone, he sat cased in gold, looking up at the concert hall which shared his name as if he was wondering too how so much could have led to nothing. 'If it's over, why are they still watching?'

'I can't believe it's finished,' Friedman said.

Brodie laughed now, but her laugh was hollow. 'You said that to me once before when we were in the Royal Pavilion.'

'And I was right,' he said. 'It wasn't over.'

'Not that time.' She pulled her knees in against her chest.

He lay back and looked up into the sky.

Brodie shivered, and then she lay back too. Above her the glow from the streetlights caught on the terracotta frieze running around the top of the concert hall, showing various figures dancing and reading. She could just make out the words '*This hall was erected for the advancement of Arts and Sciences and works of . . .*' but the letters disappeared into a sky devoid of stars.

Brodie closed her eyes and in her memory she could hear the pulse of 'The Arthur Music' beating like a broken heart.

As a car horn sounded loud and clear, a thought struck her like an electric shock.

10

The Constellation of the Phoenix

'Light pollution!'

'What?' Friedman lifted his head.

'Light pollution. In cities it's sometimes impossible to see the stars. But it doesn't mean they're not there. Just because we can't see them.'

Friedman sat up, leaning his weight on his elbows.

'I just don't know how we couldn't see it.'

'Er, see what exactly?'

'It's so obvious and we missed it.'

Friedman sat up fully now.

'The connection between the codes. Between what Elgar left behind and what Van der Essen gave us.'

'Yes?'

'The connection *isn't* fire.'

'It isn't?'

'No. Not really.'

'OK. I'm not really sure I can agree with you. Seems like the connection's fire to me. What d'you think it is?'

'Number 88.'

Friedman's face showed clearly he was puzzled. 'You're beginning to sound a lot like Hunter.'

Brodie struggled to sort what she wanted to say into any logical order. 'Maybe I am. But it's definitely number 88.' She tried to speak more clearly. 'I explained about it when we were back at the museum. The constellation of the phoenix. The Firebird.'

'What?'

'It's *not* the fire which is important. It's what *survives* the flames. Yes, Savonarola built a huge bonfire and things were burnt. People even. But it's all there in Elgar's use of words! Smithies explained it weeks ago!' She sat herself up tall and opened her hands as if she were reading words from her palms like from pages in a book. 'Smithies said there's no word in the English language for someone who's lost a child. If you lose a husband you're a "widow". A wife, a "widower". But the idea of losing a child's so terrible it just shouldn't happen. So it has no word.' She got up then and began to pace. 'But, if you lose parents then there *is* a word. And the word's "orphan".'

'Go on,' Friedman urged.

'It's that word "orphan". The fires of 1497 didn't kill Hans. They destroyed those who loved him. They *made* him an orphan. He survived. And if he survived then maybe the book he had survived too. Maybe the code-book didn't burn after all.'

She stopped pacing.

'Eighty-eight,' she said calmly. 'The number of piano keys and the number of the *phoenix* constellation. Phoenix – rising from fire. I think Elgar was talking about something which survived, not something which was lost. So maybe,' she said eagerly, 'there's still hope.'

'I knew it.' Kerrith stood up from her position on the floor, brandishing a piece of headed notepaper. To a casual observer it would have looked like she was playing a rather elaborate game. The floor was completely covered with paper and documents like pieces of an outsized jigsaw puzzle. 'Perfect.'

The paper she held was almost entirely blank apart from the heading which had the name of a Belgian hotel. Why anyone would want to holiday in Belgium was completely beyond her. The only writing on the paper was in thin purple ink. A date and the time 8 p.m.

Kerrith reached for another scrap of paper. A small receipt. On the top of the receipt was printed an address. The same address which headed the notepaper.

'Perfect. Absolutely perfect.'

She flapped the large piece of hotel notepaper in front of her face in a desperate attempt to cool off. Solving puzzles was hot work. It was also incredibly good fun. Somehow she'd forgotten.

It was as she was fanning herself with the paper that she saw it. Traces of writing. Mere shadows pressed in the fabric of the page.

She stepped carefully across the network of papers to reach her desk. She took out a pencil, sharpened it in the automatic sharpener then blew away the whispers of lead from the tip.

Then, ever so slowly, like an artist at work on a masterpiece, she began to shade across the front of the sheet.

As if surfacing from water, letters began to appear. Small, carefully formed letters.

A name.

Kerrith rocked the pencil back and forth.

Now she had all she needed.

The group met up at Door Eleven and then, after instructions from Friedman to be quick, they bundled into waiting taxis and made their way back to the Carthorse Inn.

They all piled into Granddad's room.

Brodie was the last to enter. She'd brought Smithies up to date with her idea in the taxi and Friedman had whispered something to him. She guessed it was about the chasing men. Smithies said nothing about the chase to the others but the phoenix idea he allowed Brodie to explain.

'Hans didn't die in the fire,' she blurted. 'Elgar was telling us he survived, like a phoenix. So if he lived on, then perhaps the code-book to MS 408 survived too.'

'It's not over?' asked Sheldon.

Brodie shook her head confidently.

'Excellent. What a result. Guess I'm staying, then.' He clapped his hands together and then sat himself back down, cross-legged, on the end of the bed.

'We're all staying,' offered Friedman. 'At least, we're all going.' He laughed at the bemusement of those who listened. 'All going back to Station X, where we can start looking for clues. Find out who this "Orphan Hans" was and what book he had which was so special.'

'Hold on,' said Miss Tandari deliberately. 'We're in the city of London. A place with the most books and libraries around. Why don't we start here?'

Brodie looked across at Smithies. 'What do you

think?' she ventured. Maybe he was concerned about the suited men but surely in a city the size of London the chances of being followed again were tiny.

'Superb idea,' he said. 'We could split ourselves into teams and try and pool our resources. Give ourselves a day here to do as much finding out as we can, and then go back to Station X and look at what we've found.'

'You up for that, Granddad?' Friedman said, thumping Mr Bray sharply between the shoulder blades.

'Oh, absolutely,' said the older man. 'Absolutely.'

'Fine,' said Smithies. 'We need to form teams of three or four people. Try and split the expertise.'

Tusia darted from the room suddenly, returning with a free folding map of London which she'd obviously taken from the lobby. She shook the map open and spread it across the only available patch of bedding not being sat on. 'We could try the British Library,' she said, jabbing at its location on the map.

'And the Barbican Library,' suggested Sheldon.

'There's even one here called the Shoe Lane Library,' said Tusia, drumming against the map. 'I could try there.'

There was a general mumbling as locations were discussed and allocated.

Brodie stood up and peered down at the spidery

spread of London which suddenly seemed to promise so much. Friedman moved to stand beside her. 'I reckon I should take you and Hunter with me,' he said. 'The others seem to have got it pretty well sorted.'

'Where?' Brodie asked.

Friedman scanned the map. 'Guildhall Library?' he suggested, pointing out one of the many advertising boxes edging the map.

It was decided then. Tomorrow they'd try and find out exactly who the orphan of the flames really was.

The next morning the sky was the faded grey of old uniform socks. A light drizzle of rain fell.

Friedman looked happier than Brodie had seen him for a while. 'You kids are certainly tenacious,' he said.

'We are?' spluttered Hunter through a mouthful of pastry Friedman had bought him for breakfast.

'Yeah. You just won't let go. Just like Brodie's mum. She stuck with things till the end.'

Brodie suddenly felt a heaviness in her stomach. Friedman talked as if never giving up was a good thing, but it hadn't done her mum any good. If she'd settled for not knowing the answers, then maybe she'd still be alive. Suddenly Brodie no longer wanted the rest of her own pastry.

'Shame to waste it, BB.' Hunter took it from her

and downed the last section in one gulp. 'What? It was tasty.'

They took the tube to St Paul's Cathedral then cut across to the Guildhall Library. Inside there were large signs listing the various collections kept there. Sections on clockmakers, maritime heritage and parliamentary bills. Brodie scanned the listings. There obviously wasn't a section labelled '*lots of information about someone who became an orphan because of the fires started by Savonarola*', which would have made it a whole lot easier.

'Let's go to the history department and begin with the bonfires,' said Hunter.

It seemed a good place to start so they made their way up to the second floor. They found several books on religious history, a huge volume on the development of Florence and a smaller text on the treatment of heretics in Europe.

Hunter was the first to find a section on Savonarola. 'Seems the bloke didn't do too well out of his little bonfire trick,' he said, flattening the page so the other two could see.

'Really?' said Brodie, moving closer.

'Nope. The Pope turned against him.'

'Shame.' There was a note of glee in the way Friedman said this.

'He was tortured apparently. But vitally, they didn't do anything to hurt his right arm.'

'Why?' asked Brodie, who thought it odd torturers should show any sense of consideration.

'So the man could still sign a confession,' he said. 'They get you like that. Break you down and then make you admit to things.' The sense of pleasure had left his voice now.

'So did he sign some sort of confession, then?' asked Brodie.

'He signed it all right, and was executed in the same square where he'd burnt the books and paintings just a year before.'

'So he didn't survive the flames, then?'

Hunter shook his head.

Brodie turned the page in the open book. 'So what about the ones who did survive? Anyone called Hans?'

They worked methodically, up to a point. Behind them the clock marked the passing minutes, the rhythm of its ticking broken only by the rustle of turning pages. Several hours passed since the Danish pastries and Brodie began to regret not finishing hers. Hunter wandered off for a while and returned with a stack of books on the history of art.

'Can't believe how many pictures Savonarola burnt,'

mumbled Hunter, his stomach growling. 'What was the matter with the man?'

Brodie looked over at the open books Hunter had spread in front of him. They were all open on images of birds in flight. Phoenixes in fact, when she looked more closely.

There was an open page showing a picture from something called the Aberdeen Bestiary. A bird looking a lot like an eagle appeared to be sitting on an egg surrounded by flames. 'That one looks more like a pigeon,' she said, pointing out another version Hunter had flicked the pages to.

'Almost as bad as your "chicken" effort,' said Hunter. Brodie thumped him.

'That one looks like a cockerel,' offered Friedman, who'd finished scanning the book he'd been working through.

Brodie looked across at the picture of a phoenix on top of a temple in Japan. 'That one looks most like the Firebird on the back of Van der Essen's letter, though, look.' She pointed to an open page of a book on the middle of the table.

'Does it look the same?' asked Hunter.

Brodie was just about to tell him off for not paying attention when Friedman opened his wallet and drew out a rather battered envelope.

'You still have the Firebird Code?' she said.

'Course. I was the one who got it in the first place. Smithies gave it back to me when you lot cracked the code.'

'But you've got it with you?'

Friedman's face coloured a little. 'Solving the Firebird Code set me free from something. It feels good to have it with me as a reminder.' He patted the envelope gently. 'I've lots of details on codes and code-cracking at home but they're hidden away safely. In the wrong hands, proving I was working on MS 408 wouldn't be difficult. But I keep this with me to remind myself that sometimes problems can be solved.' His voice tailed away as he put the envelope down beside the books and stroked the broken seal flat.

'Well?' said Hunter.

Brodie moved the open book closer.

'Identical,' whispered Friedman. 'They're totally identical.'

'Great,' said Brodie. 'Identical birds. Now can we please get back to the business of looking for Hans.'

'What?' Hunter sounded outraged and a strolling librarian shot him a look which could have withered someone less brave. 'Come on, BB. Think about it. What are the mathematical chances of those birds being identical?'

'Pardon?' She was really hungry now and with the best will in the world she'd no idea what he was talking about.

'Think of all the dragons in the Music Room of the Pavilion. All 185 of them.'

'You remember the number.'

He raised his eyebrows in exasperation. 'You told me the number. I never even made it into the Music Room after getting hurt, if you remember. But you told me – 185. I don't forget numbers.'

'So what about 185?'

'They were all different. That's the point. And the phoenixes too. All different.'

'And?'

'There's a billion different ways to draw a phoenix. It's not like you can sketch a real one. Some pictures are better than others. Some even look like chickens,' he mumbled. 'So if we suddenly come across a picture of a phoenix which is identical to the bird on the stamp of the letter, that must be important. Can't be chance.' Hunter concentrated, trying to back up his argument as he hurried on. 'Remember the clarinet player?' Brodie creased her forehead, thinking, but Hunter didn't wait for her answer. 'Elgar's clarinet player. You went on about him.'

'A clarinet player?' said Friedman.

'Brodie said Elgar made him play silently for several bars in order to warm up. Remember?'

'Oh yeah.'

'Well. It was crackers.'

The librarian turned and resumed her walk back between the tables towards them.

'Anyway,' hissed Hunter. 'It all comes down to details. Like with warming up the clarinet. The phoenix seal on the letter could be a fluke. But it's not very likely, is it? It's a detail. Of all the images of Firebirds Van der Essen could have chosen, he went for that one.'

'So?'

'Maybe this particular way of drawing a phoenix is important. So we need to read this book to find out what's special about this particular design of phoenix.'

'OK,' said Brodie, catching on eagerly.

They looked down.

Friedman broke the silence. 'We go with Plan B, you reckon?' he asked gently.

'Plan B?'

Hunter grinned. 'We need Granddad.'

'Granddad?' said Brodie anxiously.

'We need him, BB,' said Hunter. 'Every word in this book's in German. So we take the book back to the hotel and get your granddad to read it.'

* * *

213

'Well?' blurted Hunter.

'Well what?' Granddad leant against the chest of drawers, his arms folded across his chest.

'It's your chance to show us your skills in action. To make the Firebird sing,' explained Hunter.

Granddad straightened his glasses.

He took the book and sat down on the end of the bed.

There were moments when Brodie thought he'd made a breakthrough. He scribbled sections on pieces of paper as he worked, and now and then he underlined words he'd written, emphasising their importance.

The room was silent.

At one point Sheldon began to play his harmonica. 'What?' he asked, as most around the room lifted their heads to glare at him. 'I thought it might help.'

'Well, it doesn't,' said Granddad, rubbing his temple.

'Fine,' snapped Sheldon, slipping the harmonica back into his pocket.

Miss Tandari left the room after a while, returning with chocolate, which was shared around eagerly. Hunter had just begun to whisper about sending out for seconds, and Sicknote had just excused himself to go and get his inhaler, when Granddad stood up.

'Got it,' he said, and the pieces of paper slipped like overstuffed snowflakes to the floor.

'You have?'

'Well, I think so.'

'So come on then,' begged Friedman.

'Aachen.'

Miss Tandari frowned as if believing Mr Bray had just said something incredibly rude.

'Aachen,' repeated Granddad. 'It's a town in Germany. And that phoenix, the particular firebird Van der Essen used in his seal, is part of Aachen's town crest.'

'OK . . .' Brodie said carefully, waiting for what came next with anxious concentration.

'I've looked at the history of Aachen.'

Brodie mentally crossed her fingers that Granddad was on to something real, not just a dead end.

He peered through his glasses intently. 'There's mention in the town history of someone called Hans.'

'There is?' urged Tusia. 'It's him!'

'Hold on!' Sicknote warned. 'Hans is a very common German name. We can't be sure the Hans you've read about is the one we're looking for.'

'Very true. This particular Hans was quite well known around Aachen. Seems his father was a bit of a local hero.'

'And?' pressed Smithies.

'Hans's father was a freedom fighter. There's mention of him being interested in the arts. Stories,

215

pictures, music, that sort of thing. Apparently, the man was originally from England but he travelled to Aachen and had a son. Then, and here's the important bit, *he travelled to Florence*. Bonfire of the Vanities took place in *Florence*,' Granddad reminded them.

'So this freedom fighter guy, Hans's father, was in Florence when Savonarola got up to all his burnings?' asked Hunter.

'Precisely. He took on Savonarola's men and did all he could to try and prevent the destruction.'

'But we know he failed,' Miss Tandari said sadly.

'And in fact he was incredibly badly burnt,' went on Granddad. 'He returned to Aachen injured and terribly disfigured. His son Hans cared for him *but* he died of an infection.'

'Healthcare wasn't what it is now,' mumbled Sicknote, as if this thought alone caused his blood pressure to rise.

'Aachen took Hans's father as a bit of a figurehead and they felt sorry for Hans too. Seems the boy lost his mother during the years his father had been away. Of course there were many orphans in those times. Probably too many to mention.'

'But Hans *was* mentioned?' asked Brodie.

'Yes. He was called the "orphan of the flames" because of his father's sad story.'

'Well, that's fabulous,' said Sheldon. 'Not his dad dying or anything, but him being called a special orphan. That must mean the book's talking about the same "orphan Hans" we're looking for, doesn't it?'

'Does it say any more?' pressed Brodie.

Her granddad's eyes widened. 'It does. It talks about how this "orphan of the flames" was quite well known in Aachen because of what his dad did and because of *what he owned*.' He paused for effect. 'It seems Hans's father didn't leave him with nothing,' said Granddad. 'He signed him over to the care of the town and the town records list his possessions as being a medallion.'

'And this medallion was special?' said Tusia.

'Special enough to write about in the town records,' said Granddad, 'and special enough for us to think there must be a real connection to our code. Here's the point. The medallion had an animal on it. A bird.'

'You're saying the bird was a phoenix?' yelped Brodie. '*Please* tell us it was a phoenix.'

Granddad flicked to the picture in the book.

Brodie could barely contain her excitement. It *was* a phoenix. And more than that, it was the picture which made it look the same as the phoenix stamp on the back of the Firebird Code envelope.

'It was this particular phoenix the people of Aachen copied into their town sign,' said Granddad. 'When you saw this picture in the book and knew it reminded you of the stamp on the Firebird Code, you were looking at the phoenix of Aachen. The phoenix the town uses in their town sign. And they got the idea from Hans's medallion.'

There was a sense of anticipation in the air. They'd found their orphan. A boy who lost his father because of the fires of Savonarola and now they knew he'd lived in Germany. It was exciting and brilliant and . . .

But how would it help?

'Nothing else?' Sheldon prompted.

'Oh, yes.'

Brodie could hardly bear the wait. 'What?' she insisted.

'His father left him a book – a book no one could read.'

Smithies' voice cracked. 'In code?'

Granddad shook his head. 'Latin. The book Hans had dated from the 1400s and it was written entirely in Latin. But here's the exciting bit.'

Brodie wasn't sure she dared to breathe.

'The connection that brings the story *back to England*. The book written in Latin, which we think Hans's father saved from the fire in Florence, was printed here in London!'

11

A Journey to Aachen

It felt good to have a celebration, even in a cramped bed and breakfast room smelling of cough medicine and rather damp coats. Miss Tandari made sure there was enough chocolate to go round, and when Sheldon took out his harmonica this time, no one asked him to stop.

Brodie stood back from it all and watched. It was amazing how hours before they'd all felt so despondent, and now, because of the puzzle pieces various people had collected, a picture, if a bit hazy, was beginning to form again.

Brodie felt a sense of relaxed happiness and she realised she hadn't felt this for a while.

Over the sound of the harmonica, and Granddad's rather out-of-tune singing, she was suddenly aware of a phone ringing. Friedman caught her eye, drew a mobile from his pocket, then slipped from the room. Brodie waited. It suddenly felt like the thing to do to follow him.

'You OK, BB?'

'Fine. Just need some air.'

'Well, don't be long, then,' said Hunter. 'I've managed to persuade Smithies to buy us all fish and chips. Even I can't survive just on chocolate.' By the sugared glaze of his eyes, Brodie was pretty sure he'd made quite a good job of trying. He moved closer to whisper, 'And you should check on Friedman.'

'What do you mean? Check on him?'

Hunter shrugged. 'Don't know really. It's just odd he always wants to get away. Be on his own.'

'He's getting the chips!'

'Yeah. Well. I'm just saying. Watch him, that's all.'

Brodie clicked the door shut behind her.

Friedman was in the corridor whispering into his phone. 'I told you not to call me,' she heard him say.

She fiddled with the door handle. The last thing she wanted Friedman to do was to think she was listening in, but she didn't have to worry. As far as the caller was concerned at least, the conversation was obviously over.

'Hello? Hello?' Friedman was shaking the phone.

He caught Brodie's eye. 'Bad connection,' he said. 'It's a friend, I think, but I can hardly hear him.'

Brodie let go of the door handle. 'It's a bit mad in there,' she said, gesturing to the room they'd just left. 'Just thought I'd get some space.'

'Great idea,' Friedman said, giving up on his phone and putting it in his inside pocket. 'Let's go and get the chip supper Hunter's been banging on about.'

The light was fading and the puddles shrinking on the pavement. Brodie shivered and Friedman took off his jacket and wrapped it around her shoulders. 'Better?' he asked.

'Thanks.'

He plunged his hands into his pockets.

They walked for a while without speaking. Then at last she broke the silence. 'You're worried. About the people who followed us at the Royal Albert Hall?'

'We have to be careful all the time, Brodie. I don't think they ever stop watching us.'

'Hunter thinks perhaps you worry too much,' she said nervously.

Friedman stopped walking for a moment. 'Have you told Hunter about the men who chased us?'

'Miss Tandari told me I shouldn't.'

'Good advice,' he said playfully.

Brodie was embarrassed. 'You look sad too,' she said

quietly, and it was more of a question than a statement.

'Well, perhaps I am a little sad. But it's OK.'

'But we got away from those men. They didn't get us. Or in the explosion. Things are OK. And you looked so happy this morning when we were looking for answers, and now we've found some, you look kind of different.'

'Sometimes the hunt brings more pleasure than the kill, Brodie.'

'It's good Hans survived, though, isn't it?' she said.

'Of course.'

Now she pushed her own hands deep into her pockets. 'Can I ask you something?' she said at last. 'Do you think he ever recovered? You know, Hans.'

'From losing his parents, you mean?'

'I mean, he became the "orphan of the flames",' she explained. 'That's what he was. How people knew him.'

Friedman stopped for a moment. 'What do you mean?'

'That's what's written down about him. Whatever else he did. That's the most important thing. The detail everybody knows.'

A shadow crept across Friedman's eyes.

'Like with me. I know it's what people think about. Poor thing. Lost her mum. Never knew her dad. It's like I'm an orphan of the flames, too.'

'You're so much more than that, Brodie. It's just your starting place. It's not where you finish. It just explains who you are at the beginning. It won't be who you are at the end.'

'It won't?'

'Sure.'

'But what about Hans?'

Friedman scuffed the ground with his foot. 'We've still got to find out how his story goes on . . . and how it ends.'

'But isn't it that he just had the book?'

This time a smile reached his eyes. 'Perhaps. But maybe there's more for us to find. A thrilling story to amaze us all.'

'You really think so?'

'Of course we can't tell yet. We'll have to read on to learn more.'

Brodie was beginning to feel tired. The light was almost gone.

'Let's get the supper,' said Friedman. 'Hunter will have starved.'

They turned then and walked back in silence to the chip shop. It wasn't an awkward silence. It was comfortable.

When they approached the hotel steps, their arms laden with wrapped fish suppers, Brodie slowed again.

'There's just one more thing,' she said. 'How did your story start? Just out of interest. I mean, did you grow up with your parents?'

'No,' Friedman said. 'I was like you. Brought up by my grandparents, William and Elizebeth.'

Brodie held the food tighter.

'They were great people,' he said. 'Grandparents often are.'

The Director folded his arms across his chest. 'And you're entirely sure there can be no doubt?' he said slowly.

'No doubt at all.' Kerrith twitched a little. The new diamond bracelet she'd bought as a reward to herself flashed on her wrist.

'He was definitely there?'

'Yes, sir. He was there. His papers and receipts prove it.'

'And we can make it look good?'

'We can make it look very good.'

The Director rolled a gold-plated pen backwards and forwards across the end of the mahogany desk. For a moment it looked like the pen would fall, but he didn't allow it. 'And you think this will bring him down?'

'We can prove he's working on MS 408. And you

said you wanted him destroyed. I believe this will do that.'

The Director slipped the pen into his jacket pocket. 'Good work, Kerrith.'

The bracelet flashed once more on her wrist. 'Yes, sir. I know.'

'We have to go back to the Guildhall Library.'

'I'm not sure, Brodie,' Friedman said. 'We need to keep on the move. We've been here too long.'

'What's the matter with him?' hissed Hunter. 'Why's he so keen to get away?'

Brodie said nothing. She'd promised not to talk about the men from Level Five.

'I get the feeling the guy's got something to hide,' said Hunter, this time in barely more than a whisper.

Brodie stalled. 'We have to get the book on Aachen back at least,' she said, turning to Friedman. 'And we could see if there are any more records in the library.'

'But . . .' Friedman glanced at the window. Was he trying to show her the men with suits were here? Had they been followed again?

Smithies decided the matter. He insisted they put on their Pembroke uniforms this time as he was afraid four 'nearly teenagers' absent from school but together on a weekday could arouse suspicion. Because Sheldon didn't have a blazer, Hunter said he stood out like a pork sandwich in a vegetarian deli, so Smithies bought him a collar shirt from the Tesco across the road and made him wear Hunter's tie.

Miss Tandari led the way and bamboozled the librarian into believing Pembroke School had booked a reading room. Leaning heavily on Brodie's arm, Granddad looked very pained and Sicknote drew heavily on his inhaler, so the poor librarian became so befuddled she led them upstairs and opened the research room.

'OK, Hans, orphan of the flames,' said Smithies theatrically, 'we need to know what book it was which was so important to your father he saved it from the flames for you.' He straightened the cuffs on his shirt like a magician about to begin his most complicated trick.

'Could it really be the code-book?' said Tusia. 'To MS 408, I mean?'

'It's a possibility . . . isn't it? Elgar and Van der Essen wanted us to know Hans had it,' said Smithies. 'They left a trail of clues. It seems very likely it's a code-book, otherwise why go to all the trouble of leaving us his name?'

'But it could just be an important book, right? One

his dad saved from Savonarola's flames. It might not be a code-book,' Sheldon pointed out.

'True,' said Smithies. 'But code-breaking's all about links,' he said. 'The others have spent months working on that idea. So let's go forward on the basis that the book Hans's dad rescued at least links to MS 408 or why bother leaving us the clues about it? But . . . the book, when we find it, might not be a code-book. It might be a book that explains MS 408. Something with extra information which somehow works with MS 408 to make sense of the code in it.' He paused. 'But whatever this book is and however it helps us, it was important enough for Hans's dad to risk his own life to save it.'

'It *cost* him his life really, didn't it?' said Sicknote, obviously remembering the horrific burns. 'Hans's dad must have thought the book was more important than his own safety.'

'So we begin with him, then,' concluded Friedman. 'Hans's dad.'

Smithies began to pace.

Brodie doodled the word 'dad' on the notepad in front of her. It seemed strange to see it written down. She wasn't sure she'd written the word that often before. When she crossed it out her granddad looked at her sheepishly.

Hunter glanced down at the notes Brodie had made in her logbook in the hotel while her granddad had explained what he'd read in the German book. 'Hans's father was from England originally. The town hall records from Aachen explained that. So we need to know where he came from and when. What did the book say his name was, Granddad?'

'Benjamin Barge.'

'So we know this Benjamin Barge was in Florence in 1497,' said Miss Tandari.

'And the town hall records tell us Hans was fifteen when he was given over to the care of the town,' added Granddad. 'And that his father had been a citizen of the town for fifteen years when he died.'

'So, that suggests Benjamin Barge arrived in Aachen just before Hans was born. That puts him there in 1482,' said Hunter. Brodie had long ago decided there was no need to check Hunter's maths.

'And you wrote down here, that Hans's dad was sixty-five when he died,' said Hunter. 'So he was fifty when he had Hans. Quite old, then.'

Granddad sniffed as if suggesting that fifty was old was a totally ridiculous idea.

'So we need to find out about a fifty-year-old Englishman called Benjamin Barge who sailed to Germany in about 1482,' concluded Hunter.

'And we really know nothing about him other than that?' asked Sheldon.

'Well, there may be something else.' Everyone turned to look at Granddad. 'I'm not sure if this is his trade.'

'What do you mean?' Smithies asked.

'Well, in the book they kept making references to the name "Carpenter".'

'But his name was definitely Barge,' confirmed Tusia.

'Yes,' stressed Granddad anxiously. 'But the name Carpenter kept cropping up. It could've been his job.'

Sicknote got up and scoured the shelves marked 'Maritime history', taking down a thick shabby volume and wrinkling his nose against the cloud of dust. 'These books list sea voyages in the fourteenth and fifteenth centuries. If we're lucky it will have Benjamin Barge's name down on some ship's roll-call or boarding list. We need to find out whether any tradesmen called Barge, who were good with wood, travelled to Aachen.' He passed several more volumes down to those seated at the table, wobbling a little, before collapsing back into his chair.

'There's hundreds of names listed here,' moaned Sheldon, as Sicknote flicked through the records listing boat passengers in the 1480s.

At this point Hunter's eyes seemed to light up. 'We never said it'd be easy, Fingers,' he said airily.

'No. But it'd just be nice if some of it was,' came the reply.

They scoured the pages for ages, dust and mites filling the air as their despondency increased.

'There's loads of people listed here under the name "Suffolk",' said Miss Tandari eventually. 'Does that mean they all have the name Suffolk, or that they're from Suffolk, because there's no such job as "a Suffolk", surely?'

'Here, let me see,' said Friedman, pulling the largest book towards him and causing Sicknote to launch into a rather excessive coughing fit. 'It's more subtle, I think,' he said. 'Suffolk, or in this case the Earl of Suffolk, is their "sponsor", I think.'

'What, are they raising money for charity?' laughed Hunter.

Friedman wasn't amused. 'Sponsors paid for certain men and women to travel abroad. And set up new lives elsewhere. They vouched for them, I guess.'

Smithies reached for a book. He flicked page after page. After what seemed like hours he lifted his head. Here's a list with "Carpenter" on it,' he said, barely hiding the excitement in his voice. 'Someone called Carpenter must have been a sponsor like the Earl of

Aachen

*Local hero = Benjamin Barge

from England
travelled to Florence

badly burnt
died in Aachen

Son= Orphan of the Flames
Hans

Owned medallion with a
Phoenix stamp on

also owned a book

from the 1400s

in Latin

book printed in LONDON

Town crest
of Aachen

The wax
seal on
THE FIREBIRD
CODE!!

Suffolk. The list's dated 1482. That would fit.' He ran his finger down the list of names recorded. 'And there's one man here. Older than the others.'

Brodie detected a quiet tut from her grandfather's direction, but Smithies carried on.

'This guy's fifty.' He looked up at Hunter expectantly. 'That would make him the right age, yes?'

Hunter nodded.

It was almost too much to hope for. Granddad ran his finger along the line of the record.

'Come on,' urged Friedman. 'Put us out of our misery. Is his name Barge?'

Her granddad clapping his hands excitedly gave her the answer she needed.

'So do we think that's him, then?' asked Miss Tandari, moving closer to the table.

'We need to track the journey,' said Friedman.

'See which town accepted him,' offered Sicknote.

This search took them even longer. Brodie didn't think they could keep looking but then Smithies jabbed the pages with his thumb. 'Bingo!'

'Bingo?' whispered Tusia. 'There's really a town called Bingo?'

'No. I mean, bingo, I've found it,' said Smithies.

'What have you found?'

'Aachen.'

Sicknote passed over a tissue before he understood what Smithies had said.

'It's Aachen. The town which accepted the fifty-year-old man called Benjamin Barge who was sponsored by someone called Carpenter.'

Miss Tandari leant over to examine the document more carefully. 'What's this symbol mean?' she said, pointing more closely at the list of names.

'It looks like a letter "d",' offered Tusia.

'So what does that mean?'

'Dead,' said Sicknote, with a rather excessive amount of relish.

'Dead?'

'Yes. Deceased. Over. Kicked the bucket. No more.'

Friedman snorted from the end of the room. 'We're very well aware what the term means. We just wondered why it was there. Benjamin Barge clearly wasn't dead if he was accepted by the town of Aachen.'

Friedman cleared his throat. 'It means the sponsor was dead. Look, there's a small letter "d" next to every mention of the word Carpenter.'

'Not much of a sponsor, then,' suggested Hunter.

'No. But the estate would have been managed by someone. This Carpenter person was probably the estate manager. I guess the "d" symbol means Carpenter's managing an estate of someone who's dead.'

'So whose estate was Carpenter managing, then?' asked Smithies, peering down once more at the list.

Friedman leant over and flicked through the pages. Then he stopped.

'Well?'

'It's ridiculous,' he said.

'Why? What have you found?'

He rubbed his eyes as if hoping to make the letters on the page rearrange themselves to spell out something which made more sense. 'It looks like Carpenter refers to a certain John Carpenter.'

'I know that name,' said Hunter. 'Never forget a name, me.'

'You *have* mentioned that,' groaned Tusia.

'He was a very famous Londoner. Apparently, he was town clerk or something,' Hunter went on.

'And how exactly do you know all this?' asked Tusia.

'My parents,' he said rather mournfully. 'At one time they wanted me to go to City of London School. It's supposed to be good there. You know. For people who like maths. And your John Carpenter was the founder.'

'Well done, Hunter. He was. And he also worked for a very influential boss. And, I believe it was this boss's estate which sponsored Benjamin.'

'OK,' said Smithies to Friedman. 'But nothing ridiculous so far.'

'No. It's just the name of the boss and the owner of the estate that's ridiculous,' Friedman replied.

He took a piece of blank notepaper from the pile and wrote something down. Then he passed the paper to Smithies.

'Well,' said Smithies. 'It's certainly interesting.'

'Who is it?' begged Brodie.

Smithies cleared his throat. 'We've followed a clue left for us by a nutty Belgian professor, which led us to a nutty English composer, but I think we've reached the most eccentric twist in the tale now.'

'Who is it?' chorused Tusia and Hunter.

Smithies lowered the piece of paper for them to see.

12

Dick Whittington's Legacy

'No,' said Hunter. 'Get your mushrooms back on the kebab stick!'

Brodie peered at the name. 'Are you sure?'

Smithies put the paper on the table so everyone could see it.

DICK WHITTINGTON

Friedman rubbed his chin. 'The pantomime dude with the cat and the big red spotty handkerchief on a pole?'

Sheldon looked at Friedman as if he were exhibiting advanced stages of madness. 'What are you talking about? A man with a cat and a big spotted handkerchief? How does he fit in?'

'He can't, can he? Just a fairytale character?' Friedman looked around the room for confirmation.

'I think you'll find you're mistaken,' Sicknote said pertly. 'Whittington's not imagined! He's a vital part of our British heritage, I'll have you know.'

'Well, have us know, then.' Friedman frowned.

Sicknote didn't need telling twice. 'Sir Richard Whittington lived in the late 1300s and early 1400s and he became the Lord Mayor of London.'

'So the pantomime story's true?'

'Aspects of the story are true, though I doubt very much he found the streets of London paved with gold.'

'But was he rich, like the story says?' Tusia asked.

'Very rich and very generous. Used his money to do lots of amazing things such as setting up a hospital ward for unmarried mothers at St Thomas's.'

'There's a Whittington hospital in Islington, London,' said Miss Tandari. 'And a statue of his cat.'

Sicknote snuffled a sneeze. 'Stories say,' he continued, 'he was so generous that one day he took the list of all his moneylending and burnt it.'

'What's so great about that?' asked Tusia.

'Well, everyone who owed him money was suddenly totally free from the debt. If it wasn't written down no one knew about it.'

'A bit like the meaning of the language in MS 408,' said Brodie. 'We can't find a written record . . . so no one knows!'

'Nice story,' said Hunter, returning to the idea of the debts.

'Yep, and another link to our fire theme,' said Friedman. 'But how does all this stuff about a very nice man with a cat and a handkerchief link to Hans and Carpenter?'

Smithies had been avidly scanning the book while Sicknote explained. 'Well, it looks to me,' he said, 'like he needed an executor to carry out the wishes in his will. His money had to be spent when he died and someone had to decide how.'

'And that "someone" was Carpenter?' said Granddad.

'It was. He made all the decisions, based on Whittington's wishes, about how much should be spent on what. He spent loads of the money to rebuild bits of this library.'

Brodie looked around her. 'The Guildhall?'

'The very same. And according to what's written here his money was also used to rebuild Newgate Gaol. Carpenter was town clerk of London and had to make sure Whittington's wishes were carried out. Whittington thought up the ideas . . . Carpenter just made sure it all happened. He managed Whittington's money.'

'Like my mum and clearing up,' groaned Sheldon. 'Her idea. I make it happen.'

Brodie summarised slowly. '"d" in the records, next to Carpenter's name, means Carpenter was managing the money of a dead sponsor and the sponsor was Dick Whittington.'

Smithies tapped the book enthusiastically. 'But also – look – Carpenter used Whittington's money to sponsor people, but he had a fair bit of money for his own use which he put towards good causes. For the "betterment of the poor". Four of them specifically.' He brought his hand down against the pages of the book. 'Benjamin Barge was one of them. See?'

Brodie peered closely at the copperplate writing. 'So,' she said, with a deceptively high amount of confidence. She counted things off on her fingers. 'One, Whittington was Mayor. Two, he had a town clerk called Carpenter. Three, both of them did good things for the poor. Four, like helping support this Benjamin Barge, who, five, went to Aachen and became Hans's dad.'

'Exactly.' Smithies beamed. 'Carpenter gave him a start. Made sure he was well looked after and had a job. For a while it says Benjamin worked as Carpenter's page. But then, just before he went to Aachen, he worked at Newgate Gaol. You remember it had been rebuilt by Whittington's money.'

'So, Carpenter cared for Benjamin,' confirmed

Brodie. 'Could he be the person who gave him a book? The one we need to read MS 408?'

Smithies pushed his glasses up on to his forehead and narrowed his eyes. 'Now that's a thought! Bit of a leap – but let's follow that idea for a moment. If Whittington's money helped pay for this library, then maybe it was a book from here?'

'That *is* a bit of a leap, isn't it?' Hunter remarked dubiously.

'Maybe.' Smithies was obviously impressed with his questioning. 'But we're talking about life hundreds of years ago. There weren't many books. You couldn't buy them everywhere like we can now, from newsagents and train stations and bookshops. They cost a load of money too. Only the wealthiest people had private book collections. Most books came from libraries.'

'So why not this one?' Sheldon finished for him. 'If there's a definite link with Whittington and this place?'

There was a general rumbling of agreement.

'But if the book was from here,' said Miss Tandari slowly, 'then Benjamin Barge would have taken it to Aachen with him, saved it from the flames of Savonarola and then given it back to Hans, his son. The book won't be here any more.' She fiddled nervously with her bracelets, aware her comments left everyone in the room feeling deflated.

'I'm not sure,' said Granddad. 'Going back to the beginning of this trail . . . Elgar, one of the most famous English composers, wrote a code leading us to Benjamin Barge *and* Carpenter. I think the history's important. I think Benjamin did save the book from the flames and passed it to his son. But I think it could be quite likely Hans returned the book here.'

'Why?' said Brodie. 'If you're talking about leaps – that's a big one!'

'A sense of home,' Granddad told her. 'Think of it this way, Brodie. There comes a time in everyone's life, when they want things sort of tidied up. Loose ends tied together. If you think about it, Benjamin Barge was near to death when he passed the book he'd rescued over to his son. It seems logical to me an Englishman abroad might want things returned home.' He looked sort of wistful, Brodie thought. 'There's no chance his injured body could be returned home to be buried. We're talking about centuries ago. It wouldn't have been possible. But to return his possessions home to England – his son could have done that for him.'

'Could have done,' said Hunter. 'But we've got no proof.'

'True,' said Granddad. 'But we've got the idea a famous English composer knew about the book. Doesn't that make it *likely* the book's on British soil

241

again? All the clues we've followed have been about restoring things. Being reborn from the flames. I think we should at least consider the idea the book may be here,' he finished firmly.

No one spoke. Brodie could hear the beating of her own heart.

'That's double whipped cream great,' said Hunter. 'And I don't want to rain on anybody's barbecue, but do you have any idea at all how many books there are in this library? Any idea at all?'

Brodie looked around again. She didn't need him to tell her. Loads.

'Even if the book's really here,' Hunter continued, 'how the strawberry smoothie would we find it—'

'Hunter?'

Hunter broke off and stood up, his face screwed into deep creased lines.

'What, Hunter?'

'City of London School. I went there, right, to have a look round. And there was a statue. Of this John Carpenter. And the statue, I think, was holding a book. What if it's the book we need.'

'What was it?' Brodie asked excitedly.

Hunter's face reddened. 'I didn't look close enough to see.'

* * *

'I'm not happy.'

Both men thought the Director's statement was unnecessary. 'Sir. I'm sorry. It's just . . . London. It's difficult to do things without being seen.'

The Director clearly thought this comment was amusing. 'Not if you try hard enough.' He paused. 'No matter. There's been a change of emphasis. We are pursuing a new line of enquiry. Another string to our bow.' He turned to face the window. 'Agent Vernan will bring you up to speed.'

'I can't believe we're doing this,' groaned Brodie, pushing her hair up inside a bobble hat. 'You seriously think this is going to work?'

'It's a boys' school. You can't go in looking like you normally do.'

Tusia kicked Hunter sharply in the ankle. 'How's this?' she said, directing her attention at Brodie and sticking the last strands of curly auburn hair under her own knitted hat.

'Oh yes. Very convincing,' hissed Hunter.

Tusia kicked him again.

The plan was simple. Get inside the school. Blend and merge.

'OK. Ready?' Tusia was in charge.

Hunter winced and dragged his stilts behind him.

At a nod from Tusia he climbed up on the stilts and began to walk up and down. 'Hey, mate?' he said, calling down to a smallish boy sitting on a bench outside the school entrance. 'Want a go?'

'Sure.' The little boy looked like he'd won the lottery.

'Best take your blazer off, though. Don't want to go ripping that if you fall.'

The little boy looked a little less keen.

'My mate Fingers will hold it for you.' Sheldon stepped forward to take the offered blazer. 'Anyone else want a go? Blazer off and in the queue if you're up for it. Up for it? Get it? Up for it on stilts.'

'He can cut out the silly jokes,' hissed Tusia.

'What? He's doing OK,' said Brodie, taking the blazer Sheldon had passed to her and quietly slipping it on.

Tusia had to admit, rather reluctantly, Brodie was right. Hunter had drawn quite a crowd. She swapped her own blazer for the City of London School one and tugged her hat more firmly down on her head. 'Ready? Let's leave him to it and get inside.'

It took little less than a minute. There was a receptionist monitoring the door, but the strategy of blending and merging seemed to work. 'Keep your head down,' Tusia hissed as they moved forward with a crowd of boys keen to get to the first lesson of the afternoon.

'I can't help it,' whispered Brodie. 'I need to know how we're going to find this statue.'

'It's this way,' said Tusia, glancing up at the signs. 'Hunter said it was in the atrium. Follow me.'

They hurried along the corridor. It was weird to be in a school again, even if this one was very different to the school she'd gone to at home. They followed the route past science labs and maths rooms until they found the stairs.

Most of the boys had left them now, drifting off into classrooms or study spaces. Brodie's heart rate slowed a little. 'Where now?' she said, turning a corner and realising the three of them were on their own.

'What's that?' said Sheldon, slowing his step.

'Courtyard,' said Tusia. 'Built on top of the road tunnel running through the building.'

'Tunnel?'

'Didn't you see it from outside the building? It cuts right through the place. But what we need according to Hunter is further up than the courtyard. Come on. Up here.'

Tusia took the stairs two at a time.

Brodie could hardly breathe when she reached the top. It was oddly quiet. Deserted. A huge space with a glass ceiling. Brodie could see the skyline of London and the Millennium Bridge stretching across the River Thames. 'Wow. This is . . .'

'Focus,' growled Tusia. 'We haven't got long. Come on, John Carpenter.' She scanned the walls for signs. 'Where are you hiding yourself?'

They ran across the space towards a door to the balcony to the great hall. And there, high above them on a plinth, was a huge white statue. The man wore a long cloak. He was gazing forward, looking down on all of London.

'It's him,' said Sheldon. 'Look. John Carpenter. The school's founder.'

Suddenly Brodie's breathing came more easily. In the statue's left hand, clutched tight to his chest, was a large stone book.

'What is it?' hissed Brodie, scanning the plinth for information. 'Does it say? Does it tell us what the book is?'

'There,' said Tusia and she pointed to a name sculpted across the cover of the book.

Hunter was quite reluctant to put the stilts away. They had, though, returned the blazers they'd borrowed and Brodie had shaken her hair free of the bobble hat. Tusia kept hers on.

They gathered on the steps of St Paul's Cathedral and sat down.

'It's the "White Book",' said Tusia.

Sheldon crinkled his nose. 'Actually sort of "off-white", isn't it? I mean, not totally white, more a sort of cream.'

'No. That's what it's *called*,' groaned Tusia. 'The White Book. Or *Liber Albus* if you want to be posh. And the exciting thing is, the stuff on the plinth says, Carpenter *wrote* it. It was the very first book of English common law, it said.'

'Sounds important,' said Friedman.

Tusia passed him his phone. She'd used it to take a photo of the statue. 'It also said this really interesting thing that's apparently written inside the cover of the *Liber Albus*. Listen.' She took the phone back, slid the screen to the next photo and began to read.

The book that once was white is white no more.
Made black with grease, and thumb'd its pages o'er.
Then, while it still exists, transcribe each page;
Once gone, 'tis lost to every future age.
And if so lost – some fault of ours, 'tis time –
An me! Thou gem of greatest price, adieu!

'Amazing,' said Miss Tandari.

247

'I know, I said it wasn't really white,' crowed Sheldon. 'Even the poem says so.'

'I mean the words of the poem,' said Miss Tandari.

'Oh.'

'It's obviously a *really* important book,' chipped in Friedman. 'One Carpenter wanted to be kept safe and treasured. A *gem of greatest price*.'

'So precious, then,' continued Smithies, 'it'd need protecting from Savonarola's flames.'

'Absolutely.'

Brodie mulled the poem over in her head and spoke the words in a whisper. '*Once gone, 'tis lost to every future age. And if so lost – some fault of ours.* Makes it sound like someone thought it vital to keep the book for future generations,' she said.

'Which fits with the idea of Benjamin Barge risking everything to make sure the book passed on to his son,' added Hunter.

'And it'd also make sense of Elgar and Van der Essen trying to pass on information for future generations too,' said Brodie. 'They obviously didn't want it to be their fault if the book's importance was lost.'

Sheldon whistled as he thought. 'It all makes sense the book was important. Worth passing through history. Protecting and all that. But that doesn't necessarily mean it's a code-book to MS 408, does it?

And that's what we're really looking for.'

'Maybe it's not a code-book,' said Hunter. 'But it's got to be linked. And it's got to be what Elgar's code was steering us to.'

'So have we done it, then?' said Brodie. 'Have we found the solution to Dorabella's cipher and the Firebird Code?'

'I think,' said Smithies cautiously, 'perhaps we really have.'

'The White Book by Carpenter,' said Sicknote. 'The *Liber Albus*. The "treasure" at the end of the search.'

'So we need to get a copy,' said Friedman, standing up from the step. 'Get a copy of the *Liber Albus* and put it alongside MS 408. We have to work out why the Belgian professor needed us to find this book of all the books there have ever been. And why it links to MS 408.'

Brodie savoured the idea. Were they really one step closer to breaking the unbreakable code of Voynich's manuscript?

'This will break him.'

'That's my intention,' said Kerrith.

The man held out a battered mobile phone.

'You've made it infinitely more easy to track him down, Les. I'm very grateful to you.' She ran her fingernail across the keys on the phone. 'We'll bide our time. Take him when he's least expecting it. When he's beyond the safety of Station X or a public place. Lions do that, you know.' She paused, laughing at her own joke. 'They single antelope out from the herd and then bring them down. When he's alone and has no defences, we'll strike. And the guilt of the loss on the others will destroy the herd from the inside.'

'People like you should be ashamed,' said Les in a voice which could hardly be heard.

Kerrith closed her palm and squeezed the phone tight. 'People like you should be more careful.'

13

The Great Liber Albus

'History. History of Law. Common Law.' Tusia read out the names of library sections as if listing guests at a wedding.

It was on a middle shelf. It looked insignificant. Spine outwards, the title barely legible.

'That's it?' hissed Hunter. 'All the searching and the code-breaking and the agonising and it's just sitting there, in the middle of all those other books in the Guildhall Library.'

Smithies slid it from the shelf. 'A secret right in front of our very noses,' he said. 'The very best type.'

Once inside the Matroyska, the magnitude of what they'd done suddenly hit Brodie.

They'd found the book Elgar and Van der Essen wanted them to find. They'd actually followed all the clues and now had the book they needed and it seemed strange to glance forward at Smithies who'd refused to hand the driving over to someone else but was seated behind the wheel, the copy of the White Book balanced firmly on his lap.

The sun was setting when they arrived back at Station X, and Bletchley Mansion itself seemed to be basking in an orange glow.

'Welcome to your new home, Sheldon,' said Friedman. 'It's here we're going to finally make sense of the Voynich Manuscript.' Brodie smiled to herself when she remembered, despite all Sheldon's involvement he'd never seen a copy of MS 408. He had that to look forward to. And more than that, like them, he'd get to read it.

Smithies called a meeting in Hut 11 on the morning after their return from London.

They sat, as they'd done so many times before, around the tables arranged in a horseshoe shape, with Smithies at the front.

'So, Sheldon,' continued Smithies, 'you become an official member today of Team Veritas secret breakers.'

He passed Sheldon the reproduction copy of MS 408 and Brodie watched as Sheldon flicked through the unreadable pages. It seemed strange to see someone viewing them for the first time. Pages and pictures familiar to her as old friends, but ones which up until now refused to speak.

Smithies coughed, in an attempt to regain everyone's attention, then held the copy of the White Book in the air. 'The *Liber Albus*,' he said, 'the companion book to MS 408. Now we simply have to work out how the books work together.'

'Simple as making choux pastry, then,' whispered Hunter.

'Let's consider how a code-book works,' Smithies said, and then sat down, leaving the floor open for Sicknote, who hobbled to his feet.

Sicknote rested his hand on the head of the wooden elephant statue and began to explain. 'Initially we hoped Van der Essen had found something like a sort of dictionary when he was in Mondragone Castle with Voynich. Would have been so easy, then. A list of symbols and a list of meanings and, hey presto, we'd have made sense of everything written.' He paused. 'Then we realised that something Van der Essen found in Mondragone just led him to know there was a book out there, somewhere in the world, which once belonged to an orphan of the flames called Hans. That book could be used to help us read the crazy document his friend Voynich found.'

Brodie made notes; linked the ideas together to make order on the page.

'Elgar was in on the secret. Perhaps Van der Essen told him. Perhaps something Elgar told Van der Essen helped the Professor understand clues he'd been left. But whoever was first with the information, the two men left behind a complicated series of clues which led us to this. The White Book. The *Liber Albus*.' He paused. 'And the *Liber Albus*'s not a code-book.'

It was obvious he could see the despondency in the faces of those who listened.

'Not a code-book in a "dictionary" sort of way at least,' he explained. 'But other books can be used to break codes. We know that. We've covered that in lessons.'

Brodie hoped Sicknote didn't ask her to explain and lowered her head further, concentrating intently on the page of her logbook.

'If the *Liber Albus* is used as a companion book then this is how it would work. Words in the MS 408 could have been replaced by words from the White Book,' he said. 'Symbols and squiggles could be swapped with readable words from the White Book and suddenly MS 408 would make sense. But we'd need to know which words swap with which squiggles. And usually that method of code-writing works with numbers.'

'Sounds good,' said Hunter.

'You find a word in the White Book and you write down the page it's on and then add a full stop. Then you note the line it's in and add another full stop. Finally, you write down the number of the word counting from the left.'

Brodie struggled to see the pattern in her head.

'Here, let me show you,' said Sicknote. 'If we look at the poem on the first page of the White Book then we could encode the word GEM by writing:

1.6.4

It's the first page, sixth line, fourth word, you see.'

Brodie counted along to check.

'And of course,' added Miss Tandari encouragingly, 'you successfully used a similar system to translate the Firebird Code.'

'Our problem is,' went on Sicknote, 'MS 408 doesn't contain numbers. Nowhere in the document are there recognisable numbers. If the system worked, we'd open MS 408 and see a whole load of numbers to swap with words from the White Book. But there's no numbers at all . . . except for the name 408 given when the manuscript was handed over to the university for storage. The lack of numbers makes things tricky.'

'I'd say it makes it more than tricky,' Brodie whispered. 'Sounds to me as if it makes it impossible.

And I thought we'd done all this work to move away from impossible!'

'How can there be no numbers?' hissed Hunter. 'What sort of rubbish system is that?'

Sicknote ploughed on. 'The point is, there's odd pictures and strange letter formations in MS 408. So it's a possibility that these must represent the words from the White Book.' He steadied himself against the desk. 'So . . . next option, abandon the number system and instead try it with a code-cracking method used by Joseph Feely. Miss Tandari – you'll explain?'

'This is how Feely's method works.' Miss Tandari took over. 'First, find the most commonly used letter in the White Book.'

'Oh, OK.' The smile returned to Hunter's face. 'Things are looking up. We have to count.'

'We literally have to look through the White Book and note how many times each letter's written. When we find the most common letters, these will be called "the leaders". In most pieces of English writing, the letter E's the most common letter. It's used the most. We need to check this and find the ordering of the other letters. Of course it's made more difficult because we're dealing with Latin. But no matter, the principle's the same.'

Brodie laughed to herself. It seemed however hard

the system was, it wouldn't dare to beat Miss Tandari.

'But that'll take months?' Tusia said in alarm. 'It's not exactly short, is it? The White Book, I mean. We really have to count how many times all the letters are used?'

'Fine by me.' Hunter beamed.

'No! Seriously!' pleaded Tusia.

Smithies urged Miss Tandari on. 'So,' she continued, 'we find the leaders in the White Book and match them to the leader squiggles in MS 408. The most common squiggle would equal the most common letter. And so on. It's a case of swapping letters for symbols according to how often they're used. Simple, you see?'

Brodie was excited. But she wasn't sure she could agree it would be simple.

Smithies clapped his hands for attention. 'Come on, team. No one said it'd be easy. Or quick! We have Van der Essen, Elgar, Carpenter and even Dick Whittington to thank for this. The links were complicated and the solving of the code looks set to be complicated too. But anything worth doing often is. Who knows what secret we'll uncover if we work well?' His smile twitched a little, but his eyes were bright. 'So let's start counting and recording.'

Brodie felt more than a little dejected. She'd hoped

somehow for something dramatic and exciting and had forgotten about the slog, the hard work and the effort, involved in code-cracking.

'Normal lessons will continue,' said Smithies. 'Just work on the White Book and MS 408 as best you can in the afternoons. There's just two things, though.' Smithies glanced across at Friedman. 'If we're going to be looking so closely at MS 408 we need to be extra careful. If Level Five know we're still here, they'd have a job up until now to prove we were looking at MS 408 because we've spent so long on the Firebird Code and Elgar. We just need to make sure we hide our notes, leave nothing out on display which can be directly linked to MS 408. However good Fabyan's extra security is, we can't take chances.'

Brodie thought about the men at the Royal Albert Hall.

'Meanwhile, there's another thing,' Smithies said, trying to lift the mood.

'I'd like to see at least some of you having a go at swimming in the lake. I think it's about time we began to enjoy ourselves a little. However hard the task seems, the truth is, our quest, after all, is actually nearly done.'

'I *think* I liked that,' said Brodie as Sheldon closed the lid of the piano one morning. The piece had been weirdly haunting and in a way a bit difficult to listen to.

'It's called "Judas",' Sheldon explained. 'After the apostle who betrayed Jesus. Elgar wrote it.'

Brodie knew the story well. She'd always worried about how someone who'd been chosen to be a friend of Jesus had handed him over to the soldiers who took him off to crucify him. The story unsettled her.

'I think Elgar felt sorry for Judas,' went on Sheldon. 'Sort of understood how Judas believed he did the right thing when he handed Jesus over to be killed.'

Brodie didn't say any more. How could anyone understand something so terrible? How could anyone do something so awful to someone he claimed was his friend?

After lunch, Brodie led the way on to the lawn in front of the house. They took pages of the White Book, and counted every time each letter appeared. The counting of the squiggles in MS 408 they did well away from prying eyes. 'I don't know why we should hide what we're doing,' groaned Sheldon. 'Level Five can't really be that bothered, surely. We're kids and we're looking at a book.'

Brodie wanted to tell him about being chased in the Royal Albert Hall. She wanted to tell him about the Royal Pavilion and the explosion. But she just kept counting.

'He's getting on my nerves,' Hunter moaned to Brodie after executing an impressive swallow-dive in the middle of the lake late one afternoon after a particularly tiring session with the White Book.

'Who?'

'Frantic Friedman,' Hunter shook water from his ears.

It was true Friedman did seem a little edgy, moody even, Brodie thought, but not really any worse than normal.

'He's always on edge. Always watching his back. And he keeps moaning it's taking too long,' Hunter added. 'I don't know what his problem is. They've all been at it for years and just because we can't solve the thing in months he's having a go.'

'No one's having a go,' Brodie countered. 'He just wants to get it done.'

'We all want to get it done, B. Why's he so special?'

'I didn't say he was. But he's spent his life trying to do this. So it matters.'

'What, more than to us? I've had enough, B.' He clambered from the lake and grabbed his towel. 'Of the swimming and them thinking we're not trying. Don't they all know we lie awake at night dreaming we'll be the first to crack this thing? It matters to me just as much as it matters to anyone else. Friedman needs to lighten up a little.'

'He just wants to get answers.'

'We all do. And he unnerves me, B. Always checking if we're OK. Watching over his shoulder.'

Tusia had joined them. 'Hate to say it, but I think Hunter's right,' she said. 'Friedman knows something. And I'd say he's scared. I don't understand why he's so twitchy.'

'Course he's twitchy! He saw what they did to my house! You all saw it. And Friedman was thrown out of the Chamber. Of course he doesn't want them to find us looking at the manuscript. It's banned.'

Hunter shrugged. 'Maybe it's banned for a reason, B. All this waiting for answers is getting to me.'

'You want to give up?'

'How the peanut butter sandwich did you work that out from me just saying it was getting to me?'

Brodie wrapped her towel tight around her. 'Sounded like that to me. Giving up.'

'Great. Now you really sound like Friedman. I'm going to go for a ride on the unicycle. I need some air.'

'We've been outside all afternoon!' growled Brodie.

'*Different* air!' snapped Hunter. 'Away from people who think I'm not trying enough,' and if he hadn't

261

looked quite so cross striding off, Brodie might have called after him.

She didn't want to think about Friedman getting angry. Or giving up. And most of all she didn't want to think about the fact that maybe they wouldn't be able to do it. That they'd fail. Like everyone else had.

That night she pored over the pages of MS 408 long after Tusia was fast asleep. She stared down at the painted flowers and plants that looked like none she'd ever seen on earth. She opened out the folded map page and counted the unknown islands. Then she ran her finger across the unreadable squiggles and loops that were supposed to make everything clear but said nothing she could understand. In the silence of the night the pages sang to her but she couldn't make sense of the song. Her heart beat a little harder, her fingers trembled and tiny beads of sweat blistered on her forehead. With every turn of the page she was pulled in closer, drawn like a sailor to the rocks as the sirens sang. And when she finally went to sleep she dreamt about being shipwrecked. She reached out to Friedman to save her. He stood back and let her drown.

'Surely we've got enough to bring them in, ma'am.' The suited man was filing his report on another raid in York. In his free hand he held a dossier on Station X.

'They must be looking at MS 408. Why else would they still be there?'

Kerrith shook her head. Her lips were pursed. 'It's too soon,' she said. 'The raids in York were just small fry. Lone eccentrics playing. But at Station X they're taking things seriously. And our job is to watch and wait.'

'But, ma'am. It's clear to anyone they're breaking the ban and if—'

Kerrith cut him off with an icy stare. 'And clear to anyone that this ragbag of idiots may actually be getting somewhere. If we're going to bust their operation, let's catch them drowning in details. Let's catch them soaking in all there is to know. Not just dabbling.' She ran her finger beside her eye. She was fearful she was developing worry lines. That wouldn't be a good look. 'We have the situation with Station X under control. Let them find out all they can and then, when there's no hope for salvation, we'll break them by taking the ground from under them. They've gained their strength from the mistaken belief they are in this battle together. They believe they're a team.' She sniffed. 'Let's see what happens to the team when we take out their star player. Let's see how strong their resolve to break the rules is then.'

* * *

It took about three weeks to determine that the 'leaders' or the most commonly used letters in the White Book were E, I, T A, N, U and S.

After finding the 'leader letters' in the White Book the next stage was to compare it with the symbol frequency for MS 408. Tusia and Granddad had worked on this. They'd made a graph to show how often each symbol was used. Now the most common squiggle could be swapped for the most common letter.

This should have been the easy bit. It wasn't.

However they worked they couldn't make sense of the words the squiggles made.

'Is it because the White Book's in Latin?' said Brodie, practically tearing at her hair.

'Shouldn't matter,' said Miss Tandari. 'Even if the letter swaps lead to Latin words they make no sense. Latin or English it makes no difference. We can't read what we get.'

They were in Hut 11. On the wall next to photographs of Van der Essen and Helen Weaver and a picture of the phoenix Tusia had drawn, Smithies had tacked a piece of paper with a single sentence written across it.

when skuge of tunn'e-bag rip, seo uogon kum sli of se mosure-issue ped stans skubent, stokked kimbo elbow crawknd.

Leaders in The White Book:

E I T A N
U S

when skuge of turn 'e-bag rip, seo
uggon Kum sli of se Mosure-issue ped
stans skubent, stokked Kimbo elbow
crawlend

We're not getting anywhere!!

Smithies' violet tie lifted and fell against his stomach. 'It's the best we've got. This is what happens when we replace the squiggles in the MS 408 with the leader letters from the White Book.' He lowered his head. 'And now I'm not so sure we've got it right. I mean everything suggested we use the White Book to read MS 408. We've ploughed on, sure this would give the answer. I hate to say it, but I think we've gone terribly wrong.' He jabbed at the notice-board and the photos fluttered.

'If I may be so bold,' Miss Tandari interrupted, 'perhaps the book's right, it's just we have the wrong copy. I mean, we took a nice pristine copy of the White Book from the Guildhall Library. It's been faithfully reproduced to look like the original but really the original book was written in 1419. Chances are, it was handwritten. Caxton didn't set up the printing press until fifty-seven years later, in 1476.'

'And?' prompted Sicknote, who cradled his mug while the radiator chain clinked against the table leg.

'Well, if it was handwritten there'd have been mistakes. However good the scribes were. I'm just thinking that a tiny error could be a vital clue. A letter written differently, or once too often. It'd make the list of most common letters different. And then we'd end up with a totally different translation.' She twisted the bracelet on her wrist. 'We have to keep in mind that books in the 1400s were very rare. In 1424, Cambridge University had only 122 books. Each of them was as valuable as a farm or vineyard. We've been looking at a reproduction of the White Book which was made in 1859. This book wouldn't be the actual one saved from Savonarola's fire, would it? Perhaps if we were able to look at the original then we'd find a different pattern of letter use, and then we'd find different meanings for the squiggles in MS 408.'

'Sounds good to me. An original or imperfect version of the White Book.' Friedman looked a little wistful, Brodie thought, as if his thoughts were carrying him far away. 'Perhaps I should go back to the Guildhall and ask them if they have a damaged or misprinted version of the *Liber Albus*.'

'We should all come,' said Hunter. 'We're a team. All of us should go.'

Friedman's eyes darkened. 'We are a team, Hunter. And I'm glad you're getting it.'

'Getting it?'

'Yeah. Smithies told me when you first came here you weren't a natural leader. But I think you're beginning to understand the power of your name. That's what you are now, isn't it? A hunter of the truth. A hunter for Veritas.' Friedman smiled. 'I think it's time now you knew about Nimrod. I told you once when we first listened to the *Enigma Variations*, that Nimrod meant something.'

'And?' said Hunter suspiciously.

'It means "Hunter". And I think it's clear you're starting to grow into that name of yours.' Friedman drew in a deep breath. 'But it's best you stay here. There's really no need for everyone to go. I'll leave for London in the morning.'

Kerrith surveyed her tidied office. In the corner, the papers and pages she'd spent so many hours rummaging through lay stacked and filed in organised boxes. And on the table in front of her lay the mobile phone.

She was growing impatient. For a man who had, for so many years, avoided crowds, Friedman seemed to be enjoying the company of the group.

It didn't matter.

Her time would come. She was sure of it. She pressed redial one more time. Then she waited for an answer and hung up. The tracking team would be on to it in minutes. If he'd left the safety of the group, which she knew was back at Station X, then they'd know.

She ran her fingers down the spine of the book on her desk. She turned the cover to open it. Across the front page, stamped deep into the paper like a brand, was a stamp. A stamp showing flames towering to a peak.

Her body tingled.

The Director had made her a promise. Bring down Friedman, break up the work of Station X, and he'd explain the secret of the Suppressors' mark to her.

She closed the book and lowered her palm against the leather cover.

It felt warm.

14

A Posey of Michelmas Daisies

Brodie woke and rolled on to her side. The sunlight sliced through the bottom of the curtains. She could hear from the heavy breathing that Tusia was still asleep.

She'd been dreading today.

It wasn't just the promise of the White Book fading like cheap patterned curtains in the sun. Today would always be difficult. This day was difficult every year.

A walk round the lake did little to lift her mood. She didn't even have the energy to avoid the spluttering fountain. The splashes on her arms looked like tears.

Friedman was standing by the monument to the Polish cryptographers just inside the entrance to the stable yard. A three-sided wall edged a large black granite stand. On top was a sculpted book, pages open, glinting in the sun. He stood with his back to her, gazing down at the open pages. He held a bunch of wild daisies.

Brodie stood for a while behind him. His shoulders lifted as if he wished to shake off a weight he carried there.

She didn't know how long she'd stood there before he turned. 'Brodie?' His voice was a whisper, unsure. As if when he looked at her he saw someone else. 'Brodie?' He lowered the posy of flowers to his side.

'I thought you were going to London today,' she said.

'I am. But there's something I wanted to do first.'

'Michaelmas daisies,' she said, glancing at the flowers. 'My granddad said they were my mum's favourites.'

She saw his hands tighten on the stems. 'They were.'

'Nine years ago today,' Brodie said.

'I know.'

'I wonder what she'd have been like,' Brodie said at last. 'If we'd have got on. You know. What she'd have made of all this.'

'She'd have thought it was wonderful. And of course you'd have got on.'

'I just wonder if maybe I'm not as driven as her. Maybe I don't need to know the answers as badly as

271

she did. Sometimes I think she'd have been disappointed in me.'

'Perhaps you don't need to know the answers so much because no one's fully explained the question to you.'

'What do you mean?'

'Well, it's all about simply cracking the code, isn't it? All about the technical stuff. If you knew why it was so important to break the secret, perhaps you'd feel differently.' He glanced down at the monument in front of her, and she followed his gaze. 'Those who battled with codes during the war knew what they were up against. They were trying to right a great wrong, protect a way of life, protect life itself. It's hard for you if you don't know what the battle's about.'

'So when will I know?'

'When Smithies is ready to tell you, I guess.'

Brodie twisted a lose strand of hair around her fingers. She hadn't plaited her hair today. 'I don't think anything can be so important that my mum could've left me on my own.' She traced a circle in the dust with the toe of her shoe.

Friedman moved closer and rested his arm around her shoulder. The flowers quivered in his grasp. 'She *never* meant to leave you on your own! Nine years ago today she paid the ultimate price for trying to find the truth. But she never planned to leave you! This puzzle's far bigger than the players you see who are on your side. Other people took your mum from you. However hard, you mustn't blame *her* for not being here, Brodie!'

'I know, but if she'd loved me more than the puzzle then maybe she'd have kept herself safe . . .'

'Bad things happen, Brodie. To those we love, however much they try to protect themselves and us from them. Living on when we've lost someone can be the hardest thing. But being angry with her for leaving just eats away at her memory. Be angry with those who took her from you, Brodie, but don't be angry at her.' He took a single flower from the posy and tucked it into her hair. 'She's always with you, you know. Always.'

Then he turned again and put the flowers down on the open pages of the monument.

Brodie closed her eyes, but the white and the yellow of the flowers spread across the pages burnt in her head.

'Come on,' he said at last. 'I've that train to London to catch. I don't think taking the Matroyska just for me's such a good idea.' The petals of the flowers flickered like sparks in the breeze. 'And you. You need a break from all this.'

'I'll come with you, then. To London, to get the book.'

'I've got a better idea. Let me drop you off at Smithies' home on the way to the railway station. I know Mrs Smithies would love to entertain you.'

Brodie felt the colour rise to her cheeks.

'Look, I know Smithies took you there. I know you've some grasp of what happened. Let me take you. I don't want you to be alone today.'

'But *you'll* be alone.'

A ghost of a smile flickered across his lips. 'I'm always alone,' he said.

The taxi drew up in front of Smithies' house. 'You sure this will be OK?' Brodie asked, as Friedman paid the driver and then opened the car door for her.

'Course I am.'

Brodie lifted her gaze to the front door and saw a scooter propped against the porch, a pair of bicycle clips and knee-pads hooked across the handlebars. 'My granddad's here?' she said defensively.

Friedman raised his shoulders apologetically.

'You planned this?' Brodie said, a little crossly.

'We're just looking out for you. Best I leave you lot to it. You know I'm not good with crowds.'

'It's hardly a crowd, is it?' she asked, hoping no one

else from Station X would be inside.

'No, well . . .' He hesitated. 'Anyway, I haven't eaten at the station café for a while, you know. Gordon will think I'm rejecting his food.' He smiled as if this excuse was worth going with. 'I'll drop into the café, and grab a bite to eat before the nine o'clock train.' He straightened the flower in her hair. 'Just get through today, Brodie. Things will feel better in the morning.'

She walked down the drive. She'd barely raised her hand to the bell when the door opened and Granddad was there hugging her.

Out on the path, Friedman raised his hand in acknowledgement.

Inside the house, Mrs Smithies had prepared a buffet of breakfast rolls and biscuits. She poured tea from a spotted teapot.

'It was really good of you to come,' said Smithies.

Brodie thought it odd he believed she was doing them the favour.

'It helps when Sarah has things to do,' he explained. 'While we were away in Worcester and London, she didn't really do too well. It's always hard when I leave her.'

Brodie was sure she saw something like guilt flicker in his eyes.

'If being busy's good, couldn't she come and help us with the codes?' whispered Brodie, when Mrs Smithies had left the room to make more tea.

'Sarah doesn't know about the codes, Brodie. She's too fragile to take it all on board. For her, the grief and loss is like a place where she's trapped.'

Brodie looked up at Mrs Smithies, caught in a prison of her own making, and the way Smithies and Granddad were looking at her it seemed they believed there was very little chance of parole.

Something clicked into place in her mind – the plate Brodie had balanced on her knees slipped to the floor. The flowered pattern shattered. Shards of china flew in the air.

Brodie looked down at both her watches.

'I'm really sorry,' she blurted, scrabbling on her knees to pick up the broken pieces. 'I need to go,' she said, as they watched her in confusion. 'I've just got to . . .'

Brodie ran.

The sky was overcast. The air intensely hot, pressing against her trying to force out all energy. Her footsteps rang out and her heartbeat matched every step.

Friedman had walked to the station. It was only minutes away. She glanced at her Greenwich Mean

Time watch. Twenty to nine. If she ran, she'd just make it back to the mansion and then to the station.

She couldn't do this alone.

Brodie could barely breathe.

'I don't understand, B.' Hunter looked panicked; scared even.

'You have to come now.' The words fell over themselves.

'But where, B? I don't understand.'

'Later. I'll explain later. Just trust me.'

The fact that Tusia, Hunter and Sheldon came with her, proved they did.

Their feet pounded down the platform.

The café door was ajar. Every table inside the cafe was empty.

A lone figure stooped over the table closest to the counter. He was clearing empty plates, a damp dish-cloth in his hand.

Brodie stopped and steadied herself against the back of a chair. 'Are you Gordon?'

The man stood up, clenched the dish-cloth and balanced the empty plates in the crook of his arm. 'I am.'

'Friedman?' she blurted.

The man's brow furrowed into lines.

'Friedman?' she said again. 'Do you know Friedman? Has he gone?'

The man lowered the plates once more on to the table and checked his watch. 'People are often in here asking for Friedman. You just missed him. His train leaves at nine.'

'I know. I know.'

He peered at them. 'If you hurry you can catch him. It leaves from Platform Four.'

'But we haven't got tickets.'

'So buy them on the train. Platform Four,' he said again. 'Over the footbridge.'

Brodie mumbled thanks and made for the door.

'And, kids,' he called.

'Yeah?'

'If I was you, I'd run *quick*!'

The station guard stood beside the train. He raised a whistle to his lips, his right hand lifted like a starting judge in a hundred-metre sprint.

They raced over the footbridge and launched themselves on to the train just as the doors hissed shut.

Brodie leant her forehead against the glass window, and as the train pulled out of the station, she saw Gordon standing at the door of the café, waving. She breathed out and the glass misted.

278

After a moment she turned and moved to stand in the gangway. She led the way along the aisle.

The train jolted as it moved and the flower loosened from her hair and tumbled free, falling over the seat in front of her.

'Alex?' Friedman looked up. His eyes were red.

'No. Not Alex. Me.'

He picked up the flower. 'What are you *doing* here, Brodie?'

'I've worked something out,' she said. 'I think it makes all the difference.'

They bought tickets from the guard and then slid the doors open to the first-class carriage and stepped inside. 'OK,' Friedman said. 'You've got my attention. What's so urgent you couldn't wait 'til I got back from London?'

'You're going to collect the wrong book,' said Brodie.

'The wrong book?' blurted Sheldon. 'But he's going to collect an old or damaged version of the *Liber Albus*. We were all agreed. It's what we need.'

'Well, I think we're wrong,' she said defiantly.

Friedman smiled. 'You seem very sure. Have you explained all this to Smithies?'

'I didn't have time.'

'And your granddad? You told him, I suppose, what you were racing off for?'

'No, you see—'

'Fine,' Friedman interrupted, almost laughing. 'Despite your love for your granddad and your respect for Smithies, running off to follow me was just something which couldn't wait.'

She suddenly saw where he was going. 'You're talking about my mum?' she said.

'Maybe.'

She shrugged and folded her arms across herself. 'OK. So this seemed important and I didn't have time to tell Smithies. So you're going to listen, then?'

He frowned and tucked the crumpled flower into the buttonhole of his jacket. 'I'm all ears. Go ahead.'

'Look,' said Brodie, marshalling it all in her head. 'We followed the codes, didn't we? From Edward Elgar to Van der Essen, all the way to a boy called Hans. And we discovered Hans's father was killed as a result of Savonarola. Hans became an "orphan of the flames".'

'Yes. Are we going to get to the new bit anytime soon?' Hunter said.

'Be patient! I just want to make sure you can all see where we're going.'

'We're going to London,' Hunter said. 'On a very fast train. So you really need to get on with your story.'

'OK. So we discover Hans's father was sponsored by someone called Carpenter. And this made us think the book we needed was his book, the *Liber Albus*. But I think we're forgetting a really important part of the history. Dick Whittington.'

'The pantomime guy?' Sheldon asked.

'Yes. The pantomime guy. Somehow we all sort of ignored his part of the story and I just got to thinking perhaps it's his bit of the story that's the most important.'

'OK. We're listening. Go on.'

'Well, Whittington did a lot with his money. And we latched on to the fact that he helped set up the Guildhall Library—' she said.

'Which is why I'm going to it,' Friedman interrupted. 'To get the *Liber Albus*.'

'I don't think it's the White Book we really need,' she said. 'The White Book's about law. And look at all the work we've done, and despite everything we've tried with leader letters and patterns it doesn't work. I mean it doesn't make sense of MS 408.'

'Yeah, but now we're looking for a different copy. Like Miss Tandari said.'

'But a damaged copy will only be slightly different. It may look the same but there'll be little changes. If the book's not connected to the code then it won't work.'

'But it *is* connected,' groaned Tusia. 'Carpenter and

the statue of him holding the book. That's how we got to this point.'

'And I'm saying, we're wrong. Really. I think we are.'

Friedman didn't look happy.

'Everyone goes on and on about not making leaps. But that's what we did. We jumped to a connection when there wasn't one. What I'm trying to say is, Carpenter was a connection, I'm not arguing with that. But he was part of the story *because of Whittington*. And we forgot. We saw the statue and we just presumed the White Book was the one we needed. But we're forgetting Carpenter was only a link in the story. He's only there because Whittington died and he was carrying out his boss's wishes. And that's important, isn't it? Carpenter was doing what Whittington wanted. What if we should be focusing on Whittington? What if *he's* the important part of the story?'

Friedman leant forward in the seat as the train moved through a tunnel. 'So where do you suggest we go from here, then?'

'Prison. Not literally, but it's the part of the story we skipped over. All Dick Whittington's money wasn't just used for libraries. He rebuilt other stuff. Prisons. Don't you remember? Newgate Gaol.'

The tunnel ended and Friedman leant back once more in the seat.

Brodie pressed on insistently. 'Carpenter managed Whittington's money to restore Newgate Gaol. And we should have made a connection then, to what we knew *before*. Newgate Gaol's come up before.'

'Some of the four boys Carpenter sponsored worked in Newgate Gaol,' said Tusia slowly.

'Yes, and one of those four was Benjamin Barge, the man who went on to become Hans's father,' Hunter said.

'And he worked *there* before he went to Aachen!' added Sheldon.

Brodie nodded. 'It all connects,' she said. 'I think that's the key.'

Friedman was watching her intently, a half smile on his face.

The train trundled onwards and Brodie tried to make her arguments follow a straight path like the carriage. 'We want a way of reading MS 408 but whatever we do with the letters in the White Book we haven't come anywhere close to making any sense with them. Even if we find an older version I don't believe it's going to be different enough to make everything suddenly work. I think we need a different book. The Firebird Code made me think of it.'

'You solved that code. It led us to Elgar,' said Friedman.

'Yes. We solved it. And then we forgot everything we learned when we were working it out. And our very first lesson at Station X was that we mustn't forget anything we'd learnt.'

'So how does the Firebird help us?' Hunter prompted.

'I remember that when we were trying to solve the Firebird Code, we had to look for a story written by "one the world rejected". And it meant Thomas Malory. The famous writer who was sent to prison several times. And what was the prison he was sent to?'

Tusia clapped her hands together. 'I remember! Newgate Gaol.'

Brodie could see Friedman processing the information as if the cogs in his brain were twisting and turning the details so they fell into place. 'So after all this,' he said quietly, 'you think we just need to refer to something written by Malory like you did for the Firebird Code?'

'Yes and no. I mean, maybe it's something Malory wrote which was at risk from Savonarola. Something Benjamin Barge would've rescued from the flames. Not a book *about* the law like the *Liber Albus*. What about a book which *broke* the law? So, one

Savonarola wanted to burn.'

Friedman raked his hair as if trying to force the information inside his mind. 'So we look for something written by the prisoner Malory and then passed on to Benjamin Barge, Hans's father?'

'Maybe.'

'So then why are we still racing across the country on our way to Guildhall Library?' Hunter wanted to know.

'Taking things home. That's what Granddad said. Taking things home at the end when the battle's over. Newgate Gaol was in London. Whittington paid to have it rebuilt. And he paid to have Guildhall Library rebuilt as well. London was home. To Whittington, to Malory and to Benjamin Barge.'

'So there's a chance this Malory book could still be at the Guildhall,' suggested Sheldon.

'Well, I know it's a leap . . .'

Friedman turned to the window. 'I should turn round and take you all back,' he said. 'We can't be sure of any of this.'

'But let's try,' she pleaded.

He turned to look out of the window. Her stomach was in knots. It'd make today somehow bearable if it was the day they found the code-book. She looked across the carriage at Friedman. His mobile phone was in his hand.

'Well?' she said.

'I've just missed a call from a friend,' he said. 'Keeps trying to contact me. But he'll have to wait.'

'He will?'

'I believe us five are on a mission,' Friedman said. 'I'll ring Smithies and explain.'

She watched as he deleted the missed call sign and tapped in a new number. Then he lifted the phone to speak. 'Smithies,' he said. 'It's Friedman.' There was a pause as the voice at the other end asked a question. 'No. They're OK. They're with me.' Again he paused. 'Yep. We're all fine. But we do have important news.'

15

In the Depths of the Earth

Kerrith slipped elegantly into the back of the black cab.

She looked down. A small chip glinted in the newly polished paint on her longest nail. Her jaw tightened. She brushed her hand against it. The chip didn't matter. Not now. Not today.

Friedman was on the move. And best of all, he was on his own.

According to the data she'd received, he'd purchased a single ticket from Bletchley Station. He was on his way to London.

The train pulled into Euston station. Brodie hardly had time to get her bearings before Friedman hurried them across the concourse.

Outside the British Library, Friedman hailed a cab.

'You sure you be wanting the Guildhall Library?' the driver asked, munching loudly on his chewing-gum. 'Guildhall's going to be heaving, what with the Lord Mayor's Show and all. I'll get you just as close as I can.'

'Lord Mayor's Show?' Friedman said anxiously.

The taxi driver looked up into the rear-view mirror. 'Fabulous procession. Sets off from the Guildhall. Circular route so you're bound to catch some of it.'

As close as they could get to the library, Friedman passed over a twenty pound note and waved away the offer of change.

They pushed their way through the crowds of people who'd begun to line the route and hurried up the steps to the library.

Friedman took the copy of the *Liber Albus* he'd tucked safely inside his jacket and put it on the counter. 'We want to return this book,' he said.

The librarian pursed her lips. 'Was that all you needed?' she said.

'Actually no,' began Friedman. 'We're really after something by Sir Thomas Malory.'

The librarian broke into a broad grin. 'Beautiful work. We've several copies. The man was a genius,' the librarian continued, 'although of course he was terribly badly treated by the establishment. Wrongly imprisoned on totally trumped-up charges.'

Brodie felt her spine prickle.

'It didn't stop him writing, though. Despite all they did to him.'

'They did more than lock him up?' Tusia asked, nervously.

'There are far worse things than taking away your physical freedoms, you know.'

'There are?'

'Of course.' This time the librarian's voice was loud and she seemed to surprise even herself. She spoke more quietly as she continued. 'They tried to take away his creative freedoms. His freedoms of belief. That can do people much more harm than locking them up, you know.'

'Who are these "they" you keep talking about?' Hunter said.

'More than my job's worth to explain,' she said.

'The truth's that important?' asked Friedman.

She looked away.

He took the crumpled flower from his buttonhole and held it out towards her. 'You'd make us very happy if you shared what you knew.'

She blushed and her glasses seemed to steam. Then with a giggle she took the flower and held it tightly. 'Quick, round here,' she said.

They followed her round from behind the counter to a small ante-area where a trolley of books waiting to be restacked was positioned. She clung tightly to the flower. 'Malory was one of the ones on *the list*,' she said at last.

'The list?' said Sheldon.

'The list of those they wanted.'

Friedman chose his words carefully. 'And you were going to tell us who "they" were,' he said.

She leant forward and this time her whisper was strained. 'The Suppressors,' she said. 'They banned and destroyed certain works.'

'And Malory wrote things the Suppressors wanted to destroy?' Friedman added helpfully.

The flower wobbled in the librarian's grasp.

'Could you show us some of these works?' Brodie asked.

The librarian's fingernails pressed into the stem of the flower and the head leant forward, about to fall. 'No one's allowed into Section Nine of the basement,' she said. 'I've already said more than I should. It's against the rules to talk about the Suppressors. I'm really sorry. Ministry of Information's very hot on that. Part of our contract of employment here.'

Friedman touched her gently on the arm. 'Don't worry,' he said reassuringly. 'We understand.'

'So what do we do?' Brodie's mind was bursting with questions. 'The Suppressors. These people she wouldn't talk about. Who are they?'

'Do you think they're the reason Savonarola fought to burn the book and why Benjamin Barge, Hans's dad, fought to keep it safe?' said Tusia.

'Maybe?' said Friedman.

'And do you think the book by Malory we're looking for, which could work as a code-book, is down with the other books on "the list" in the restricted section?' pressed Hunter.

'Maybe.'

'And so what do we do, if the book we need is one we can't get?'

'We find a way,' he said. Friedman's eyes were wild but his face furrowed into deep lines of concentration. 'We're so close. Everything you worked out, Brodie, and everything the librarian told us makes sense! We need that book. So I have to go and get it.'

'But the librarian said—'

He didn't let Sheldon finish. 'It'll be OK,' he said.

'I'll go,' Brodie said. She didn't like the hunger in Friedman's eyes. It almost scared her.

Friedman looked at her sharply.

'I'll go,' Brodie pressed on. 'It's safest.'

'How exactly?' demanded Hunter.

'You lot stay here. Keep the librarian talking and distracted if you need to. That way I can get on with finding this Section Nine she talked about, without being disturbed.'

'But it's too dangerous.'

'It can't be! We're in a library.'

'Brodie, have you learnt nothing over the last few months? People have lost their lives searching for and protecting books. What it comes down to is that nothing about this search is really safe. You mother learnt that lesson.'

Brodie forced her mouth into a smile. 'Then I'll do it for her. To prove that what she did wasn't wasted. I'll carry on 'til we find the answers she was looking for. Friedman, please – let me go and look!'

'It's really a bad idea,' Hunter said, sighing deeply.

'It's the best idea we've got,' Brodie snapped. She was still sure going alone would be easier but Friedman bluntly refused. 'You three keep the librarian talking so she's distracted and Friedman and I try and find Section Nine.'

'And if anyone else finds you?' Tusia said. 'You could be arrested or something. How are you going to get yourself out of that?'

'We'll just say we're lost.'

'You've got fifteen minutes,' Hunter said at last. 'Just fifteen and then if you haven't come back I'm coming down to find you.'

Reluctantly, Brodie agreed. 'Just trust me,' she said.

'I do trust you – totally,' Hunter said. 'Just don't want to see you get hurt.'

Brodie and Friedman followed the signs past the clockmakers' museum and the maritime records towards a service lift in the corner. The sign above said it wasn't for public use. It seemed most likely this would take them down to the basement. Friedman pulled open the metal door and they climbed inside. The door was criss-crossed metal like bars of a cage, and as Brodie pressed the button to descend, the brickwork of the lift shaft was still visible. A light above her head flickered as the lift began to fall.

The air in the shaft was cold. The light cross-hatched by the bars of the cage. Brodie felt her stomach falling and suddenly it had nothing to do with the movement of the lift.

With a quiet hiss, the lift stopped. She swallowed and pulled open the door which concertinaed behind her, then she and Friedman stepped out into a dark basement with low ceilings. The air was icy.

Peering into the semi-darkness they tried to make sense of the space in front of them. Rows and rows of floor-to-ceiling bookshelves stretched in every direction. The air smelt vinegary and above their heads was the metallic hum of an air-conditioner.

Brodie stepped forward. As her foot touched the ground a light came on above her head. A thin sepia light, which hummed a little, cast a soft yellow glow around her feet. She waited, then stepped forward again. More light, soft and yellow. Braver now, because of the light, they walked on, and with each step the tunnel of brightness grew and stretched. But glancing over her shoulder, Brodie saw the light behind her had faded and died, and the opening to the lift was lost in darkness.

'You go back and stay near the lift,' Brodie urged. She was sure it'd be possible to be lost forever in the vast underground city of books.

'What?'

'We can't lose the way out.' Her voice was shaking.

'I'm staying with you!'

'But someone needs to stay near the lift. Help the other person find the way back.' In her head she could see the story of Hansel and Gretel and the breadcrumb trail back to safety.

'We're not splitting up!' Friedman said firmly.

'But it's better if you stay – like a guide,' she pressed. 'Please!'

Friedman's eyes sparked in the flickering light. 'You make sure you come back to me,' he said at last.

'And you make sure you're there when I need you,' she said.

The light bounced for a moment, forward and back as Friedman walked towards the lift. He was swallowed by the darkness.

The maze of shelving stretched like the arms of an octopus in all directions. Brodie took a deep breath and then strode forward into the labyrinth.

After moments of walking, a pattern began to emerge. The shelves were labelled with letters and numbers, the numbers falling in descending order. Every now and then, Brodie was aware of section signs suspended from the ceiling. According to the signs, Section Nine was getting nearer.

It happened very suddenly. Brodie became more aware of the weight of books pushing in around her. The walkways seemed to narrow, the ceiling feel a little lower, the pools of light a little weaker. She walked to the centre of the stacks and the air was thinner and harder to breathe. When she reached Section Nine, what air there was seemed to leak from her lungs.

Stretched across the stacks, under a chipped sign

labelled Section Nine, was a metal grille, fastened securely with a padlock and chain. Beyond the grille, Section Nine stretched into darkness. There was no way in.

Brodie sank slowly down to her knees. She was cold. She was tired and she was sad. And the book they'd come for was out of reach.

From her position on the floor, Brodie looked up at the lights on the ceiling. The bulbs flickered and buzzed. If the lights went out, she figured, she'd be lost. And it was this thought that made her lean back against the grille and close her eyes.

The grille moved.

Not enough to open. Not so much that she could walk between the bars. But enough so a gap opened beneath. Just big enough for a child to crawl through. Brodie lowered herself to the ground, the concrete floor like ice against her chest. She pulled in her stomach and pushed herself under the bars. It was tight. The metal hard against her spine. She could barely breathe. But with fingers clawing against the ground, she made it through.

She was inside Section Nine.

The shelves this time were filled with boxes. Large cardboard boxes. Illegible handwriting, now faded, had been scrawled across them. And a stamp. A large circular stamp showing tongues of fire swirling and dancing. She knew this stamp. She'd seen it only once before, but she knew it. And she knew what it stood for. She knew this without being told. Because of the flames. It was the mark of the Suppressors.

Brodie ran her fingers along the edge of each box, working her way through every part of the alphabet. She traced every letter, her heart pulsing the beat of her steps. And then, when she was close to giving up, her hands stopped against a box pushed up high on the furthest shelf marked with the letter 'M'.

She took the box down and lifted the lid.

Inside, crammed tightly against the cardboard edges, were several thick leather-bound volumes. Brodie ran her finger along every spine. And found it. Barely visible in the fading light, was a book by Malory.

She lifted it out carefully as if it was made of material as delicate as butterfly wings. She held its weight in her hands and turned the pages.

The words were what she could guess now was Latin. But every now and then, as if added by mistake, were tiny squiggles between words. Glyphs. Symbols. Like in MS 408.

She flicked to the back and there, attached to a wispy strand of ribbon, was a small golden disc. Hans's medallion of a phoenix in flight.

She'd found it. The code-book to MS 408. This time she'd really found it.

Pools of light far away in the darkness showed her she was no longer alone.

Brodie closed the book as in the distance light grew in stretches from the edge of the darkness towards where she stood, framed in her own pool of light. Hiding was futile. They'd see her pool of light as she saw theirs. They'd find her. The only choice left was to run.

She forced herself under the grille, the metal digging deep into her back. She scrambled to her feet clutching the book and ran past the towering columns of books, away from the voices which echoed and bounced on the leather volumes for a moment keeping her hidden. She ran harder and faster than she'd ever done before, back towards where Friedman had promised to wait.

She could hear voices. Friedman's and others. Friedman was shouting.

Brodie ducked behind a shelf. There was the sound of metal folding. The door of the lift being opened and the noise of a struggle.

Then a whirring noise as the door of the lift slammed shut and the lift began to climb.

Brodie staggered out of the light. She flung herself

against the door of the rising cage. Three people were inside. Friedman and the suited men from the Royal Albert Hall.

Friedman looked at her through the bars.

'They've taken him!' Brodie shrieked.

Hunter held her arms to steady her.

'Two men. They took him. He was—'

Tusia cut her off. 'Friedman went with them willingly, Brodie,' she said.

'No!'

'He came out of the lift and he wasn't struggling and he didn't resist and he went with them. We saw.'

'No! They took him! He wouldn't have gone with them! I've got to help him.'

She pulled out of Hunter's grasp and rushed down the steps towards the exit, her fingers still clutching the book.

And it would have been so much easier to follow Friedman and his captors out into the street if it hadn't been for the giants.

Two towering figures made of wicker moved slowly on wheels down the road past the library. Each held silver spears. One held a shield. Swarming around the giants were men and women dressed in red and black.

'The Lord Mayor's Show,' screeched Tusia. 'It's Gog and Magog.'

'Who?'

'Guardians of the City of London! The giants. This is the Lord Mayor's Parade.'

Brodie didn't care whose parade it was. Even if the idea of the Lord Mayor made her think of Dick Whittington and the very reason they'd come back to London in the first place. She shoved the book into her bag. 'Which way?' she shouted.

'B, please, we—'

'Which way?'

Hunter pointed down the street away from the giants. Brodie could just make out two suited figures moving through the crowd, Friedman between them.

She pushed against flag-wavers as she ran. 'Oi, watch out, kid. We've been here hours to see the show.'

Brodie didn't even look back. She ploughed on, following the men in suits – Hunter, Tusia and Sheldon hard behind her.

The parade rounded a corner and a gap appeared in the metal railings holding back the crowd. 'Hurry!' she yelled over her shoulder. 'We're going to lose them.'

Hunter rushed behind her, darting along the road despite yells telling them to get back.

Horses were moving towards them. A marching

band, its music drowning the shouts to get out of the way. Brodie fronted the charge, fighting against the flow.

Next, a group of dancers, and Brodie led the weave amongst them, trying to make it look like they belonged. She shouted for Friedman but his name was lost in the swirl of the drums, the clash of the dance sticks and the beat of the hooves.

Floats rounded the corner. Speakers pumped music. Brodie's head was thumping. She was suffocating in the noise, panic swelling in her stomach. She scanned the crowd. A kaleidoscope of colour and movement. She couldn't find the suited men.

'There!' shouted Sheldon, pointing to his right. 'Up that back street.'

Tusia vaulted the barrier and held her hand out. Brodie grabbed hold and clambered after her. The men were at the end of the alley. They were about to turn out of sight.

They raced up the alleyway, left, then right. The men in the suits hurried Friedman onwards. He didn't look back.

Suddenly a sea of feathers and white netting engulfed them. Dancers from the Central School of Dance spilling into the street laughing and calling to each other. A cacophony of legs and arms and voices.

'This way,' yelled Sheldon, pushing through them. 'Don't stop.'

Brodie's legs were shaking. Air couldn't find its way to her lungs. But Sheldon steered them onwards.

She saw the sign. 'Phoenix Place'. The road was wide. The building on the left enormous.

'It's some sort of post office,' yelled Hunter. 'Mount Pleasant, look.'

The men were making for the side of the building.

By the time Brodie and the others rounded the corner, the men had gone.

'Where? I don't understand. They were here and . . .'

Hunter pointed. A doorway blocked with struts of wood. Two struts had been removed. The opening was just big enough for a man to climb through.

'What is this place?'

The air was dank. The light low. A sheeting of dust filmed everything.

The crack in the door had led into a wide barny space filled with shelves and tables. The shelves were empty. Signs showing letters of the alphabet hung from the ceiling.

'An abandoned library?' whispered Sheldon.

'No. I told you. It's the sorting office. Where the post comes,' said Hunter.

'But there's nothing here.'

Brodie stepped forward. A cloud of dust lifted. The sign hanging over her head swung to the side, creaking as it moved.

'It's not used any more, then?' said Tusia.

'Can't be. Looks like no one's been in this part for years.'

'Except them,' whispered Brodie.

The suited men were ahead of them. They were walking towards a huge bulkhead doorway like Brodie imagined was used inside ships to keep the water out, or banks to keep the money in. Friedman walked between them still. His head was lowered but he didn't struggle.

'B, I really think we're out of our depth here. We should get help.'

'Where from? In case you hadn't noticed the rest of the team are back at Bletchley. We're on our own.' One of the men was turning the lock. The bulkhead door began to swing open. 'We have to follow them!'

'How? They'll see us. Whatever reason they've got Friedman with them can't be good.'

Brodie scanned the room. 'Time for your speciality, then.'

Tusia's face fell. 'Really?'

'You distract them and us three will find out

where Friedman's going.'

There was no time for Tusia to argue. She pushed the empty post trolley hard against the table as the other three darted down behind the shelving.

Dust clogged Brodie's nostrils. Tusia was doing well. Some rambling story about being lost and being scared of the giants. One of the suited men at least was falling for it, but the other one had steered Friedman through the door to a flight of stairs stretching downwards, labelled 'TO THE RAIL'.

'We can't do it,' said Sheldon. 'However good she is, she can't block three of us from sight.'

Brodie knew Tusia was good. But Sheldon was right. 'There,' she said, pointing to what looked like a spiral mail chute.

'We don't know where it comes out, B!'

Brodie waved madly at the sign above it. 'MAIL TO RAIL. We have to try!'

Brodie darted out of the cover of the shelving. The suited man was gesticulating madly at Tusia, directing her towards the broken slats of the doorway. Now was their chance.

Brodie clambered up on to the chute. It felt like the top of a slide at a water park. The opening was huge, big enough for bags of post. Big enough for the three of them.

Hunter squeezed in front of her. 'Me first,' he said. 'To break your fall. Ready?'

The air was cold against her face as she tumbled down – darkness overwhelming. Her arm caught against the side. Her feet jarred as she landed. And for a moment she wasn't sure if she was broken.

'You two all right?' Hunter's voice was shaking. They'd landed, but the ground wasn't still. They were moving.

'It's a conveyor-belt,' said Sheldon. 'We've set it off.'

The belt was moving them onwards, like a river towards the rapids. Above them Brodie could just make out a giant crane. Its arm was creaking. Years of non-use now spluttering into life. The crane was swinging towards them. At the end of the belt was a plummet over the edge. Above them was a metal claw. Brodie closed her eyes.

'Jump!' yelled Sheldon, pushing against her. 'Jump off the belt!'

She wasn't sure when she made the decision. Wasn't even sure if she did. Suddenly the ground rose up to meet her and she rolled across hard, unyielding concrete.

Hunter helped her up. Lights above them flickered but it was difficult to see.

But when her vision was clearer, Brodie didn't like what she saw.

It was some sort of railway station. A sign on the wall, flaky and old, said 'MAIL RAIL'. Two tracks ran parallel towards a tunnel. A small train stood on each track. One had open carriages – no doors, just rows of seats for passengers. One was made up of cages with metal lids.

Friedman was on the first train. The suited man sat beside him. He reached up and pressed a button that hung from the ceiling. The train began to move.

'Hurry!' Hunter sprinted for the other train. He flung open the lid of the metal cage and clambered inside. Brodie went to follow.

'You need to stay here, Fingers!'

'What?'

'One of us needs to press that button. Start the train. We can't wait for Tusia to catch us up! It has to be you!'

Sheldon's face was wild.

'Please, Sheldon.'

Sheldon hurried over to the starting button. 'Ready?' he yelled.

There was no time to answer before the train began to move.

It careered towards the tunnel. The lid of the cages banging above them. The air grew colder still. The tunnel swallowed them; the light a flickering spark.

Then the ground fell away! The train hurtled downwards, gaining speed all the time. Air crushed against the sides of Brodie's lungs. Tears stung in her eyes.

'It's OK, B!'

But it wasn't. They were falling. The train was out of control.

In the flickering light it was possible to see they were gaining ground on the other train. Sparks shot from the wheels.

Brodie pushed open the lid of the cage. 'Friedman,' she yelled into the semi-light. 'Please!' She was desperate for him to hear her. Desperate for him to turn.

The train lurched to the right. It lifted on its axle, the squealing of metal on metal. Sparks lit the air like fireworks.

'We need to get on his train,' yelled Hunter. 'I need to jump across.'

'No!' yelled Brodie. 'I should do it.'

'What?'

The trains were drawing closer, thundering together through the darkness.

'Hold me. Keep me steady. Let me move across.'

'You're crazy, B!'

Brodie looked into the spark of Hunter's eyes.

The carriages were a breath away from each other.

The beginning of their train next to the end of Friedman's.

'I can do it from here!' Brodie yelled, stretching out to reach the end carriage.

'B, really I think . . .'

Brodie didn't hear what Hunter thought. The tunnel was thickening and the two tracks about to diverge. It was now or never.

Brodie launched herself on to the other train. She felt Hunter's hands slip from hers. His train careered into the distance.

Brodie held her breath.

The train she'd boarded was slowing down. It was pulling uphill. She clambered across the seats of the carriage, climbing nearer and nearer to the front.

There was a scream of metal against metal. A grating noise like the air was being torn.

Brodie cradled her head and braced herself for impact. But the train juddered to a stop.

Friedman and the suited man got out.

Waiting on the platform was a woman dressed in red. Brodie recognised her at once from the Royal Pavilion. She wore the same high boots, the same cold look. Brodie knew her now as Kerrith. At the Royal Pavilion she'd just been the woman who'd stolen a dream and been there when Brodie had opened a box filled with ash. She knew her now as a worker from the Black Chamber. As one who wanted to see the operation at Station X shut down. She knew her now as the enemy.

Brodie's heart raced but even through her panic she could hear Kerrith speaking.

'We're taking you in, Friedman.'

Friedman said nothing.

Brodie crouched down behind the seating so she couldn't be seen.

'Time's an amazing thing,' Kerrith said. 'If you wait long enough, things turn up.'

'Long enough?'

'Like nine years perhaps. Ironic, don't you think? Nine years to the day and we track you down. How amazing we can make an anniversary of it.' She swept her hair behind her shoulders dismissively. 'Mobile phones are wonderful things for tracking. Your call to Smithies confirmed where you were going. I have to say, it's worked out rather well.' She sighed. 'Part of me would've liked to see the girl's face as I took you in. I've a feeling I'd have enjoyed the dawning understanding of misplaced trust, but this way I can imagine it later, when you don't return to Station X and she gets to appreciate the reason why. Imagine what Brodie would do if she knew you'd been with her mother the day she died. If she'd known you'd been at the wheel of the car. If she'd known that perhaps if you'd stayed after the accident and not run for safety yourself, then maybe her mother wouldn't have died.'

Brodie feared she'd fall. The words seemed to bang inside her brain. Words about her mother. About death. And about Friedman. In the confusion she couldn't be sure whether the words she heard next were from Friedman or simply bouncing inside her head. 'You've got it wrong.'

'What can be wrong?' Kerrith's voice cut through the fog. 'Are you denying you were in the car with Alex Bray nine years ago when it crashed?'

Brodie saw him shake his head.

'I think I've got enough now, Friedman, to send you down for a very long time,' Kerrith said. 'So keen for Brodie to know her mother's death wasn't an accident, weren't you? You should have left well alone. The truth has a way of coming out, so they say.'

Brodie heard him then. 'You've got it wrong.'

'I don't think so, Robbie. You and Smithies got it wrong when you decided to take on Level Five. We'll bring you all down. One at a time until there's no one left to consider MS 408. One at a time. And you're the first to fall.'

But it was Brodie who fell. Crumpled inside the carriage of a train which had taken her on a journey she wasn't supposed to take.

Put it was Brodie who fell. Crumpled inside the carriage of a train who had taken her on a journey she wasn't supposed to take.

16

Shadows on the Wall

Brodie wasn't sure how she got back to Euston station. After an eternity she'd clambered from the train carriage and fought her way above ground. This time the boarded-up exit led out into a street beside Paddington station. It was raining. Thunder rumbling across the sky. Brodie was soaked to the skin, but it didn't matter. Nothing mattered any more.

She wasn't sure where the others were, or how they made their way back to Bletchley. She'd never felt more alone. So she clung to the book from the Guildhall. It belonged to a time when things were certain and full of hope. Before she'd seen Kerrith lead Friedman away.

He'd turned for just a second. She was sure he saw her. Knew she'd heard every word.

* * *

The café at Bletchley was still open. Gordon was upturning chairs and stacking them on tables. 'Hey, what's up with you, princess? Look like you've seen a ghost.'

Perhaps she had.

'Robbie not with you?' he said.

No. It seemed after all he wasn't. Not with her, or on her side at all.

It suddenly felt to Brodie as if she heard the 'dark saying' of their work on the Dorabella Cipher. An untold message suddenly screaming in her ear. Friedman wasn't what he seemed. A character hidden by the music of teamwork now exposed for what he really was. A Judas hidden in the clothes of a saint. A betrayer.

Gordon's face was lined with concern. 'Here.' He passed her a jammy doughnut and a can of cola. 'Looks like you could do with some sugar,' he said.

The doughnut tasted like cotton wool in her mouth; the sugar like salt on her lips. 'Sorry,' she said. 'I can't.'

'You want me to ring Smithies? Come and get you?'

Brodie's thoughts began to unravel, like fraying fabric. She dug her hand in her pocket and checked her purse. 'No,' she said and then she walked back along the platform to the ticket office.

* * *

Mr Bray stood at the window. It was dark. 'We should call the police.'

Smithies rested his hand on the older man's arm. 'Gordon said he saw her.'

'Then why isn't she here? Why hasn't she come home?'

'Maybe she *has* gone home?' said Tusia. 'I mean, to your old house. You said when things were over, people needed things to be brought home.'

There was a spark of hope in the old man's eyes. 'To the rubble of the explosion? You think she'll go there?'

'No.' It was Hunter speaking. His voice was dry. 'She won't go home to the rubble. And she won't come back here.'

'Then where?'

All eyes were on him.

'I reckon where she felt safe. That's what home means. Where Friedman showed he believed in her. Where we heard "Nimrod".'

'To the music room here?' said Sicknote, remembering the night the Firebird Box had first been played.

Hunter shook his head. 'No. The place where she first learnt about Elgar's friends. Where we hid when it

314

seemed it had all gone wrong. Where she first heard Variation IX played properly.' He walked towards the door. 'I reckon she'll go back to Station IX.'

Brodie sat with her back against the wall in the corner of the room.

Somehow she was managing to breathe. One breath after another. In and out as if this was all her body could do. She'd never had to think about that before but now she was scared that if she didn't concentrate her body would forget. That she wouldn't have enough air.

It had taken longer to get here than she'd thought it would. The train had only brought her so far. And the walk through the overgrown grounds had been difficult. She was wet, her clothes were torn. A line of blood ran down her leg.

It wasn't difficult to get inside. The boarding was easy to prise away from the window now she knew the areas of weakness. Her arm had caught against the shattered glass, but that didn't matter. Nothing did.

She'd slipped the large black disc from the sleeve, lifted the needle on the radiogram and lowered it into the groove. And the disc had spun as the ridges cut in the circle released their song.

She pulled her knees up close to her chest and closed

her eyes. And concentrated only on breathing as the music played.

As Variation IX began, the door opened and a chink of light cut across the room.

Brodie lifted her head slowly.

Hunter stood there, framed by the morning light. He walked across the room and sat down beside her.

The music of 'Nimrod' crashed around her.

They all travelled back in the Matroyska, the windscreen wipers slicing across the screen, the yellow curtains tapping against Brodie's shoulders like angry moths around a flame.

As Smithies drove, Brodie found she could explain everything she'd heard. About Friedman, about Kerrith and about her mother's accident. One thing after another.

No one else said a word.

Being soaked in the rain led to a heavy fever. Brodie dreamt of fires and tunnels and pods of green water connected by tubes and pipes which led one from another into the darkness. And shipwrecks.

On the third day, the fever left her.

She washed and dressed and then Hunter walked with her to the music room. Sheldon was at the piano.

His fingers moved slowly across the keys.

'It's by Elgar,' Tusia explained. 'It's called "Sospiri", which means "the sighing".'

Sheldon played on. Hunter put his hand on Brodie's shoulder.

That was when she began to cry.

The next morning, Brodie made her way over to Hut 11 where the rest of the team were waiting. She stood for a while, steadying herself against the large table, her fingertips finding her mother's initials carved in the wood.

'You OK, Brodie?' Tusia asked as she eventually slid into her seat beside her.

Smithies was standing, his hand resting on top of the Jumbo Rush Elephant. 'This is a sad day,' he said slowly. 'A day when one of our number's been taken from us.' He held a piece of paper. A notification of Friedman's arrest. Brodie imagined Kerrith's delight as she wrote it.

'He betrayed my mother.' Brodie didn't remember opening her mouth to speak. 'He betrayed us,' she added.

'Brodie, I know you're upset,' Smithies began.

'I thought he was on my side. Like, part of the team, and all the time he was lying. I went with him to

London to get the code-book.'

She could hear the tension stretch across the room.

'See, it's here,' she said, and she held out the small leather-bound volume. 'My mother lost her life because of this thing and Friedman was there. I don't want anything to do with it.'

Smithies and Granddad stood in the doorway. 'Let me talk to her,' Smithies said. Mr Bray nodded sadly and went back inside.

They stood outside Hut 11, as the sun weakened in a patchy evening sky. 'You can't leave,' he said.

Brodie's answer was equally clear. 'I'm going to. I said I don't want anything more to do with all this.'

Smithies sat down on the step and patted the ground beside him. She didn't respond.

'Brodie,' he said at last, 'before a man's sent to prison, the evidence about him's discussed. Don't you owe it to Friedman to consider all the facts?'

'She said he was there when my mother died. He didn't say he wasn't.'

'Kerrith knew all she needed to see Robbie locked away. Level Five's corrupt. It just wants to be in control. Surely you see that.'

'I've seen all I need,' Brodie said tightly.

'But what if you haven't seen the whole truth? The

truth, the whole truth and nothing but the truth. Something we don't know yet. Like the language of MS 408. We can't see it clearly.'

'I'm not going to wait around 'til the picture becomes clearer. Until I know all the gruesome details.'

'You have to. If that's what it takes to get to the truth,' Smithies responded quietly.

She continued to look away.

'Brodie, you've seen pieces of a puzzle only. Sections of blue you've been told must make the painting show a sky.' He hesitated. 'But what if there's more? Different pieces, with greens and purples and whites. What if when you see the whole picture it's not of the sky at all? But of the sea. An ocean deep and wide and teeming with life.'

Brodie concentrated on watching the sun edging the mansion roof, as if lining the tiles with orange ice. 'You're telling me there's an excuse for what Friedman did? He abandoned my mum and somehow that's OK?'

'No. I'm saying we have to know everything before we judge. We need to know the meaning of every squiggle and brush stroke before we read the code.'

'It's not about the code!' Brodie yelled. 'Not any more. It's not about pictures and puzzles and letters and books. It's about my mum! You're always saying we mustn't take leaps. We find the links and the connections, you said. Well, I saw them and I ignored them. I heard you talking about how my mum had been let down and I didn't ask who did that. I saw Friedman so keen to get the answers and I thought it was because he wanted what we all did. Answers. Now I know he wanted to take what he could from us before I knew. *There's* the connections and the leaps I should have made! He was never on our side.'

'Life's complicated, Brodie. It's not clean and simple and about sides. It's not full of good and bad. It's more difficult.'

'It's not difficult. Friedman's the enemy. That's simple.'

Smithies sighed. 'Do you remember once, I told you a story Plato told? Do you remember how Plato spoke of people in a cave who saw only shadows moving across the walls?'

Brodie's hands balled into fists.

'What the people saw wasn't reality but distorted reflections. A prisoner escaped one day and saw the world for what it really was but when he returned with the truth, no one would listen. For Robbie's sake, don't you owe it to everyone to look outside the cave? You're seeing only shadows. If I know anything it's that Friedman loved your mother. Always. There's more to the story than we have. We've got to believe that.'

'He let my mother die,' she said. 'How is that love?'

Smithies didn't answer.

'I thought this was a game. Some sort of puzzle to solve. I thought we were searching for answers to a code.'

'Well, we were. We are.'

'But my mother died and Friedman was there! So it's all different . . . it's like . . . the rules keep changing.'

He waited a moment before he spoke. 'In a way they do. We have to adapt.' He paused. 'I know you think you can't trust anyone now. But you can. You can trust your friends. Hunter and the others.'

Brodie turned and looked at him. The sun slid finally behind the mansion, leaving only shadow.

After a while she sat down on the step beside him.

'It's true,' he said softly, 'what you're involved in is far bigger and deeper than we first explained. Perhaps I should've told you from the very beginning. Perhaps we should've made the risks clear. The thing you're involved in, Brodie, is huge. Over five hundred years of history have led to here and now. Lives have been lost along the way. Not just your mother's. Other innocent lives. Some have been destroyed and corrupted by the search or damaged. There's lots I need to tell you, about the enemy and the battles we'll face if we continue. I don't know what happened the night your mother died. But I know things are rarely what they first seem. If you really believe you want out, of course you should go.' He sighed. 'Your grandfather will understand. We'll all understand. It has to be your decision, Brodie. But I'd like you to consider the friends you'd be walking out on.'

She snapped round to face him. 'That's not fair! You make it sound like I'd be letting them down. Betraying them.'

'We'd understand. But you'd be leaving when they needed you.'

'You're twisting things. Making me sound like him. There's no one who'll *die* if I leave. It's not the same. It's not life and death. What do I add anyway? Only stories.'

'And aren't stories life and death?'

'It's not the same!'

He looked as if he'd say no more. When he spoke it was just a whisper. 'Like I said, Brodie. It's your decision.'

Brodie pressed the keys of the piano. First black then white. It wasn't music. Just noise. How could Sheldon do what he did? Take the ebony and the ivory and mix them to make sound that made sense? Melody.

She ran her fingertips along the keys. She pressed every one of the eight-eight separate notes. And each one echoed with her heartbeat.

Epilogue

It was morning. Too early for breakfast. The air still chilled.

Hunter sat beside her, his feet dangling in the lake. 'Well, B? You decided?'

Brodie watched the ripples spill out from around his feet. 'Smithies said if I stay he'll tell us *everything* now. He's promised he'll tell the truth. Nothing hidden.'

'And what about Friedman?'

'Smithies says I should wait. Before I judge.'

'And you agree?'

Brodie shrugged. 'I don't know,' she said honestly. 'I'm not sure of anything any more.'

Hunter's feet moved in the water. The ripples grew. 'We want you to stay, Brodie.'

They watched the ripples stretch across the lake.

Bigger and bigger circles reaching for the shore.

'Maybe I owe it to Smithies to try and let him help me understand. And I've been thinking I owe it to Elgar and Van der Essen and Dorabella to use Malory's book to solve the code of MS 408. And maybe there's other people I owe too.'

Hunter lifted his feet from the lake and dried them on the grass. 'One step at a time, then?'

'One step at a time,' she agreed.

'Well, time's what we've got lots of,' Hunter laughed, pulling her up. 'I mean, especially you with your two watches and everything.'

At the doorway of Hut 12 the others were making their way in to breakfast. Tusia was walking between Sheldon and Miss Tandari; Granddad was chatting with Smithies, while Sicknote gulped keenly through his inhaler.

'You've only called me by my proper name once before,' she said. 'At the Royal Pavilion when we thought we were going to lose the Firebird Code.'

He blushed. 'Maybe I use your name when I'm scared of losing you,' he said.

'I'm not going anywhere,' she said at last. 'At least, not yet.' And with that they made their way over to Hut 12 to join their friends.

AUTHOR'S NOTE

VERITAS: The search for Truth

True stories were my inspiration (again!) when writing Orphan of the Flames. The codes and mysteries are genuine, the libraries and museum the team visit are real; the statue in City of London School really exists and Carpenter, Dick Whittington and Savonarola were actual people! The Lord Mayor's Show is a parade through England's capital city which dates back to 1535 and takes place every year.

STATION IX

Station IX is another real place, in a large mansion called The Fythe, in Welwyn, about 30 miles north of London. It used to be a country hotel. Just before World War Two, the building was taken over by the British Military Intelligence and it became a secret factory where all sorts of weapons were made. Civilian scientists and members of the services worked in the building and in huts around the grounds. After the war, Station IX was taken over by commercial researchers and eventually by GlaxoSmithKline. In 2010 the building was sold to a property developer but at the time of writing Orphan of the Flames it remained empty, making it the perfect secret hideout for Team Veritas!

THE MAIL RAIL

Underground locations are vital to Secret Breakers and the Mail Rail really exists! The driverless train system was built to carry letters and parcels beneath the city streets. Trains ran using electricity and carried huge sacks between nine stations underground. The largest station was underneath Mount Pleasant. The tracks were built about twenty-one metres underground but the stations were higher up. The track had to slope down quickly to make the trains accelerate and then slope up to make them slow down, just like I describe in the story. It's also true that the track splits into two at certain sections. The rail system ran from 1927 until 2003 when it was suddenly closed in the middle of the night. The track and trains were simply left as they were, abandoned and now unused, hidden under the streets of London.

ELGAR AND HIS CODES

The composer Sir Edward Elgar is central to Orphan of the Flames. 'The Enigma Variations' is probably his most famous work. Each of the Variations are based on Elgar's friends and I loved the idea that the language of music could talk about people (and even pet dogs!). No one really knows who is hidden by Variation XIII and I wanted to explore the story of Helen Weaver. My favourite Variation is Nimrod. This is Variation IX and this made me even more certain that the team should take shelter in Station IX. Nimrod was named after Elgar's publisher Jaeger and I realised that he was a very important person in Elgar's life. The fact that the word 'Nimrod' is connected to the name 'Hunter' was another really exciting link. Truth proved stranger than fiction again! And as for Dorabella – it was great to find her Variation matched the number of Station X. Her 88 symbol cipher really was sent on the back of a letter by Elgar. There have been lots of attempts to read those 88 symbols and as I'm fascinated by firebirds rising again from the flames, I was thrilled to find out that MGC 88 is a spiral galaxy in the Phoenix Constellation. It seemed to me that all these strands of stories and codes were meant to come together as I wrote Orphan of the Flames.

Discover the world of the Secret Breakers.

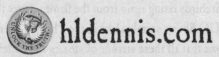